Tales

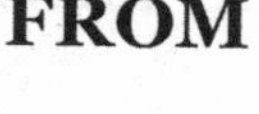

BOOKS BY GARRETT DENNIS

Port Starbird

Port of Refuge

The Port Fee

Tales From Port Starbird

Tales From Port Starbird

The Storm Ketchum Tales

by

Garrett Dennis

Copyright © 2018 by Garrett Dennis. All rights reserved under International and Pan-American Copyright Conventions. No part of this text may be reproduced in any form or by any means without the express written permission of the author.

This is a work of fiction. Storm Ketchum and the other main characters are fictitious unless otherwise noted. Businesses and organizations, locales, scientific and religious references, and historical figures and events are real, but may be used fictitiously.

TALES FROM PORT STARBIRD
ISBN: 978-1721218097

This book is dedicated to the memory of Jack, my faithful companion for many years and one of the stars of these stories. As I told you every day, you are the best puppy – still, and always.

2003-2017

The Outer Banks of North Carolina

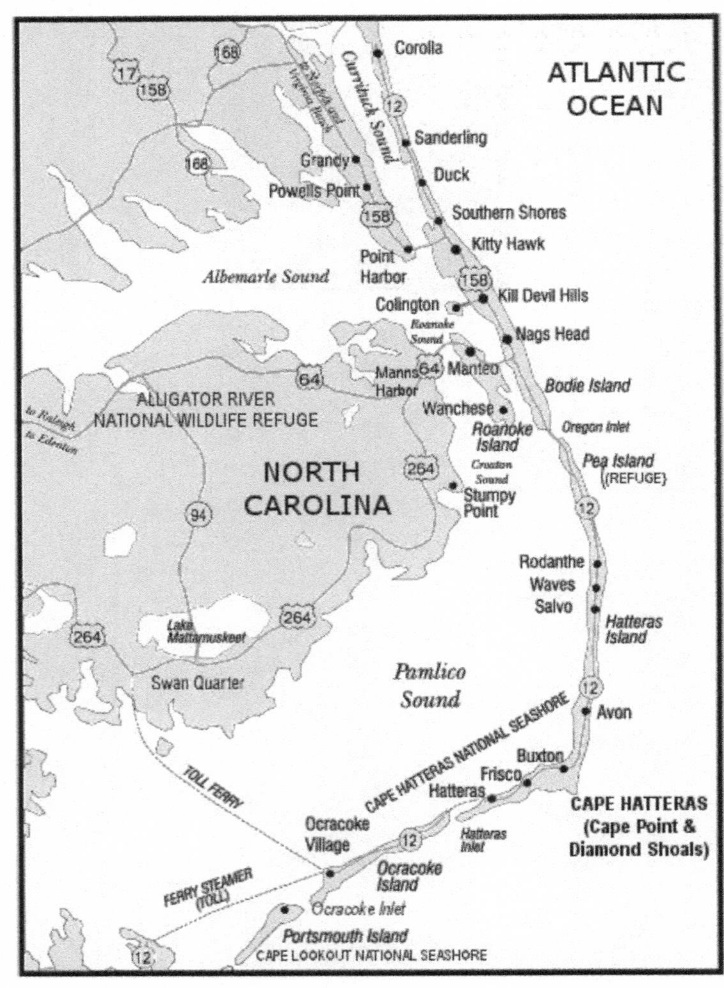

CONTENTS

Tales From Port Starbird

Introduction

Greetings, and welcome to my world! I'm the author of the **Storm Ketchum Adventures**, a series of Outer Banks mysteries and adventures that begins with the full-length novel ***Port Starbird.*** My stories are fictional, but they reference real historical, cultural, and ecological events that have occurred on the Outer Banks.

The **Storm Ketchum Tales** are short stories that accompany the Storm Ketchum Adventure novels. This book is a collection of those short stories. They can be read along with, or independently of, the full-length Adventure novels. The Adventure novels are not included in this book.

Chronologically, the settings of these short Tales fall before, between, and after the Adventure novels. Here's a timeline to help you keep things straight:

An Olde Christmas Carol (Tale #1): January 2010

The Sad Blue Boat (Tale #2): April 2011

Cora's Tree (Tale #3): October 2012

PORT STARBIRD (Adventure #1): June 2013

PORT OF REFUGE (Adventure #2): September 2013

Dixie Island (Tale #4): October 2013

The Wayward Mariner (Tale #5): February 2014

THE PORT FEE (Adventure #3): June 2014

Pharaoh's Treasure (Tale #6): August 2014

Route 101 (Tale #7): September 1925

No, the date for Tale #7 is not a typo! That Tale is set in the past for a reason that will become apparent after you've read the other Tales – and for that reason, it's presented last in this book.

Please visit **www.GarrettDennis.com** if you want to learn more about the Adventures, the Tales, and Ketch's world. That site also contains information on how to connect with me on social media and by email, and on how to sign up for my Port Starbird VIP Reader List.

And now – sit back and enjoy!

Garrett Dennis

June 2018

AN OLDE CHRISTMAS CAROL

DESCRIPTION

In Storm Ketchum Tale #1, a stolen item is recovered and a Victorian lesson is relearned.

Ketch, a new and damaged emigre to North Carolina's picturesque Outer Banks, simply wants to be left alone. Now that he's finally where his soul belongs, he thinks he doesn't need anyone but his dog. But in the tradition of Scrooge, he learns otherwise at the annual Banker celebration of Olde Christmas.

Join amateur sleuth Storm 'Ketch' Ketchum and his loyal dog Jack as they embark on a winter journey of self-discovery and redemption on historic Hatteras Island, where intrigue (and Old Buck) could be just around the next corner.

NOTE: The Kinnakeet Boatyard and the Sea Dog Scuba Center are fictitious.

January 2010

Ketch gingerly eased himself into the rickety old rocking chair on the front porch. It held, so he draped the afghan he'd dragged outside with him across his lap. Although he was fully dressed and the temperature here on Cape Hatteras was nowhere near as low on this early January morning as it had been back North where he'd come from, that number alone was deceptive. There was no snow on the ground, but he was surrounded by water, so the air here was always damp – and when the sea breezes blew, it was just as capable of chilling one to the bone as an upstate New York winter.

Jack didn't appear to be bothered by the weather, but Ketch figured that could be due to the dog's interest in the plate of buttered toast he'd set on a nearby stand. The two-year-old beagle-lab mix he'd rescued from a shelter a few months back on a whim was already intensely loyal, and unexpectedly well-behaved and atypically polite (for a dog) when it came to food. He didn't think he'd ever before met a dog as intelligent and empathetic as this one.

Though he wasn't looking for friends, Ketch appreciated the dog's silent camaraderie, and more saliently the calming effect the dog's presence seemed to have had on his own fevered mind, something the human therapist he'd grudgingly engaged for a time hadn't been able to achieve. Ketch fed Jack a well-deserved slice of toast before digging in himself on the remaining two. He saved the last crust for the dog and then washed his breakfast down with a glass of orange juice.

He was still cold, so he stood and wrapped the afghan around himself like one would a bath towel, then sat back down. It probably didn't help that he was hungover. Contrary to popular tales of alpine rescues, and in spite of the false burn it created on the way down, alcohol lowered the body's core temperature and wasn't really an effective way to get or stay warm. It also didn't permanently solve any problems, a fact he'd always known but had lately chosen to ignore. The dog, satisfied now, curled up on the throw rug under Ketch's stockinged feet and allowed them to rest on his back.

Warmer now, Ketch sat back and took in the view this Buxton cottage provided. Though it wasn't a waterfront property, he could make out the Cape Hatteras lighthouse with its distinctive black-and-white barbershop-pole day marker in the dawning sun and hear the breakers from here. Since this was just a relatively inexpensive ninety-day rental whose purpose was to shelter him and Jack while he house-hunted in Avon, and since he was finally on his beloved Hatteras Island for good regardless of anything else, that was enough for him.

For the first time in as long as he could remember, there was nothing he absolutely had to do today. Although the thirty-first was his official retirement date, he'd been able to take the Christmas holidays and this entire month off due to accrued vacation time. He'd already sold his old house, and the few belongings he'd decided to keep were in a self-storage unit not too far away. And he'd shopped at Conner's grocery after checking in here, so he had adequate provisions – which was good, since this island's economy was predominantly tourism-driven these days and the restaurants were all closed off-season. And he didn't have enough laundry to bother with.

So what should he do today, with this bounty of free time – drink some more? No, he thought not, though he still felt justified in considering it. Maybe play a little more guitar and then do a bit of beachcombing after the temperature had risen some, or perhaps a mini-hike through part of the nearby Buxton Woods Reserve? It was the largest remaining stand of maritime forest on the Outer Banks, and its trails extended all the way south to Frisco. The reptiles and insects there wouldn't be too troublesome at this time of year.

He remembered reading that there was a trailhead not far from here, near the small cemetery past the lighthouse. The British Cemetery held the graves of two sailors from across the pond whose bodies had washed ashore after their vessel was torpedoed by one of the German U-boats that prowled the East Coast during World War II. He'd always meant to visit there, but had never gotten around to it on his previous visits to the island. Well, he had plenty of time to do that now, and more.

He also knew today was a Christmas of sorts and there'd be a celebration of that up in Rodanthe, as there was every year. But although that did admittedly pique his interest from a cultural perspective, a tranquil day by the sea with his always accommodating canine companion was more appealing at the moment. There'd probably be a lot of people at that shindig, and he'd had enough of people.

He'd never himself attended despite numerous vacations taken on this island, but Ketch knew from his readings that Old Christmas, or Olde Christmas to the more nostalgic, was a holiday born of miscommunication and stubbornness, and maintained as much out of winter island boredom as tradition. The story was, the Pope decreed in 1582 that the inaccurate Julian calendar be replaced by our modern Gregorian calendar. The Catholic European nations went along, but by the time Protestant England came around, almost two hundred years had passed and there was an eleven-day difference between the two calendars that had to be dealt with.

Before the Calendar Act of 1751, England had celebrated Christmas on January 6, a practice begun in medieval times. Dropping the extra eleven days moved Christmas back to December 25. By their nature resistant to change, the people of the isolated Outer Banks communities initially ignored the new date when they heard about it several years later, and continued to celebrate on January 6.

Then, realizing the potential for additional partying, to which they were always amenable, the Banker colonists decided to extend their holiday. They started observing both the 'official' Christmas on December 25, and what came to be called Old Christmas on January 6. On Hatteras Island nowadays, folks congregated at the community center (which the locals simply referred to as the community building) in Rodanthe on the Saturday closest to that day each year to celebrate Old Christmas.

Ketch wasn't a religious man, and Christmas had never really meant that much to him even in the secular sense after his wife and son had moved on and left him behind. But Old Christmas wasn't a religious event, and since he desired to know his new island home and its history as intimately as possible, he supposed he should experience it at some point – but he'd just stay put here for today, he again decided. Having no family left to speak of now, his traditional Christmas had been a solitary affair, and he didn't see why this particular day needed to be any different. Maybe next year...

The temperature had risen a bit now, and he found he was quite comfortable under the afghan. The fur-coated dog seemed content as well beneath his feet. He could clearly hear the gulls down toward the beach, making their contributions to the soul-soothing cacophony that was the sound of the sea. That and the pleasantly salty air, chilly but still this morning, and the rising sun suffusing his seaside vista with the glow of the new day were all working their magic on him just as he'd remembered, and had hoped they would again. He wondered if he could maybe just close his eyes and rest here for a little while before he did whatever else he'd end up doing today – and then he realized yes, of course he could if he wanted to, why on Earth not?

~ ~ ~

Now what was that boy doing hitchhiking in this day and age? There'd been a time when Ketch might have picked him up, and when he'd thumbed a few rides himself to get home from college for a weekend, but those days were long gone. This one couldn't be more than twelve, and his clothes didn't look clean. Ketch didn't stop.

After he'd passed the boy, he couldn't help but glance back one time in the rearview mirror. But he still didn't brake. No, it was simply too risky these days. He refocused on the road ahead and left Buxton, and the boy, behind.

This was one of his favorite stretches of Highway 12, the two-lane road that ran the fifty-odd-mile length of the island. The landscape from the outskirts of Buxton north to Avon was still almost pristine, and when he approached the haulover, an especially narrow part of the slender island where the old-time Hatterasmen had once hauled their wooden boats between the sound and the sea, he'd be able to see both Pamlico Sound to his left and the Atlantic to his right.

He wasn't enjoying this ride as much as he usually did, though, maybe because a part of him wanted to turn around and pick up that poor boy. There likely wouldn't be much traffic today, since the winter population here was only a small fraction of the summer one, and who knew what that kid's personal situation was and why he was hitching in the first place? Maybe he could legitimately use a lift. But helping folks like him was what Ketch liked to call an S.E.P. – Somebody Else's Problem. Weren't there government programs and charities and such for people like that? Ketch's pickup hadn't broken down and his dog hadn't died, but otherwise he was almost a walking country-song disaster himself. He didn't have the time or the energy to worry about everyone else.

But Jack was enjoying himself, ears up and snout poking out into the olfactory feast whizzing by his half-open window. It was so easy to please a dog, easier than people, and almost always more gratifying to boot. Dogs were inarguably more transparent than people.

They reached Rodanthe in a surprisingly short time, considering it was about five miles from Buxton to Avon, and then almost another twenty after that. And with some more unspoiled scenery in between, which Ketch didn't remember consciously noticing today, oddly enough. Too much daydreaming, he supposed.

The community building was on the sound side of Route 12, across the road from the Chicamacomico Lifesaving Station. The restored station was a museum now, commemorating the heroism of the nineteenth and early twentieth century surfmen of the U.S. Lifesaving Service, and later the Coast Guard, whose job it had been to rescue shipwreck victims from the treacherous waters of what became known as the Graveyard of the Atlantic. He wanted to spend some more time there, but not today.

He pulled his truck into the parking lot of the community building, found a place to park, and let Jack out. He hoped it would be all right to bring the dog in with him, as he didn't want to leave the poor guy in the truck. He supposed he shouldn't have brought him along, but he hadn't thought about that earlier. Though Jack was exceptionally well-behaved and it wasn't really necessary, Ketch leashed him to be on the safe side. He figured seeing the dog restrained would reassure any Nervous Nellies that the wild animal was under control, and Jack didn't seem to mind.

The building was a repurposed historic schoolhouse set atop short pilings that didn't look high enough to allow the building to ride out a major storm surge. Well, maybe they'd rebuild with more freeboard if and when. As Ketch made his way toward the building, he wondered if there'd be someone taking money for admission? He didn't recall reading about how one paid for one's food and drink at this event. But he soon saw someone sitting at a long folding table with what looked like a cashbox, so that would be the first roadblock he'd have to get the dog past.

The jovial matrons at the table didn't say anything about Jack, so he guided the dog toward the playground behind the building. He could see that some people were inside, but it looked like most of the action was out here. He figured those inside were probably involved in preparing supper, which if he recalled correctly from his reading would likely feature a traditional stewed chicken dish with pie-bread. He hadn't brought anything for Jack to eat, so he'd share some of that with the dog later.

There were, of course, oysters a-plenty as well, they being one of the centerpieces of the Old Christmas celebration (the other would make its appearance after supper). Ketch and Jack had fortuitously arrived at the conclusion of the afternoon's traditional oyster shoot adjacent to the playground, and the targets from the last of several rounds were now being judged to determine who'd receive the prize for this round, which was of course a bag of oysters. Ketch was glad Jack hadn't had to weather the afternoon's squalls of gunshots, another thing he hadn't thought of when he'd loaded the dog into his truck.

There were bushels of oysters in the process now of being roasted over a fire as well. As soon as a batch was ready, the mollusks would be shoveled – literally, as in with a large flat spade – onto wooden tables and the cycle would repeat, and the people would indulge to their hearts' content through the remainder of the afternoon and evening.

Ketch was also glad he'd worn a jacket over his light sweatshirt. His dashboard thermometer had read fifty-six the last time he'd looked at it, but it was still chilly out here near the sound, as evidenced by the heavier coats and flannels worn by the natives. It was said the blood thinned down South. Whether or not that was true, it was true that the long-term residents he'd encountered couldn't tolerate cold as well as he could. But he imagined that might change after he'd lived here for some time.

Ketch got a beer for himself and Jack a bottle of water, which he poured into a Solo cup for the dog to lap from. He'd never been particularly fond of oysters in the past, but he thought he might try one of those roasted ones later. The other revelers all seemed to be enjoying them. They also seemed to mostly know one another, which jived with what he'd read about Old Christmas being a time for family and friends to gather, rather than a religious occasion. He didn't know anyone here, and he hadn't even recognized anyone in passing so far. But he had Jack, which was all he thought he really needed.

It sounded like the band was tuning up inside, so he decided to take Jack in and have a look around. Again, no one challenged the two of them.

The main hall was tastefully decorated, with festive red streamers and tiny white lights strung throughout, and an old-timey band was indeed warming up on a stage at one end of the main hall. There was already a dessert table, and the kitchen workers were starting to set out the entrees as well. There were some other people milling around, but most were still outside. Ketch claimed a couple of the folding chairs that lined the walls of the room, left Jack leashed to one of them, and picked up two plates of stew.

The band began in earnest then, which was apparently a signal as more people started filing in from outside. There was suddenly a rapidly growing food line. He and Jack had gotten in just under the wire. Ketch decided to feed the dog and give him another drink before he went to work on his own plate.

He was just about to start eating when a woman pulled up a chair uncomfortably close to his own and purposefully dropped onto it. Jack didn't seem at all alarmed, and continued to lie on the floor next to Ketch where he'd decided to settle with his pleasantly full belly. In fact, he appeared to be having trouble keeping his eyes open. Ketch took his cue from the dog and tried to politely ignore the interloper – but then she spoke his name.

"Hello, Storm," she said, in a voice that was still familiar to him even after all this time. Ketch looked up in surprise and nearly dropped his plate.

"You know I hate that name," he automatically replied. Of all the things he could have said, why in the world had he said that? He set his plate back down on Jack's empty chair and rubbed at his eyes. When he opened them again, she was still there.

"What are *you* doing here?" he blurted, turning to face her.

"Oh, I just wanted to check on you and see how you're making out. I heard you were having some problems."

Ketch was flabbergasted at this. "How would you know anything about that," he said, "or anything about me at all? We haven't spoken in years!" About eight, to be more precise, and they'd gotten divorced before that. And they hadn't even lived in the same state after the divorce. "How did you know I'd be here? How did you get here?" he demanded in astonishment.

She smiled and ignored his questions. "So, you had something like a nervous breakdown, you retired early, and you decided to move here. I'm not surprised, I know you always loved coming here. And this, I take it, is your new therapist?" she asked, motioning to the now-slumbering dog. "How's that working for you? Are you drinking less now?"

"What?" Ketch spluttered, at a loss for words. Though the music was filling the room now, he'd heard everything she'd said quite clearly. And now he felt guilty about the cup of beer on the floor by his chair. The old anger he'd felt years ago started to rise to the surface again. How dare she?

She held up her hands. "I'm sorry. That didn't come out quite right, did it? I don't mean to criticize. That's not why I'm here."

Then why *was* she here? "Is Rollin all right?" he inquired, the anger abruptly replaced by concern. Ketch hadn't spoken with him, either, in almost all of those years.

"Oh, I'm sorry!" she said again. "I didn't mean to scare you. Don't worry, your son is fine."

Ketch breathed a sigh of relief. Then he defiantly picked up his cup and downed a healthy gulp. What did it matter what she might think about that?

"How was your Christmas this year, Ketch?" she gently asked. "Did you do anything special?" When he didn't answer right away, she answered for him. "No, you didn't. You were all alone on Christmas morning, just you and your dog. And I know you didn't go to church, and you didn't go to any parties, either, did you?" Ketch just shrugged. "Do you remember what Christmas was like years ago, when we were all still together? Here, let me help you remember." She pulled a small photo album from her purse and opened it facing him.

"Now, you wait just a minute," he started to protest. He needed to ask her something, but he didn't know quite how to put it. "Are you, er, deceased?"

She laughed. "You think I'm a ghost? Well, I'm not."

"Well, what are you then?"

"We were joined together once. I'll always be a part of you, whether you like it or not," she cryptically replied. "Now look, here's Rollin's first Christmas," she said, leafing through the album, "and his second, and here are some from the first one where he really understood what was going on. Do you remember that one?"

Ketch did remember – the joy and wonder on the boy's face, his trusting and guileless innocence, his delight at the decorations, the tree, the gifts, all of it. They'd annually made a pilgrimage to a tree farm and cut their own starting with that Christmas, for a while anyway. He remembered how the boy had looked forward to that, until Ketch had gotten too busy and decided it was too much bother.

"And look here, Ketch," she was saying. "Here are my parents, and your parents, and your friends – you used to have some back then – and some of Rollin's friends. They were important to him, you know, since he didn't have any brothers or sisters, and not even any cousins. But one is enough, and kids adjust when you make them move to new places, right Ketch?"

Ketch was finding it increasingly difficult to speak. This was getting downright hurtful. "Why are you doing this to me?" he finally managed to eke out.

"I was sorry to hear about your father passing last year, by the way," she went on. "And so soon after your mother. I always liked them." She flipped another page. "Look at these now. Do you notice anything odd about them?" Ketch obeyed, but he couldn't discern anything out of the ordinary. "You look happy in these pictures, Ketch. Do you know why? It's because after you take away the religious trappings of holidays like this, and the commercialism, what's left is family. And you were with your family."

"I have no family now," he croaked. "You took that away from me, in case you forgot."

"Is that what you think?" She cocked her head at him. "I had my faults, of course – but you didn't understand me, Ketch, and you didn't understand our son. You didn't know what we needed, because you didn't know what *you* needed. You were always working toward some future point in time when everything would align and your world would be perfect. You were waiting until then to allow yourself to be truly happy, and while you worked and waited, you pushed us farther and farther away."

He fidgeted uncomfortably in his seat. He didn't know

what to say.

"But Ketch," she continued, "the thing is, that time never comes. It's just a carrot that dangles in front of you, always out of reach, to make you keep racing. Instead of chasing that carrot, you need to make the most of each day as it comes."

He realized he couldn't argue with her. As painful as the admission was, he knew everything she was saying was true. He sighed, and she waited patiently for him to catch up.

"When did you get so wise?" he finally said, with a hint of a rueful smile.

She laughed again. "I don't know, but it sure took me long enough, didn't it?" Then she got serious again. "It can happen to you, too, Ketch, if you let it."

"Why did you come here?" he asked again.

"I wanted you to know some things," she answered, "before it's too late."

"Too late for what?"

She just smiled. "I wanted you to know that old wounds can be healed, you can make new friends, and family can be anyone if you let them know you well enough." She returned the album to her purse and glanced around the room. "I need to find the facilities. Go make a friend while I'm gone." She rose from her seat and placed a hand on his shoulder. "You can be happy again, Ketch," she said, and then she bustled off.

Somehow Ketch knew she wouldn't be coming back. He looked down at Jack and saw that the dog's eyes were now open. "Well, she's gone," he said. "Why didn't you say hello?" Jack's eyes started to close again. Say hello to whom, Ketch imagined he might have asked if he could talk.

It looked like some among the crowd in the hall were done eating and starting to dance. He finished his beer and decided to get another to wash his probably cold dinner down with. "I'll be right back, boy," he said to the dog. "You stay here and be good."

He left the dog leashed to the chair and wended his way through the dancers to the drink table. When he turned to leave the table, full cup in hand, a woman accidently jostled his elbow and made him spill some of his beer.

"Lordy, I am *so* sorry!" she exclaimed. "Are you okay? Did you get all wet?"

Ordinarily, her clumsiness might have annoyed him. But he felt different now than he had yesterday. "Oh, just my hand – and my sneakers, I think," he replied, looking himself over. He smiled at her. "But they'll live. They've seen worse."

"Well, you come on over here," she said, leading him to one end of the table, "and I'll get you some napkins and some more beer. There you go. You just stay put now, hear?" Ketch set his half-empty cup – or half-full, depending on one's outlook – on the table and shook some beer from his hand.

She returned shortly, with napkins and two more cups. "I got one for myself, too," she said. She set the cups down and passed him a wad of napkins. "Here you go. There's some wet wipes in there, too."

"Thank you," Ketch said.

"No, thank *you* for not rippin' me a new one!" She drank some of her beer while Ketch cleaned himself up. "So Ketch," she said when he was through, "are you on vacation again, or are you finally doin' the deed and stayin' here for good?"

Ketch was taken aback. How did she know his name, for starters? And what his plans were? He took a closer look at her. Slender but muscular, auburn pony tail, green eyes, mid-thirties maybe... He didn't know her name, but she did seem familiar to him.

"I'm sorry, but do I know you?" he asked.

"You stopped by my shop one time last year. The Sea

Dog Scuba Center, in Avon?"

She was right. He remembered the place now, a nondescript old wooden building just off the highway on the north end of town. But had he told her his name, or that he'd been thinking of moving to Avon?

"Oh, yes, I did stop there once," he said, and let the rest go for now. He also diplomatically refrained from mentioning that in past years he'd patronized a competitor of hers down in Hatteras village when he'd wanted to go diving.

"You know, you don't have to go all the way to Hatteras when you want to dive," she said, making him do another double-take. It was as if she'd read his mind. "I hooked up with a charter captain over at the Kinnakeet Boatyard. He's a good old boy. With just a twelve-pack and a compass, he'll take you anywhere he can!" She laughed at her own joke.

Ketch politely smiled, then said, "Well, I am in fact moving to Avon. I just arrived this week."

"No kiddin'! Where're you stayin' at?"

"I rented a place in Buxton until I can find a house to buy."

"Well hey, I live in Buxton! I have an apartment there."

"How about that?" Ketch picked up both of his cups. "Well, I brought my dog with me, and I should get back to him, so..."

"Oh, that's your dog over there? I have one, too, but he's back home. He's gettin' pretty old now, and he was too tired to come. So okay, let's go. Mind if I set with y'all? We ought to talk some more. I might could help you out."

There were more dancers out on the floor now, but they were able to make their way through the crowd without spilling any more beer. The dog acknowledged the presence of the woman this time, standing and wagging as they approached. Or was he just wagging at his master, Ketch wondered?

"Well hey there, you!" she said to the dog. "What's his name?"

"That's Jack."

"Hey, Jack! Good boy!"

They sat down, and she talked while Ketch ate. Jack lay next to Ketch again. He stayed awake this time, though, in case of a handout.

In short order, Ketch learned there was a house for sale on the sound near that old boatyard that might be just perfect for him, and that it was reasonably priced (relatively speaking, as waterfront property was never cheap these days). He also learned the winter hours for her shop in case he wanted to come by sometime, and a little more about the semi-retired captain who docked at the boatyard.

"But he hadn't got back from Florida yet, that I know of," she was saying. "He goes there in the winter and doesn't come back here 'til springtime, but I called him on Christmas and he said he was sailin' back early this year on account of some family thing he's got goin' on. He's got a condo in Hatteras. Anyway, I bet you and him would get on just fine."

"I imagine so," Ketch said, wiping his mouth.

"You know," she said, "Mama was kinda disappointed when you didn't show for Christmas dinner. But she made a right nice toast to you anyway."

"What?" he said. What was she talking about?

"Hey, you done eatin'?" she asked. Without waiting for an answer, she jumped up and said, "Come on, let's go outside and get some of those oysters. I could use some fresh air, and I bet Jack might could use a break, right? And I want to check on Timmy."

"Okay," he said, playing along and untying Jack's leash from his chair. It had certainly been a strange day so far. Could it get any stranger? "Come on boy, let's go out. Who's Timmy?" he asked on the way.

"Oh, he's that kid that was hitchin' out on 12 before. You know, the one you didn't stop for?" Ketch didn't know what to say to that. Had she been behind him on his way up here? "Well, I picked him up, and I'll take him back with me later on." It was dark now, and she stopped at a strategic vantage point to scan the grounds. "I hope he got himself somethin' to eat. I paid his way in."

"Why?" Ketch asked.

"'Cause it's Christmas, silly! Some folks aren't as fortunate as me'n you, you know. He lives with his grand-dad in an old shack down at the end of my road, and they don't have much. The old man fishes, mostly for mullet, and Timmy does what he can to help out. You might see him ridin' his pony sometime, lookin' for bottles and cans to turn in. He thought he might could pick up a bunch of 'em around here today."

"I guess I could have picked him up and helped him out," he said. He felt bad now about not having done so.

"Why? Aren't there programs and charities for folks like them?" she replied with just a hint of acid in her voice.

But that isn't enough, Ketch thought. "He sounds like Taffy," he observed.

"Huh? Who's that?"

"The main character in a novel for young readers, *Taffy of Torpedo Junction*. It's said to be a classic in these parts."

"Oh yeah, I read that, a long time ago."

"Isn't it dangerous for him to hitchhike? He couldn't be more than twelve, maybe even ten."

"I know he doesn't look it, but he's fourteen. But yeah, it's still dangerous, and I spoke to him about that. I called his grand-dad, too, to let him know what was goin' on. Oh, there he is. Hey Timmy!" The boy waved back, and they joined him at one of the oyster-covered tables.

"Timmy, this is Ketch," the woman said. "How'd you make out?"

"Pretty darn good, ma'am! I stuck two big bags in the

back of your car, like you said, next to your cooler. Here's your keys back. Nice to meet you, sir," the boy said. Ketch nodded at him.

"Thanks, Timmy," she said. "You locked it back up, right? Don't want somebody takin' my oysters!" she explained to Ketch.

"Why do you have oysters?" he asked.

"Oh, I won me a bag in the oyster shoot. Well, not exactly," she laughed. "I entered every round'n lost every dang one of 'em. But they felt sorry for me and gave me a bag anyway at the end, for effort I guess."

She'd been here for the oyster shoot? But that had been over with when he and Jack had arrived, and she had to have picked up the boy after he'd passed him by.

Before he could give that some more thought, his cell phone alerted him of an incoming message, a rare event for him these days. "Excuse me," he said, "I should probably see what this is." He stepped away from the table and left the woman and the boy to munch on roasted oysters.

The caller ID didn't say where the message had come from. And there was no text in the message, just some attached photos. He tapped on the icon and watched.

He pieced together the story from a progression of grainy black-and-white shots. It began with a rather startling and gruesome image. Someone had died in a grubby room somewhere, and from the looks of the body, it hadn't been found for some time. There was a dried-up Christmas wreath hanging on the wall. The police and a coroner were called and the body was transported to a morgue. After a cursory autopsy, the body was taken to a funeral home and cremated. The ashes were then scooped into a cardboard box, which was driven to a cemetery and buried without ceremony. There was no service of any kind, and there was no one at the grave but the workers. Finally, a simple wooden marker was stuck into the freshly turned ground.

There was a name on the marker, and two dates with a dash between them. He couldn't quite make them out, so he zoomed in on the marker. It was fuzzy, but now he could decipher the first date – which as it turned out happened to be his own birthday. The other date was past the edge of the screen. With a strong sense of foreboding, he scrolled up until the date was gone and he could see part of the name.

The first name of the deceased was 'Storm'. He blinked a couple of times and looked again, and it still read the same. He scrolled right far enough to see that the surname was indeed 'Ketchum'.

He felt as though he'd been punched in the chest. Was all this supposed to represent some future Christmas of his? If so, it was apparently a time when he was completely alone in the world, and there was no one at all to care whether he lived or died. Was this meant to be some kind of warning about what awaited him down the line if he didn't change his ways?

He resumed breathing. Who would send him something like this? And why? This was beyond cruel. He found himself tempted to scroll down to read the other date, but he decided to turn the phone off instead. Though it was probably just a prank, he didn't want to know, just in case.

There was some sort of commotion now over by the oyster tables. When he turned to see what was going on, he beheld a monstrous-looking apparition lurching along between the tables, occasionally bumping into them as well as any people who got in its way.

"It's Old Buck!" someone shouted. "Can't be, *I'm* Old Buck!" another voice called back. But it did indeed look like Old Buck, except that there appeared to be only one person under the blanket instead of the usual two Ketch remembered reading about. And this Old Buck was early, and he was in the wrong place.

Ketch knew about the legend of Old Buck, a bull that had purportedly come ashore from a shipwreck and run wild on the island back in the eighteen hundreds, when there'd been cattle here. In addition to terrorizing the island folk until he was finally shot, it was said that he'd impregnated every cow on the island during his rampage. His spirit was reputed to live on in Trent Woods, the southern end of Buxton Woods, and now he traditionally visits Rodanthe at Old Christmas each year – in the form of a bull skull on a wood frame supported by one or two men and covered with a blanket. The twenty-fifth was for Santa and church; today was Old Buck's day, and his appearance was the highlight of the celebration.

But if Ketch remembered right from his reading, Old Buck wasn't supposed to make his entrance until at least nine o'clock, and he was supposed to appear in the dance hall. Ketch watched until the legendary bull disappeared around the corner of the community building.

"The cash box, where's the cash box?" one of the women manning the cash table started demanding of anyone who'd listen. "It's gone, where is it?" she wailed.

Some of the men went to her, and some others ran around the corner of the building where Old Buck had last been seen. Those men returned with just the skull and the blanket.

Two Dare County sheriff's deputies had stationed themselves in the parking lot a while earlier, probably in case any brawls broke out, Ketch thought. After drinking all afternoon and into the evening, it had also become somewhat of a tradition at this event for some of the local fishermen to settle any differences they might have had during the previous year through fisticuffs. But there hadn't been any such occurrences so far today. The deputies briefly conferred with the people at the cash table, and then one returned to their cruiser and got on the radio while the other retraced the route the ersatz Old Buck had taken.

Timmy and the woman from the dive shop rejoined him then. Ketch still didn't know her name, and he kept forgetting to ask her for it.

"Somebody up and stole the cashbox," she said.

"So I heard," Ketch said. "I'm thinking it may have been two people working together. That Old Buck act was probably a diversion so the other one could make off with the cashbox."

"That's what they think, too. Hey, you're pretty good at this!"

"But who would do that?" Ketch asked. "I thought you pretty much all knew one another here."

"Yeah, we mostly do, but we always get some outsiders. Some folks come over from the mainland, and some drive down from up the beach."

"Has anyone driven anything out of here since this happened?"

"They don't think so, but the robbers could have parked a getaway car out by the road. They're gonna block off the lot for a while so nobody can leave. The sheriff's office is sendin' a cruiser down from Manteo to watch the bridge at Oregon Inlet, and they're gonna watch the ferry docks in Hatteras. Those are the only ways to drive off the island."

"Well, that won't help if they don't leave the island right away, or if they've got themselves a boat," Timmy contributed.

"That's true, Timmy," Ketch said. "But what if they didn't go anywhere? What if they're still here?"

"What do you mean?" the woman asked.

"Well, if I were the one trying to steal that box, I don't think I'd just run off with it. I could get caught that way. I'd probably hide it somewhere and come back for it later after everyone's gone, or at least wait until they gave up on looking for it. And if that's what's happening here," he mused, "the next question is, where might they have hidden it?"

"Well, I don't rightly know – but your dog might could find it," Timmy interjected.

"That's right!" the woman said. "I know he's not a police dog or a bloodhound, but you said he's real smart, right? Let's put him on the case!"

Had he said that? But it was true that Jack was probably the smartest dog he'd ever known. Ketch took his wallet out of his pocket.

"I don't think this will work," he said, "but I guess it's worth a try." He led Jack to the table the cashbox had rested on. The crowd there was dispersing, and no one questioned what they might be doing. The dog sniffed around the table some, and then Ketch pulled some bills from his wallet and let the dog sniff them as well.

"Now remember, we don't want to tip our hand, in case they're watching. Just act like we're taking Jack for a walk," Ketch directed the other two. Then he crouched by the dog. "Find it," he discreetly commanded him. "Find the money." He let the dog off the leash. "Go on, boy."

Jack seemed to understand what was expected of him. Nose to the ground, he meandered around the table for a minute or so, then set off on a deliberate path along the side of the building. Ketch wondered if the dog was tracking the scent of the money, or if he'd picked up on something else?

Ketch didn't think it would be possible to hide anything under the community building, especially if one were in a hurry. There wasn't that much space under the building, and the slats nailed across the pilings would preclude easy access to the crawlspace. Sure enough, Jack continued on past the building to a nearby structure that appeared to be some kind of gift shop. This building had more freeboard and no slats between its pilings. The dog ducked under the building, and a moment later Ketch heard him give a little yip.

"I think he found it!" Timmy stage-whispered. He wanted to go to the dog, but Ketch stopped him. He quietly called Jack back and leashed him.

"Good boy, Jack, good boy!" Ketch praised the dog. He scratched him behind both ears at the same time, something Ketch knew he especially enjoyed.

"But don't we want to go get that box?" Timmy asked.

"No," Ketch answered. "Keep walking."

"What are you up to, Ketch?" the woman asked.

"I think we should set a trap. Then we can return the money and catch the thieves as well."

Ketch led the group on around the perimeter of the community building, and laid out his plan while they walked. When they'd returned to their starting point, he sent Timmy back alone to verify what Jack had found under the building. In the meantime, he finally tried a roasted oyster. It wasn't bad, he decided, but nothing to write home about. He still preferred his shrimp and crab cakes.

When they next saw Timmy, Ketch could tell the boy was consciously working at controlling his excitement.

"It's there, all right!" he said. "Behind a pilin', under some sand and eel grass."

"Good work, Timmy," Ketch's other new friend said. That's right, he'd made not just one, as he'd been instructed, but two so far. Thinking of the pictures on his phone, he wondered if that would earn him any points.

"I'll go have a talk with the deputies," she continued. "I know one of 'em. Maybe they can get most of these people back inside and set up a little ole stakeout. Then maybe those robbers'll get cocky enough to go for that box."

Ketch, Jack, and Timmy went inside while she went off to speak with the deputies. "Did you get any supper?" he asked the boy.

"Yes sir, I did. But I hadn't made it to the dessert table

yet."

"Well then, let's go check that out and see what they have," Ketch said with a smile. The boy still looked only about as clean as he had out on the road earlier, but there was more to him than met the eye, Ketch now knew. He found he was pleased rather than embarrassed by the boy tagging along with him.

The woman rejoined them after they'd found a place to sit, carrying two more cups of beer and a soft drink. "Well, it's all set. Now we just have to wait," she said.

They ate and drank and talked as the hall filled with people. There were more dancers now than ever, and Ketch was glad he'd found their seats when he had. He was also relieved that the woman didn't seem interested in dancing, something he wasn't especially fond of doing himself.

It wasn't too much longer before they were approached by two men, one of the deputies and someone from the staff of the community building. The scoundrels who'd hidden the cashbox had indeed gotten cocky, and they were now in custody.

"Thank you so much!" the staffer said to the woman. "Is there anything we can do for you in return? You want some oysters to take home?"

"Oh, I didn't do much," she said. "It was Ketch had the idea of the box bein' hidden, and to set that trap. Besides, I already got me a bag of oysters at the shoot."

"Well, how about a bag for me, and one of those delicious pies?" Ketch said. "And two chicken stews to go?" He stopped then, his face reddening. "I'm sorry, is that too much?"

The staffer laughed. "Surely not, it's the least we can do! I'll have somebody box up that pie and stew for you, and I'll send word down that you'll be pickin' up some oysters."

"And then I think I should get Timmy on home," the

woman said.

"But you're gonna miss Old Buck, then," the staffer warned.

"Oh well! Been there, done that," she laughed. Timmy went off with the staffer, so he could carry the box back. When he was out of earshot, the woman regarded Ketch with a new kind of interest.

"I thought you said you didn't like pecan pie," she said. "Nor those oysters all that much neither."

"Timmy and his grandfather will like them. It's all going to their place, if you don't mind carting it there for me."

"I thought so," she said, "and I don't mind one bit. It'll make a fine Sunday dinner for them, a lot finer than they're used to." She looked up at him approvingly. "So, you gonna stay for Old Buck? The real one, I mean?"

"Yes, I think I will. I haven't been there and done that yet."

"All right then. Say, seems like you might be good at solvin' mysteries," she said with a twinkle in her eye. "You ever thought about bein' a private eye? Since you're retired now, you could hang a shingle and see what happens. It'd give you somethin' to do."

Well, he didn't know about that. And had he said he was retired? He didn't think so.

"Anyway, here comes Timmy now. Hey, don't be a stranger, hear? Come on by the shop sometime. And don't forget to bring my Jacky-boy!" she smiled.

"I will, I promise," he said, and meant it.

After she and Timmy had left, he sat back down, drew the dog to him, and gave him a big hug. "You're the best dog I ever had," he told him – which Jack apparently appreciated, as he started licking the man's face and ears and neck, and kept licking, and licking...

~ ~ ~

And licking, though it was actually Ketch's hand and arm. He woke with a start and sat up straight in the rocking chair.

"Jack?" he said. He looked around in puzzlement at the initially unfamiliar landscape that surrounded him. The sun was fully up now, but he could tell it was still early. He must have dozed off for a little while.

"What is it, boy? Was I talking in my sleep? It's okay, I'm okay now." He petted and reassured the dog, settled back in the rocker, and tried to think.

Though it was already dissipating, as his dreams always did, he focused hard and managed to retain considerably more of it than he was typically able to before it could completely slip away – enough to acknowledge that he'd probably owe Dickens a nod if the man were still living. And enough to be reminded and cognizant of the spirits' lesson therein.

This one had been a dilly, for sure. Was Timmy real, he wondered? His ex-wife, of course, was a real person, and so was that woman from the dive shop. He'd stopped in there once a while back, and he remembered seeing her there. Well, if he ever did encounter a boy like that around here, he resolved to not just arbitrarily ignore him as he might have before. In fact, if he saw anyone like that up in Rodanthe later, he might pay their way in to the Old Christmas celebration if it looked like they needed someone to.

Ketch rose from the chair and stretched, then went back inside the cottage to the kitchen. He bagged all the liquor bottles but one and tossed them in the big black trash barrel outside. Now that he was finally where his soul had longed to be, it wouldn't do to drink that away. He kept the few beers that remained, though, and a lone bottle of tequila, in case he got in a parrothead mood sometime. He didn't think he needed to get *too* monkish.

Then he went to the bathroom to shave and shower. Yes, he and Jack would drive up to Rodanthe today after all, so he guessed he should try to look presentable.

He realized he didn't really want to lead the solitary life of a monk or hermit. As Mister Buffett had once sung about a friend of his, some of it was magic and some of it was tragic, but he'd had a good life at one time and it could be good again. Although this particular pirate was looking at fifty-five rather than forty, he decided to take the view from now on that any day he wasn't six feet under was a good day.

When they were ready to head out, he thought maybe they'd drop by that pleasantly bohemian boatyard first and see if there was anyone around who might want to join them in Rodanthe. That place was real, too, and he knew where it was, and he'd spoken to a couple of people there in the past. And while he was in that neighborhood, he could take a quick look around and see if there happened to be a soundfront house for sale somewhere around there. That would be something, if there was, though he wasn't superstitious enough to think it would mean anything.

All told, it might not seem like much to most. But it was a plan, and it was what he could do today. And it was a start.

THE SAD BLUE BOAT

DESCRIPTION

In Storm Ketchum Tale #2, Ketch's Sunday morning hike is enlivened by the discovery of a modern-day shipwreck on the beach.

It appears to be a refugee boat, a rare occurrence in these parts, but there's no one on it. Where did it come from? Were there people on the boat, or is it just a derelict? And if there were people on the boat, what happened to them?

Join amateur sleuth Storm 'Ketch' Ketchum and his loyal dog Jack as they uncover the mystery behind the sad blue boat on historic Hatteras Island, where intrigue always seems to be just around the next corner.

NOTE: The Kinnakeet Boatyard is a fictitious setting.

April 2011

Ketch rose from the hammock on the side deck with a sigh of self-satisfaction. It had been a long time coming, but he was finally here, in his favorite place on Earth – and for good this time. That still hadn't quite sunk in yet, he didn't think, even though he'd been in this house for exactly one year today.

He couldn't see the sun break over the eastern horizon from this location. The house was soundfront and not tall enough for that, being basically just a four-room bungalow on stilts with enough freeboard to park a car under. But though the sunsets here on the sound side of the island were the gaudier of the two, the sunrises held their own charm. He didn't need to be at the beach to appreciate the nascent light of the new day as it crept across his allocated part of the sky and the still water of the sound, stealthily permeating the surrounding landscape.

Over the past year, weather permitting, he'd gotten into the habit of waking before sunrise and watching it happen while he half-dozed in the hammock that had come with the house. Though he now did it by choice, it was actually a continuation of a routine that had been forced on him when he'd holed up in a Buxton rental while house-hunting here in Avon. Apparently quite a few of the locals there kept chickens, and the crowing of the roosters had woken Jack at the crack of dawn every day – and thus Ketch, since the dog had then needed to go out.

He'd come to enjoy doing it, though, and the feeling it gave him that he was getting a jump-start on the day ahead. But they were nearing the end of April now, and it wouldn't be too much longer before the mosquitoes came out in force. It would be nice if he didn't have to spray himself with Skeeter Beater every morning this summer. He resolved to make screening in this side deck his project for the coming week. Since he was retired now, he could do things like that whenever he chose – and since he was only fifty-six, he was still physically able to do them.

He was also alone and obligated to no one. That still rankled some from time to time, but he'd learned to deal with it over the years and it wasn't on his mind this morning. And he wasn't completely alone. Suffused with good will, he fed the last piece of the buttered bagel he'd brought outside with him to Jack, who'd been snoozing on the deck next to the hammock.

The three-year-old hound mix had been with Ketch for a little over a year and a half now. He couldn't have asked for a better dog. Since he'd been past the puppy stage when Ketch had picked him out at the shelter back North, he hadn't even had to housebreak him. The faithful canine had quickly become Ketch's best friend, filling a void in his life and helping him stay anchored in reality.

"Well, boy," he said to the dog, "we'd better get going. Would you like to go to the beach this morning?" Ears at attention, Jack wagged and gave a yip of assent. Playing in the back yard and the sound was fun, but the beach was better. "Okay then, let's go in and get ready."

The dog knew that meant a little bathroom time (though not much, since Ketch only occasionally had to trim his closely cropped beard and he'd just done it yesterday), and then a getting-dressed time, and then a backpack-filling time. Since he'd already eaten his breakfast, Jack curled up on a throw rug in front of the fireplace in the living room to patiently wait out these events. Although they weren't using it much anymore, the fireplace was still his favorite spot in the house.

When Ketch started loading the canvas backpack he always carried on their outings, Jack got up and stretched and went to the front door. Ketch shortly joined him there and they headed out to the truck.

Ketch paused along the way to straighten the life preserver he'd hung on one of the porch posts by the front steps when he'd decided on the new name for the house. A remnant of Hatteras Island's blustery winter winds must have blown the ring askew during the night. Maybe he'd slept through a storm – though that would be unusual for him, and Jack would have been restless in that case as well. It didn't look like it had rained here, but there could have been a storm at sea that had generated some winds.

He backed away and critically eyed the preserver. It looked straight now, but the words 'PORT STARBIRD' that he'd crudely painted in red on the white ring last summer had been faded by the sun and sandblasted by the wind since then and could use some touching up. Another little project to take care of some Saturday – which was every day now, to him. Though he was aware that today was actually Sunday, that fact didn't have any special significance for him.

Ketch held the driver's door open for Jack, who lithely jumped up onto the seat, hopped over the center console, and took his customary place by the passenger window. Ketch tossed the backpack onto the back bench, started the truck, and lowered the dog's window so his friend could ride with his head out to savor the upcoming mobile olfactory feast. He cranked his own window down as well. A dose of salt air in the morning was good for the soul. Well, for his anyway.

"Okay buddy, off we go," he said, putting the truck in gear. "We're going to Buxton today, just so you know." And the furry fellow probably did know now, Ketch thought. He'd developed an impressive listening vocabulary, for a dog, during his time with Ketch.

Ketch could have taken him to a beach access ramp he knew of just north of the outskirts of town, and hence closer to where they lived, but he'd decided on the lighthouse beach instead. They could hike along the shoreline to Cape Point from there, if Jack was up for it. Buxton was only about five miles south of Avon and it was still cool enough for hiking at this time of year, especially this early in the morning.

They drove slowly down North End Road, then turned onto Harbor Road. There was no need to rush and Ketch always enjoyed the passing scenery in this part of town. The houses here, while well-kept, were older and less glitzy than the modern developments that had sprung up elsewhere around town in recent decades.

Avon was still a small town and was nowhere near as developed as the northern towns like Nags Head up the beach, due to the mostly fortunate intervention of the National Park Service. The establishment of the Cape Hatteras National Seashore, which extended from Bodie Island south through Hatteras Island and then Ocracoke Island, prevented development outside of the few existing small island communities, but new construction seemingly everywhere it was allowed had still radically changed the faces of this town and the others, too. Today's Avon looked almost nothing like it had when Ketch had first started visiting the island back in the late Seventies, except for here in the old Avon Village (or Kinnakeet, as it had originally been known).

That was why it was his favorite part of town, and why he'd only house-hunted here. It saddened him to know that most folks who visited Avon were completely unaware of the existence of the old village and its historic harbor, though Avon Harbor had once been the nucleus of the village and was still the source of the freshest and cheapest seafood in town. They didn't know about the harbor's resident pelicans, its generations-old population of feral cats, and its incredible views of the sunsets over the sound. Located at the sound end of Harbor Road, it wasn't that far off the highway and wasn't too hard to find. But then again, maybe it was a good thing this area didn't attract more attention.

When they reached the traffic light (the first of the two

that Avon now sported in these modern times), Ketch rolled the dog's window halfway up. Highway 12, the only one on the island, was just a two-laner. But traffic would soon force them to pick up their pace, especially after the second light at the south end of town, and that much wind wouldn't be good for Jack's eyes and ears. He could still stick his nose out, though.

They headed south out of Avon on a largely pristine stretch of highway, with the Atlantic dunes alongside them on their left and Pamlico Sound a stone's throw to their right. They passed the haulover, where the Hatterasmen of old had manually hauled their primitive fishing boats between the ocean and the sound. Then came Canadian Hole, a favorite spot on the sound for wind sports. Too soon for Ketch, they entered Buxton and turned onto Lighthouse Road. Bypassing the iconic Cape Hatteras Lighthouse, they diverted to the parking lot that bordered the public beach.

There was only a handful of other vehicles in the lot – early beachcombers or surfers, most likely, and perhaps a surf caster or two. None of the vehicles were running, so Ketch didn't leash Jack when he let him out of the truck. Dogs were allowed on the beaches of the National Seashore, though technically they were supposed to be leashed.

But Jack was obedient enough to be trusted and Ketch knew he wouldn't bother anyone or anything he wasn't supposed to, including any designated sea turtle or seabird nesting sites, God forbid. Ketch had heard that the NPS had started to protect what it arbitrarily considered to be threatened species more militantly in recent years, perhaps excessively so at times, and running afoul of the park rangers could prove costly. Jack immediately began wandering and investigating, but stayed within what he'd learned was Ketch's preferred range.

As he walked past the parked cars, Ketch belatedly

noticed that one of them was a Dare County Sheriff's cruiser. He wondered if something out of the ordinary might be happening on the beach this morning. If so, perhaps he should leash Jack after all, just in case.

"Jack, come!" he called. The dog appeared surprised at the sudden command, but he left off what he was doing and dutifully returned to Ketch. "Good boy," Ketch said as he hooked him up. "Looks like something's going on out there this morning. Let's go see what it is."

They quickly passed between the dunes and onto the beach, Jack vigilant at Ketch's side. He steered the dog toward a small knot of people down at the shoreline. He had to squint against the bright early morning sun despite his shades to determine that there was a small boat at the water's edge, its bow wedged in the sand.

As they got closer, he learned from the burgeoning hubbub of conversation that some beachcombers had discovered the boat earlier this morning, and that it had been unoccupied.

"Probably refugees from somewhere," somebody said. "Wonder where they done got to then?" someone else asked. "There's some gas cans in there, but there's no outboard," another remarked. "And no mast and no sail, so I don't see how anyone could have gotten anywhere with it. Maybe it's just a derelict."

"Well, my station just got off the horn with the Coast Guard, " the deputy said. "They don't know anything about it."

"Why would they?" one of the onlookers asked. "If they'd found it at sea, they'd have rescued it and whoever was on it, wouldn't they?"

"Not always. If they catch refugees at sea, they usually pick 'em up and send 'em back to where they came from, and they mark the vessel as interdicted and set 'er adrift."

"Really? Are you serious? That's cruel!" a woman in the crowd protested. Ketch knew that such refugees weren't always deported, but to avoid it they had to present an acceptable case for persecution in their homeland and apply for political asylum. But it looked like even that tenuous strand of hope hadn't been in the cards for whoever had been aboard this boat.

"I don't see no markin's t'all anywhere on 'er," a man observed, "but there's some kinda paddle."

So maybe they'd managed to paddle in to the beach... Or maybe there *had* been a storm out there and the boat had been blown ashore. Either way, where were the people now? Had they been lost at sea? That was unfortunately often the case when a non-interdicted craft like this ended up here.

And where had the boat hailed from? Most likely Cuba, Ketch figured, though he knew Haitian refugees were almost as common, at least in Florida. If this was a refugee boat, it must have been carried by the Gulf Stream considerably farther north than originally intended, perhaps after losing its engine if there'd been one.

He didn't know any of the people on the beach, so Ketch ignored the ongoing conversation in front of him and focused on examining the boat as closely as possible from his current vantage point at the back of the group. It appeared to be about a twenty-footer or so constructed entirely of wood, including a small makeshift covered bridge-slash-cabin that looked like it had been cobbled together from scrap.

The boat was obviously old, and what remained of the hull's blue paint was peeling where it wasn't gone entirely. It had apparently been painted white before the blue, a long time before from the look of things, and there was bare wood showing where some of the white had worn away as well. The mostly plywood cabin was unpainted and mildewed, and its cutout windows were glassless.

Ketch moved back a bit to a patch of the beach that was elevated enough to allow him to see over the gunwales. In addition to the gas cans, he could also see some empty plastic jugs, a couple of life jackets, and a trash bag. The boat had a square-ended stern, and he could see that part of the transom was missing and the planking there was splintered and stained. There probably had been an outboard engine of some kind, and the wood must have been too rotten to hold it in place. It had likely vibrated itself loose at some point during the journey. So this boat had been a 'chug', a motorized vessel in Coast Guard parlance, before it had become a derelict.

A wooden boat, and probably a fishing boat, originally – but wooden fishing boats of any size were an anomaly here these days, at least in his experience. Building boats from local timber had been one of the main occupations of the old-time islanders, but the only wooden boats Ketch had ever seen around these parts other than small skiffs and rowboats had been either lovingly restored classics, or flotsam in a museum or rural yard. Even the old Whaler Montauk he'd recently picked up for potting around in the sound was made of foam-cored fiberglass. He reminded himself that he needed to come up with a good name for her soon.

Ketch knew this had happened occasionally in the past. Every now and then some seagoing raft or boat jury-rigged from homespun materials such as barrels, tires, and tarps would wash ashore here, though with nothing like the frequency that Florida saw. And as far as he knew, they'd always been unoccupied when they'd ended up here. This boat was several steps above those others, though, in quality and reliability.

He realized this was not only his first refugee boat, but his first shipwreck as well – that is, the first time he'd personally seen a boat of any kind foundering in the surf, despite this island's long history of shipwrecks. If they'd been living in the nineteenth century or early twentieth instead of the twenty-first, the people gathered here this morning might be trying to work out salvage rights.

'Wrecking', or salvaging shipwrecks, had been another occupation of the islanders at one time, back when shipwrecks had been much more common here. Treacherous conditions created by the confluence of the warm Gulf Stream from the south and the colder Labrador Current from the north had earned this part of North Carolina's Outer Banks the moniker 'Graveyard of the Atlantic'. With the advent of modern weather forecasting and navigational aids, shipwrecks nowadays were few and far between – but back in the day, the frequent shipwrecks had been major events, sometimes akin to the contents of a modern-day department store washing up on the beach, and some folks had made their fortunes through wrecking.

No one's fortune would be made here today, though, not from this sad old tub. And it *was* sad. Sad that it had outlived its use, whatever that had been in its younger days, and was now just an anachronistic old wreck on the beach... Sad that it had seemingly failed at its final mission, whatever that had been... Sad that, if it had carried refugees, they'd been desperate enough to trust this aged and diminutive hulk with their lives out on the vast open sea in hopes of a better life in a new place... Sad enough all around to dampen Ketch's formerly buoyant mood. Aware that he himself was aging as well, and having already failed at some missions of his own, Ketch felt an unwelcome kinship with the unfortunate relic.

Well, at least she'd ended up in an appropriate place, he thought. The Diamond Shoals off Cape Point had been especially notorious back in the wrecking days, as that was where those major ocean currents actually met – and Ketch was standing pretty much square in front of them right now, where North met South, and South met North. Maybe that was one of the reasons he felt drawn to this place, he reflected, this unique spot thirty miles out to sea where North and South came together, like he himself and the island he loved...

A sudden yank on the leash broke Ketch's reverie. Jack looked back at him apologetically, then put his nose back to the ground and resumed straining against the leash. When Ketch failed to respond immediately, the dog looked back again and yipped at him. Realizing Jack wanted him to follow for some reason, Ketch started walking, letting the dog lead the way.

They exited the beach and returned to the parking lot. Did the dog want to go home already? When Jack led him past their truck without even glancing at it, Ketch knew the answer to *that* question. Well, where were they going then, and why, he wondered?

Ketch tried to apply the brakes when Jack wanted to cross Lighthouse Road, but the dog insisted on extending the retractable leash to its maximum length and continuing forward. Ketch acquiesced and finally, about a half-mile from where the boat had washed ashore, they came to the edge of the Buxton Woods Coastal Reserve. This time, Ketch did make the dog stop.

"No, we can't go in there today, boy," Ketch told him. He faithfully administered an effective flea and tick repellent to Jack once a month, but he himself was only wearing shorts this morning – which, since there was no cleared path at this spot, would expose *him* to ticks – and sandals, which wouldn't be any help if he accidentally stepped on a cottonmouth. "What are you after, anyway? Come on now, let's go." But when he tugged on the leash, Jack sat down and refused to budge. Then he barked at Ketch.

This was unusual. Jack didn't normally argue with Ketch, nor disobey this willfully. But rather than attempt to discipline him, Ketch gave in. He'd had several dogs in his lifetime, and one thing he'd learned along the way was to take them seriously when they felt strongly about something. Like the time back North years ago when a rare tornado warning had been issued and his dog had been hell-bent on spending the night in the basement. Ketch had joined him there – and though nothing had happened to their house, he'd heard on the news the next day that a small twister had touched down nearby and damaged a couple of homes.

What *was* the dog after, and why was he being so obstinate about pursuing it? Ketch knew there was a surprising variety of wildlife in these woods, including some species that were virtually unheard of on most barrier islands. Maybe a fox or raccoon had wandered near the boat in the wee hours before the boat had been discovered – or could it be that one or more occupants of the beached boat had made their way inland?

But if so, why would they try to hide in the woods? If there were refugees and they were Cuban, they'd likely be aware of the U.S. government's 'wet foot, dry foot' policy. If Cuban refugees were caught at sea or while wading to shore, back they went – but if they made it onto dry land, they could stay. Ketch didn't know what the policy was for Haitians or other nationalities, though.

Fortunately, Jack didn't plunge directly into the woods when Ketch again gave him free rein. He instead sniffed furiously back and forth along the edge of the woods for a while, taking full advantage of the extendable leash, and finally settled at a spot a little farther along. When he caught up with the dog, Ketch was relieved to see that there was a narrow path into the woods there. It wasn't one he was familiar with, nor was it one of the documented entry points to the reserve, but it should be at least marginally better than lumbering through possibly tick-infested bush.

It was obvious that the dog wanted to follow the path, but Ketch again hesitated. Buxton Woods was the largest remaining stand of maritime forest on the Outer Banks, and though you'd eventually come out somewhere if you kept walking in the same direction, it might not be until you got to Frisco miles later, and you could get lost in there. But he again gave in to the dog.

He didn't release Jack from the leash, because he didn't want the dog to range too far ahead and lose his way in the woods – though when he thought it through, Ketch realized that with his super sniffer, Jack was less likely to get lost than his master. Still, he didn't want to lose track of the dog.

They continued on down the path, with Ketch trying to stay in its center and away from the brush that bordered it. After a few minutes more tracking by the dog, they came to a marshy area near one of the small ponds that dotted the woods. Jack stopped at that point, apparently uncertain of where to go next. The ground was wetter here, and Ketch figured that might have caused the dog to lose whatever scent he'd been onto.

As they both stood there trying to figure out what to do next, some noises from behind a nearby stand of salt-twisted live oaks put them both on high alert. It sounded like something was trying to move quickly and clumsily over boggy ground and through some brush. Ketch was glad he hadn't let Jack off the leash, since the dog's instincts probably would have kicked in and he would have taken off after it, whatever 'it' was. There were some deer in these woods, Ketch knew, and they could be dangerous to a dog if they decided to stand their ground instead of running away. But they didn't generally make that much of a racket.

There was also a generations-old legend of alligators in these woods, though it was entirely based on anecdotal evidence. There was to this day no known photographic or video evidence to verify the reptile's presence here – but since he and Jack were near water, Ketch fished his cell phone out of its belt holster just in case and activated its camera.

And then he put it away. If it was an alligator, he

decided the sensible thing to do would be to turn around and head back the way they'd come. And it suddenly occurred to him that if there were in fact people from the boat hiding in these woods for some reason, perhaps it was because they were terrorists or some other kind of criminal.

He started retracting the leash and pulling Jack back toward his position, but stopped when he heard voices. Jack heard them, too, of course, and he began to strain at the leash again in response. Though the voices were subdued, Ketch could tell that there were two of them – and after another moment, that they sounded like children.

He couldn't make out what they were saying, and he soon realized that was because they weren't speaking English. Before he could learn more, Jack barked and the voices went silent.

Ketch decided to give Jack his lead again, but he kept him close as the dog pulled him off the path and toward the trees. He tried to watch his step as he went, which wasn't easy as Jack was eager to finally reach the object of his search. But if there were any snakes around, Ketch thought, they were probably fleeing the scene. Despite what those who unreasonably fear them believe, snakes generally try to avoid unnecessary and potentially risky confrontations, as do most wild animals. As long as they didn't directly tromp on one, they should be okay.

They made it to the stand without mishap. Jack then directed Ketch toward a nearby thicket, where he could see what appeared to be a mound covered by a damp blanket, beneath which some whispers and an occasional fidget were occurring.

"Hello?" Ketch called, and Jack barked again. He allowed Jack to extend on the leash, and the wagging dog went to the mound and began pawing the blanket to uncover what was sitting under it. Two young faces were shortly exposed, despite their best efforts to remain hidden. Jack's entire body was wagging now, and his mouth was open wide in a big doggy grin.

"*Av, smotret', a shchenok! Idi syuda, shchenok*," said a small boy with messy blond hair.

"Sergey! *Net*!" his companion exclaimed, jumping to her feet. Her long blond hair flying, she quickly reached behind her for a hefty stick she'd apparently picked up for self-defense. She didn't try to hit Jack with it, but rather brandished it at Ketch, her eyes wide with fear.

She appeared to be somewhat older than the boy, and it looked to Ketch like she meant business. She glanced down uncertainly as the dog licked the boy's face while the boy put his arms around the animal. Then her gaze returned to Ketch and she said, "*Ostat'sya nazad*!" in an authoritative tone, swinging the stick through the air like a baseball bat for emphasis.

Ketch set the leash reel down on the ground and raised both hands as though in surrender. "It's okay," he said, "we won't hurt you. Do you speak English?" The girl stood her ground and regarded him quizzically. "English?" he repeated, but again she didn't answer.

He wondered what language or languages they *did* speak, if not English. He knew that *net* ('nyet'), the only word he'd understood so far, was Russian for 'no'. But if they'd come here from Cuba, maybe they knew some Spanish – though that wouldn't help him much at the moment, as his knowledge of that language was almost as sparse as it was with Russian.

But he thought he should check anyway. "*Espanol*?" he asked. Still no response. A few years ago (quite a few, actually) he'd traveled to Moscow one time on business in his former life, and to help pass the time on the interminable journey he'd memorized some key Russian words and phrases from a guidebook. He'd have to struggle mightily to retrieve them after all this time, but it was the best he could do right now.

"*Angliyskiy*?" he inquired, recalling the Russian word for 'English'.

"*Net*," the girl said, shaking her head. "*Russkiy*."

So it would definitely have to be Russian, then. Ketch couldn't remember how to ask if he could help, but he did manage to come up with the word for 'help'. If he added inflection to it, that should suffice.

"*Pomogite*?" He belatedly noticed that the children's lips looked parched and cracked, despite a nearly full bucket he now saw resting on the ground behind the boy, next to three cinched duffel bags. Maybe they'd gone to the pond for water – and though he knew there were some freshwater ponds in these woods, perhaps this one was brackish. He had bottled spring water in his backpack. He tried to think – 'water', 'drink'...

'Drink', he could do. "*Napitok*?" That piqued the interest of both kids, though the girl still looked suspicious. Ketch finally remembered to smile as he took off his backpack, crouched, and pulled out a couple of liter bottles. They were still cool to the touch. He set them on the ground, stood up, and moved back away from them.

Jack was now sniffing around the girl. He was still wagging and thus apparently not a threat, so she ignored him in favor of keeping her eyes on Ketch. She warily advanced, picked up the bottles, and retreated to her original position. She passed one to the boy, then set her stick down and opened the other for herself – watching Ketch all the while. With her eyes still fixed on him, she took a long and obviously satisfying pull from her bottle.

"*Akh*," she said. "*Spasibo*."

"You're welcome," Ketch replied, still smiling. He couldn't remember how to say that in Russian.

"*Gde my*?" she then asked. When she saw that Ketch didn't understand, she spread her arms wide and looked left and right.

Ketch figured she must be asking where they were. "Hatteras Island," he said. When that didn't seem to mean anything to her, he said, "Ameereeca," pronouncing it the Russian way to be sure she got it.

"*Akh, Amerika,*" she said, relieved. "*My sdelali eto,* Sergey."

"*Amerika*!" the boy exclaimed with a tired grin. "*Ura*!" Though he couldn't have any idea what they were saying, Jack caught the mood and joined in the celebration by licking the boy's face again, and then the girl's free hand.

Ketch decided it was time for introductions. "Jack," he said, pointing at the dog. And then, "Ketch," pointing to himself (not 'Storm', since he'd always disliked that name).

"Jack, Ketch," the kids parroted. Then the girl said, "Svetlana," and, pointing at the boy, added, "Sergey."

Ketch repeated their names aloud ('Svyetlana', 'Syergyey'), smiling at each child in turn. He didn't know how to say 'pleased to meet you', so he settled for a simple 'hello'.

"*Zdravstvuyte.*" It occurred to him then that they might be hungry as well as thirsty. The decent, and to him 'American', thing to do would be to take them somewhere to feed them, if he could convince them to accompany him. Logically speaking, they'd have to eventually go someplace other than here, so they should cooperate – he hoped. And then what, after they'd eaten? Well, he'd worry about that later.

"*Pitaniye*?" he asked, 'food' being the only relevant word he remembered how to translate. He slipped his backpack onto his shoulders with what he hoped was a sympathetic smile and picked up Jack's leash. "*Pitaniye,*" he repeated, motioning for the girl to follow him.

She looked uncertainly at the boy, who then left off petting Jack and stood up. "*Ya goloden,* 'Lana. *Poydem*!" Though Ketch didn't know the words, it sounded to him like Sergey was ready to go. Ketch watched as the girl considered and made her decision.

"*Khorosho, zabrat' svoy meshok,*" she said to the boy, "*I odeyalo.*" Sergey immediately picked up the blanket and one of the duffels and slung them both over his shoulders, hobo-style. Svetlana took the other two duffels. The kids pocketed their water bottles in their cargo pants, and they were on their way.

Though they dragged a bit now and then, the children followed dutifully behind Ketch as Jack led them all back to the truck. They must indeed be tired and hungry, Ketch thought. He noticed that Svetlana had left her stick behind. That was a good sign.

As they approached the parking lot, Ketch saw that the deputy's cruiser was still there. He knew he could easily avoid further entanglement and inconvenience by handing the kids over to the authorities right here and now, but he didn't want to turn them in – not just yet, anyway. They should be given a chance to get themselves back on track before that happened. But it *would* have to happen sooner or later, he knew. They couldn't just remain undocumented aliens. But he felt he had to at least help make them comfortable first, by feeding them and giving them a chance to get cleaned up and recuperate from their ordeal. Who knew when all that might happen if government bureaucracy got into the mix at this point?

And they could stand some cleaning up. He wondered where he could take them, looking the way they did. Their clothing appeared to be mostly dry, but their shirts were stained with sweat and salt, their faces and hands were dirty, and their hair needed washing.

He didn't have much to offer them at the house, as he'd been procrastinating with the grocery shopping of late, and there were no drive-through fast-food burger joints anywhere in all seven villages on this island, not even a McDonald's. It was one of the things he ordinarily appreciated about this laid-back, simpler place, where despite the summer tourist traffic one could still 'live the salt life' at one's own pace. There was a Dairy Queen in Avon that had a drive-through, but he knew that particular franchise served only hot dogs and ice cream, and not this early in the day anyway. There was also a Subway, but it was probably not open yet, either, and it didn't have a drive-through.

In fact, most of the restaurants between Avon and Frisco wouldn't be open yet, as they only served lunch and dinner, and sometimes only dinner. There weren't too many places within reasonable driving distance that served breakfast. There was Sonny's down in Hatteras, which was an informal kind of place, but he didn't want to go that far. The Gingerbread House in Frisco and the Froggy Dog in Avon offered breakfast, but he didn't know how they'd take to him bringing in what appeared to be a couple of street urchins. But he didn't want to drag the poor kids around Conner's grocery or the Food Lion, nor leave them in the truck while he shopped...

An exceptionally vivid dream he'd had early last year on Old Christmas day came to mind. In the dream, he'd initially forsaken a bedraggled boy who'd been down on his luck like these two here, only to learn later that one shouldn't judge a book by its cover. And he remembered now one of the resolutions he'd made in the aftermath of that unsettling dream.

That settled it. He wouldn't hold the downtrodden look of these unfortunate kids against them and let it interfere with anything. And he wouldn't allow anyone else to, either. He'd take them to the Froggy Dog and get them a decent meal, appearances be damned. It was close to home, and he knew the owner – and he remembered that Tatyana worked there.

She was one of the numerous and largely Eastern European foreigners who came to Hatteras Island as temp workers each year, mostly in the summer when the restaurants and shops couldn't find enough local help to cover them in the height of the tourist season. Some were itinerant wind worshippers (kiteboarders and windsurfers and such), but most were exchange students wanting to hone their English language skills. Tatyana, though, was neither a student nor a devotee of the wind sports – she'd simply wanted to travel and had signed up for a work program that specialized in East Coast beach placements.

She and a friend were renting one of the old houseboats at the Kinnakeet Boatyard, just around the corner from his house. He'd run into her around the boatyard a few times, and his friend, the Captain, had recently invited both girls to one of the parties he occasionally gave there on his charter boat. Ketch also knew her from the restaurant, and he knew she was Ukrainian. He also knew that the Ukrainian language was similar to Russian, and he remembered reading somewhere that most Ukrainians also spoke Russian.

It would certainly be a stroke of luck if she happened to be at the restaurant this morning. Maybe she'd be willing to translate, and he could get some answers about what had happened to these kids and their sad blue boat.

When they reached the truck, Ketch stowed the children's gear in the capped bed. Jack jumped into the cab and assumed his usual position riding shotgun in the front seat, and Ketch ushered the children to the back bench of the king cab.

The kids chattered to each other in the back seat while they drove back to Avon. Ketch, pondering what to do with them later on, didn't pay much attention to them. He wouldn't have understood what they were saying anyway. They might be discussing the sights, recapping their journey so far, or missing their parents. Maybe the girl was instructing the boy on what to do if the old man turned out to be a lecher or something. Jack's guess would be as good as his.

It didn't take long to reach the restaurant. It wasn't too hot to leave Jack in the truck, but Ketch still rolled the windows halfway down for him. "You be good, boy. We'll be right back," he told the dog. "I'll bring you a hushpuppy."

When they went inside, Ketch steered the kids to the rest rooms before taking a table. He mimed washing his hands, and they seemed to understand. They both went into the ladies' room before he could stop them, but he guessed that would be okay. The morning rush had come and gone, and there were hardly any customers here now.

He quickly washed up himself, then scanned the restaurant to see if he could spot Tatyana. As luck would have it (for a change), she was indeed working this morning, as evidenced by the distinctive black pixie-cut hairdo he spied between some hanging pots in the kitchen. He tracked her down and asked if she could do him a favor and wait on their table, briefly explaining about the children and their language barrier problem.

He made it back to the rest rooms in time to catch the kids coming out of the ladies' room. He noted with approval that they'd not only washed their hands, but their faces as well, and at least one of them must have had a comb. Except for their weathered outfits, they now looked semi-presentable – not that it mattered to him anymore. He led them to their table, and Tatyana soon joined them.

Not knowing what foods they liked to eat, and prudently keeping the fare on the simple side so it wouldn't upset their digestive systems, he ordered scrambled eggs and toast all around, with milk and water for the kids and a side of hushpuppies to share with Jack. It wouldn't do to return to the truck empty-handed – Ketch had made him a promise, and that dog didn't forget.

The children occupied themselves while they waited by pointing at and commenting on various elements of the restaurant's trendy nautical décor, which they seemed to find fascinating. The busboy soon brought their order out, and Sergey tucked into his meal with gleeful abandon. The girl was more reserved. Before Ketch could start eating, Tatyana returned and took a seat at the table.

"So," she said to Ketch, "these *Russkiy* children shipwreck on beach? How strange!"

"Yes," Ketch said, "and please don't tell anyone about it yet, okay? I want to give them some time before I contact the authorities. Can you talk to them now, or should we do it later?"

"Now is good, I take break. What are the names?"

Ketch told her. The girl looked sharply at him when she heard her name mentioned, but the boy was oblivious to everything but his food.

"*Privet,*" Tatyana began, "*menya zovut* Tatyana. *Ya iz Ukrainy.*"

For Ketch, it was all downhill from there. He leisurely picked at his food while Tatyana and Svetlana conversed in rapid-fire gibberish. At one point he tore open an end of the paper-wrapped straw that had come with his drink and blew the paper at Sergey. The boy briefly paused to grin at him, and then continued to chow down. It looked like nothing was going to deter him from cleaning his plate.

When he'd done just that, Ketch caught him hungrily eyeing the hushpuppies. He was apparently too polite to grab for them without asking, though. Ketch considered ordering more eggs and toast for him, or giving him the rest of his own order, but he didn't want the boy to overdo it. So he pocketed two of the hushpuppies in a napkin for Jack and slid the rest of the plate over to the lad.

Tatyana decided then to take a break from her conversation and give the girl a chance to finish her breakfast.

"Well," she said to Ketch, "now we know the story."

"Oh?"

"Yes. They come from Moscow. Father is businessman.

They go to Cuba for business and holiday. Mother is, how do you say, not wanting to be married?"

"Do you mean, she wanted a divorce?"

"Yes! Divorce. Mother has Russian friends in Miami. She wants to go to America, but father does not. She buys boat to escape. Friends are expecting her. They say they will help her."

Although the Cuban community was larger and got most of the press, Ketch knew there was a substantial Russian community in the Miami area as well. In fact, he'd recently seen a magazine article about a new 'millionaire's row'-type development that was turning out to be predominantly Russian.

"I see," he said. "So where is their mother now?"

"Soldiers chase boat. Mother jumps in water. Soldiers catch her, children escape."

So, Ketch thought, the mother decided to defect, and she took the children with her – both without her husband's knowledge or approval, no doubt – and to enable their boat to reach international waters, she had to do something to distract what was probably a Cuban gunboat trying to thwart their escape before they could cross that line. And now the mother was probably being detained, though Ketch imagined a substantial enough 'fine' paid by the father would probably secure her release. It sounded like he might be wealthy enough to do that. But still – what a can of worms, and he had a feeling it was going to get worse before it got better.

He recalled the case of Elian Gonzalez, which had ended up being somewhat of an international incident. Just before the turn of the century, Elian's mother and her boyfriend had attempted to leave Cuba for the United States on a small boat with a faulty engine, along with a dozen other people, and they'd taken the six-year-old boy with them without the knowledge of his mother's ex-husband. The engine failed, and when a series of ten-foot waves sank the boat, the passengers took to inner tubes they'd brought in case of trouble. Elian and two others survived the storm. The rest drowned in the cold and turbulent seas, including Elian's mother. The survivors were rescued by two fishermen, who turned them over to the Coast Guard.

The Immigration Service placed Elian in the custody of relatives in Miami. But his father, backed by the Cuban government, demanded that the boy be returned to him in Cuba. The relatives' petition for asylum was denied, and despite local protests and resistance on the part of the Cuban community in Miami, government agents seized Elian and reunited him with his father in Cuba. It was quite the political brouhaha at the time, but it turned out well for Elian, who'd said all along that he wanted to be with his father in Cuba. Ketch hoped things would turn out in these kids' favor as well once the dust settled.

"Svetlana has mother's bag from boat," Tatyana went on. "In bag is telephone number and address and money, U.S. dollars." She chuckled. "She said she knows how much money, so no, how do you say, funny business. But I said you are nice man and she can trust you."

"Thank you. What else did you learn?"

"There is big storm last night, motor falls off, wind blows boat here."

So they'd gotten caught in the Gulf Stream, which had carried them north past Florida, way beyond their intended destination. How had their mother expected them to navigate to Florida in the first place? She must have instructed and trusted the girl, who certainly did seem to be the resourceful type.

And she must have felt strongly that they'd be better off here, strongly enough to risk their lives. Maybe there was more to this story than simply wanting to defect – maybe the father was abusive? Maybe he could find out about that later, as he didn't think he should bring it up right now.

And if the family was well-off financially, why had there so far been no English lessons for the children, which Ketch knew would be unusual in that case? Perhaps because the father knew of the mother's proclivities and refused to encourage them?

"They are in boat for two weeks. Mother brings food and water for two weeks, but no food yesterday, and no water until storm comes."

So that was why they'd been trying to drink pond water. And no wonder they'd been hungry. Ketch noticed that Sergey had finished the hushpuppies. Ketch hadn't eaten much of his own food yet, so despite his earlier misgivings he pushed his plate across the table between the children for them to share. A little more eggs and toast wouldn't hurt them, he hoped.

They'd been lucky. After Cape Hatteras, the Gulf Stream turned eastward before resuming its northern tack. If that storm hadn't come up last night, the current might have carried their boat to northern Europe, or possibly Iceland. And of course, they never would have survived such a journey.

But still, two weeks... They didn't appear to be dangerously sunburned, as one might expect. The girl must have had sense enough to keep them both out of the sun during the days, probably under the roof of the boat's makeshift cabin. Maybe she'd covered the cabin's open back with that blanket they were carrying.

It must have been terrifying to be out there in the middle of the ocean all alone... Knowing what he knew now, he'd be willing to bet the girl had kept up a good front and stayed strong for her little brother's sake. And she must have been the one who'd rationed their supplies, judging by the way that boy ate. He looked across the table at her, politely finishing her own meal while allowing the boy to pilfer at will from Ketch's plate, with a new level of respect.

"So that is why they are so hungry," Tatyana said, and then she chuckled again. "She said where is vodka. I said no vodka for children in America, and food here is good."

Ketch had to smile at that. The Russians he'd worked with in Moscow had insisted on a shot of vodka before and after each meal, supposedly to kill bacteria in case the food was tainted. But he knew that vodka was typically eighty to a hundred proof, which isn't enough alcohol to kill microbes even in the mouth, let alone in the gut. What he didn't know was whether they'd actually believed it worked, or they'd just given that excuse for his benefit.

"How old are they?" he asked.

"Sergey is eight years. Svetlana is thirteen years."

Thirteen going on twenty-five, Ketch thought. She was obviously mature for her age, to have gotten herself and her brother this far.

"Thank you, Tatyana," he said. "Now can you please tell them some things for me before you go?"

"Yes."

"Good. Tell them I'll take them to my house, I'll call their mother's friends in Miami for them, and we'll find a way to get them together. They can stay at my house until that happens." And he wouldn't involve the authorities on his end after all – the Miami people could handle that, as they'd apparently been prepared to do.

Tatyana spouted another stream of gibberish, and the girl nodded. "Oh, and one other thing," Ketch added. "Do they know about ticks? They have long sleeves and long pants." Another wise decision on the girl's part? "But they should check each other for ticks when we get back to my place. I don't think I should check them myself – you understand, right?"

"Yes, okay." She passed that information along, and then stood to leave. "May I come to your house after my work is done?" she asked Ketch. "I can help you until the friends come."

"Why yes, of course!" Ketch replied in surprise. "That would be great! I'll pay you for your time."

"I do not need money. I will see you later. Bye!" She turned to the children. "*Proshchay, uvidimsya,*" she said to them with a smile and a wave of her hand. She left their check on the table before she moved off.

A Russian – well, Ukrainian – turning down an offer of money? Another stereotype bites the dust, Ketch thought. Regardless, he'd give her something later anyway for her trouble.

It looked like the boy was finally done eating, and the girl as well. Ketch got out his wallet and left enough money on the table to cover the bill and a generous tip. When he stood up, the children also got up out of their seats, as if on cue.

Sergey came to him then and hugged him, to Ketch's surprise. "*Spasibo*, Ketch," he said. And then to his even greater surprise, Svetlana did the same. It was a welcome change from being threatened with a big stick, he had to admit.

He wondered what would happen to them, since both of their parents were now in Cuba. Would the Russian government get involved this time? Maybe their mother would try to defect again – and if she succeeded, what then? It seemed to him that a custody battle, even though international in this case, would probably be decided in the mother's favor. But then again, when politics are involved... Well, he guessed time would tell.

For now, he'd take them home and run hot baths for them. Then he'd let them rest, and sleep or watch TV if they wanted to, while he laundered their salty belongings and made up the guest bed for them. When Tatyana arrived later, maybe she could watch them while he finally did some grocery shopping. And then maybe they'd take the kids to that big tacky beach shop out on Route 12 and let them get some new clothes, and maybe some souvenirs, or toys, whatever they wanted...

And then tomorrow they could go down to the boatyard and meet the Captain. He'd certainly get a kick out of all this – though on second thought, they might not be too excited about spending time on another boat just yet. Maybe he should invite the Captain over to the house instead. And he should take them out on the Avon Pier, they might like that. Maybe the boy would enjoy helping him pick out materials and assisting with screening in the side deck?

Slow down, he told himself, don't get too far ahead of yourself. It had been a long time since he'd had a child to take care of, but these weren't his kids. Things hadn't turned out that well with the one that *had* been his, so he was probably subconsciously looking at these two as a second chance, which he knew he shouldn't do. Besides, he hadn't spoken with the Miami friends yet. Maybe they'd be starting on a road trip tomorrow to meet them halfway, who knows?

But they were here in the moment, and he could enjoy them while it lasted. He smiled down at the kids, tousled their hair, and said, "Okay, let's go home. *Khorosho, glavnaya.*" He didn't know where 'home' would ultimately turn out to be for them, but for the time being it would be *Port Starbird* – the only Russian refugee camp he knew of on this island.

CORA'S TREE

DESCRIPTION

In Storm Ketchum Tale #3, an outing on Halloween night turns eerie for Ketch.

On his way to a costume party at the Captain's place, Ketch detours to take in a tourist attraction he's never before visited - the Cora Tree, a legendary old live oak that was allegedly split by lightning and branded with the name 'Cora' three hundred years ago during an attempt to execute an accused witch. While Ketch examines the tree, a peculiar woman approaches and relates Cora's tale to him, and then disappears as suddenly as she appeared.

Was she just a solicitous local - or was she something else, on this night when pagans believed the spirits of the departed could return to roam the Earth?

Join amateur sleuth Storm 'Ketch' Ketchum as he experiences the mystery of Cora's Tree on historic Hatteras Island, where intrigue always seems to be just around the next corner.

NOTE: The Kinnakeet Boatyard, the Sea Dog Scuba Center, and HatterasMann Realty are fictitious.

October 2012

It was Halloween again – and for the first time in a long while, Ketch actually had somewhere to go tonight. Somewhere, that is, where he'd been invited and people were expecting him. Who knows, some of them may even be looking forward to his arrival, he thought, though that might be stretching things a bit. He'd made numerous acquaintances since he'd moved here, but there were only a handful (if that) whom he could legitimately count as friends.

He'd done his civic duty earlier regarding the neighborhood trick-or-treaters – all eight of them, as it had turned out – and he'd been generous with the handouts, but the candy bowl was still half-full. It was only a little after seven now, but no one had come to the door in the past half-hour. He guessed he could bring the leftover candy to the party. He certainly wouldn't leave it out on the front porch, as he might have back North. That would be asking for trouble in this climate, specifically of the cockroach variety.

There were safer alternatives to begging treats door-to-door these days, like trunk-or-treating and indoor events at schools and churches. Plus it was no longer tourist season, and since many of the neighboring homes hereabouts were vacation rentals, children were simply scarcer at this time of year. Though hundreds of thousands of vacationers typically visited the Outer Banks annually, that mostly happened during the summer. The permanent, year-round population of Hatteras Island numbered maybe four thousand, tops, in all seven island villages combined. So tonight's paltry turnout wasn't surprising.

He wanted to be at the party by eight or so, and it would take at least twenty minutes to drive down to the Captain's condo in Hatteras village, so he supposed he'd better get going. Jack had gone outside just a short time ago and was set for the evening, and Ketch was already wearing most of the pirate costume he'd rented for the occasion.

He quickly double-checked his appearance in the dresser mirror. His salt-and-pepper beard was closely cropped the way he liked it, and he saw nothing that could be potentially embarrassing except for maybe his hair. He started to lift his comb to rectify that, but then made like the Fonz and put it back in his pocket. He'd decided to wear the bandana that matched his sash (the tricorn hat that had also come with the costume being a bit over the top, in his opinion), so why bother? Jack, who was lying on a nearby throw rug, raised his head and gave him a funny look.

"Don't worry, boy," he said to the dog. "I'm okay. I'm just happy, that's all. *Happy Days*, remember? You've seen that old show." He smiled and gave his most faithful friend a quick rub on the head. He'd found a marathon on one of those rerun channels last week during a storm, and he'd left the TV on for most of that rainy day while he'd puttered indoors.

He really *was* happy, he realized. In the past, he'd felt this way so infrequently for so many years that it had been almost shocking when it had sometimes happened. But after being here in Avon for two and a half years now, he was starting to take the feeling for granted. No, two and a half years in this house plus three months of house-hunting before that, so two years and nine months. Finally moving here for good had been one of the best decisions he'd ever made.

With the candy bowl in hand and a light jacket tossed over his shoulder, Ketch turned off all the lights save one for Jack, and bade the dog farewell. He didn't really need the jacket right now, but he supposed it was possible he might want it later. He hadn't been living here long enough yet for his blood to thin like that of the natives, and he was plenty warm in his long-sleeved swashbuckler shirt, knee breeches, and Caribbean pirate boots.

Working the pedals with those oversized boots on his feet was a tad problematic at first, but he managed to navigate his pickup down North End Road and then Harbor Road. By the time he reached Highway 12 at the end of that road, he'd gotten the hang of it.

There was hardly any traffic, so he allowed himself the luxury of a leisurely drive to Buxton, the next village down the island's one and only two-lane highway. Driving well under the speed limit with his window rolled down, he breathed deeply of the salty air from the Atlantic just beyond the dunes to his left while enjoying the nighttime views of Pamlico Sound to his right. This was a narrow part of the island, and the water was only a short walk from the road in both directions.

After passing the iconic Cape Hatteras Lighthouse, he drove through Buxton, which had been called Cape in the old days, and continued on toward Frisco, which had originally been known as Trent. The names had changed with the coming of postal service in the late nineteenth century. His town, Avon, had once been called Kinnakeet – but Hatteras village, his ultimate destination tonight at the southern end of the island, had kept its name.

Along the way, he thought of Svetlana and Sergey, the children he'd aided a year and a half ago after Jack had ferreted out their makeshift refuge in Buxton Woods. They'd been part of a Russian family that had traveled to Cuba on business. Their mother had attempted to desert her abusive husband and escape with them to America in an old boat she'd bought on the sly, but her plan had fallen apart at the seams. She'd ended up in custody back in Cuba, and the boat with the children on it had been carried by the current and blown ashore on the beach near the lighthouse. The desperate and frightened children had been lucky to survive the journey, and luckier still that Ketch had been the one who'd found them.

They hadn't been able to speak a word of English at the time, but Ketch knew they'd been learning, as he'd been getting a postcard from them once a month for the past year. The mother's well-off friends in Miami's Russian community, whom Ketch had contacted in lieu of the authorities, had taken them in and managed to hang onto them during the minor political storm that had followed. He'd spoken with the hosts by phone several times and followed the progress of the case on the news. Their resourceful mother's second escape attempt had succeeded, and improbably as it had seemed to him throughout, they'd all been granted asylum in the end despite the protests of the father, the Cuban government, and even the Russian government, which had also gotten in on the act.

He'd recently learned that the three of them, along with their Miami hosts, would be vacationing in Washington, D.C., during spring break – and that they were planning on a brief stayover in Avon on the way, at the kids' insistence. He'd assured them that he'd provide accommodations for them, but he didn't think he could handle that many houseguests at *Port Starbird*, at least not in the style to which they may have become accustomed in Miami. And there were no hotels in Avon other than the Avon Motel, which was modest at best.

So he was planning on renting one of the newer beach houses for them all. Five bedrooms would be adequate, so it wouldn't need to be one of those ten- or twelve-bedroom monstrosities, and it shouldn't be prohibitively expensive at that time of year. But even if it was, it would be worth it to see those two little troopers again.

He should probably make those arrangements sooner than later, he decided, and give some thought as well to choosing a couple of historic sites to show them during their visit. The lighthouse was an obvious choice, as was the Chicamacomico Life Saving Station and museum up in

Rodanthe, where the old-time surfmen had bravely rescued shipwreck victims from the Graveyard of the Atlantic at great personal risk – though that might be too time-consuming, especially since he'd of course have to take them to the Graveyard of the Atlantic Museum in Hatteras, where their sad blue boat was on display outside.

Speaking of tourist attractions, he was now approaching the housing development at Brigands' Bay in Frisco. That put him in mind of the Cora Tree, which was a sizeable old live oak at the center of that community that had been split by lightning a long time ago. The tree was in the middle of a street there, and he'd heard the road divided and went around the tree – and as was often the case hereabouts, there were local legends that also swirled around that tree.

Oddly enough, despite the many times he'd vacationed on this island before he'd retired, and even though he was now living here full-time, he'd never gotten around to visiting the tree. But he had looked up its location one time online, and he thought he could remember how to find it.

So why not just make a quick stop right now? He knew there was nothing else to see or do there beyond the tree itself – and he also knew that it probably didn't much matter what time he showed up at the party. Knowing the Captain, there would be plenty of other guests. Truth be told, he doubted he'd be missed right away, if ever. And though it was dark out now, the moon was almost full and there might be streetlights, and he had a flashlight in the glove box in case he needed one.

He slowed and kept his eyes peeled for Buccaneer Drive, which he'd have to make a right turn onto off Highway 12. And after that came, what was it? Ah yes, Snug Harbor Drive was the road the tree was on. Okay, there was Buccaneer...

Ketch had no trouble finding the correct street – but when he did, he saw that there was more than one big tree occupying the median between the two lanes. He drove down one side of the street and back up the other. It must be this one right here, he thought. It was the only one that looked like it could have been struck by lightning. He parked the truck, retrieved his flashlight from the glove box, and stepped out.

Legend had it that an accused witch named Cora had caused her name to be burned into the tree back in the early seventeen hundreds. And Ketch remembered reading that after all this time, it could be difficult to spot what remained of the name. Ambient light or no, he was glad he'd brought the flashlight.

It didn't seem to help much, though. He panned the light around the tree's trunk a couple of times without success. Was the name smaller than what he was expecting to see? Did he have the right tree? He moved closer to the trunk and squinted mightily as he slowly panned again.

"Would you be looking for the famous Cora's name, sir?" a voice behind him demurely inquired.

Startled, Ketch quickly turned, almost dropping the flashlight in the process. A woman had apparently crept up behind him without him noticing.

"Why yes, er, miss, yes I am," he said. Her face, at least, which was about all he could see of her, looked to be on the younger side. She was wearing a plain gray ankle-length dress with long sleeves. The dress was fronted by a white apron, and a plain white bonnet covered her head.

"Would you be wanting me to show you it, sir?" she asked. Ketch mutely nodded and she moved closer to the tree, forcing him to step aside. "Stand a wee bit farther back, sir, and aim your torch here," she said, touching a spot on the trunk.

He did as she instructed, she traced the outline with her finger – and there it was, plain as day now that he knew where to look and what to look for. It wasn't smaller than he'd expected, but rather larger. And though it had apparently faded significantly or some of the bark had grown back, it was definitely there.

"Thank you," he said.

"You are most welcome, sir," the woman responded with a slight curtsy. "Do you know the story of this oak, sir?"

He thought he did, but he also thought it might be interesting to hear a local tell it. "Some of it, yes, but I'd like to know more," he said. The woman seemed pleased.

"'Twas in the year of our Lord 1705," she began. "Cora came carrying a wee babe with her. She stayed at a hut not far from this very spot. Folks here left her be, but there came misfortunes. She touched a cow and it went dry, a boy who laughed at her babe fell sick, and no fisher save herself could catch enough fish."

Ketch was listening, but he was somewhat distracted by the woman's manner of speech. He hadn't heard anything quite like it on the islands, except for perhaps the old Hoi Toider brogue that was still spoken by some on Ocracoke, the next island down the Banks. But it wasn't exactly like that, either.

"Well," she went on, "along about that time came Captain Eli Blood of the town of Salem in the colony of Massachusetts. His brig, that were named the *Susan G.*, foundered on the shoals, and he and his crew stayed here to await word from the brig's owner. While he waited, a dead man washed up on the beach with the Mark of The Beast burned into his forehead, and there were womanish footprints nearby. And then when the Captain learned of Cora and her misdeeds, he decided to test her to see if she were a witch."

Now *there* was certainly a stroke of bad luck for old Cora, Ketch thought. The digits '666' on the dead body's forehead (he hadn't heard that bit before), plus the arrival of a man who'd probably been present at the Salem witch trials of 1692, was a recipe for disaster if there ever was one.

"First he had her bound with ropes and thrown in the sound, and then he tried to cut her hair. She floated in the water, and he said he were unable to cut because the hair were tough as wire rope, and that were two signs of witchery. Then he pricked his own finger and stirred his blood in a bowl of water, so as to read it. The blood in the water, too, said she were a witch."

"That's ridiculous," Ketch said.

"I heartily agree, sir! And then the Captain remanded her to this very tree to be tied with her babe in her arms, and kindling were bundled to burn them. But another captain by the name of Tom Smith said he could not abide such an execution and the mainland court should rule instead."

"So there was at least one sensible person, then," Ketch remarked.

"Indeed, sir. And then while Captain Smith and Captain Blood discussed, they say the babe became a cat with green eyes and red mouth, and ran off into the woods. And the sun were covered by a great dark cloud and lightning struck the tree and there were smoke. When the smoke cleared, Cora were gone, leaving behind the rope and kindling and her name burned into this tree. And so the story ends," the woman concluded.

"Do you believe that ending?" Ketch asked her. She only smiled in response. "Poor Cora," he said. "It's a shame women used to be treated so unfairly. It's always amazed me that people would turn on their midwives and healers and such the way they did, when they had such need of their services back then. But I guess that's what happens when you combine ignorance and superstition and religious zealotry... I wonder what really happened to Cora, if there was such a person."

"Oh, there were, sir, of that I am certain. And she were a cunning woman, as you said, but she were not witchy.

And though she did not burn that day, she surely did in a time to come."

"You're probably right." Ketch thought for a moment. "But you know, I've heard another story, one that says this name was carved into the tree by the fiance of a girl named Cora who lived here fifty or so years ago. But that story isn't quite as interesting, is it?" he smiled.

"No, sir, it is not. Nor is it the truest tale."

"Are you going to a Halloween party?" Ketch asked her. "I'm on my way to one down in Hatteras," he added by way of explaining his own outlandish attire – which she so far hadn't remarked on.

And she didn't now. "I am sorry, sir, but I know not of what you speak." She looked past him over his shoulder then and said, "Oh! I must take my leave now. Good eve to you, kind sir."

Ketch swiveled for a moment to see what had caught her attention. When he turned back around, she was gone.

He looked about in consternation. She was nowhere in sight. Where could she have gotten to so quickly, and so soundlessly? He recalled that he hadn't heard her approaching earlier, either. Had she ever really been here at all? Had he imagined the encounter, or hallucinated it? Was there something wrong with him – or with her?

The hairs on the back of his neck suddenly standing on end, he beat a hasty retreat to his truck, fired it up, and took off. He wasn't panicked enough to drive recklessly – especially tonight of all nights, when there might still be trick-or-treaters afoot in the dark – but he didn't start to relax until he was back on Highway 12 and had put Brigands' Bay in the rearview mirror.

And now that he had, he felt silly. He wasn't a superstitious man, and yet he'd allowed himself to be spooked by that woman. He thought again about her peculiar speech and mannerisms.

'Good eve', she'd said to him, he recalled. Tonight was

Halloween, or All Hallows' Eve, the one night of the year when pre-Christian pagans had believed the souls of the departed could return to their homes seeking hospitality. Hence the tradition of 'guising', now called trick-or-treating, in which people had disguised themselves to represent the souls of the dead and gone begging from house to house, where they'd received offerings of food given in hopes of good fortune from the spirits.

Atypically distracted from the island scenery and starry skies he ordinarily enjoyed so much, he autopiloted the pickup toward Hatteras village. She'd also spoken as if she were taking what had supposedly happened to the eighteenth-century Cora as a personal affront, and she'd seemed quite certain that Cora had in fact existed and been mistreated by that demented ship's captain from Salem, as well as perhaps by the legal system of that era. Could she have been that Cora herself, returning on this night to her former home in search of succor? She'd seemed satisfied at the end of their encounter. Had his sympathetic reaction to her story appeased her spirit?

Although Ketch didn't consider himself superstitious (he again reminded himself), he did believe that there was more to life, the universe, and everything (to paraphrase a favorite author of his) than met the eye. We don't know everything yet, he thought, not by a long shot, and we probably never will. Maybe there *are* such things as ghosts...

But tonight, back there at Cora's Tree? Nonsense, he decided, until proven otherwise. As a former scientist, he was conditioned to search for a logical explanation first and foremost, rather than automatically resorting to the supernatural.

So how could the woman's sudden disappearance be rationalized scientifically? Well, maybe she'd been wearing soft shoes or slippers (he hadn't noticed) and she'd simply hurried off when his back had been turned, and he hadn't been able to see her in the dark. But the moon was almost full tonight, so why hadn't he been able to see her? Maybe his pupils had been dilated by the flashlight he'd been using, so his surroundings had temporarily appeared darker to him. Yes, that was probably all it had been. Still, it would be interesting to hear what his friend the Captain might make of it.

He had a name, this friend, but Ketch just called him 'Captain'. He was a semi-retired charter captain who berthed his boat at the Kinnakeet Boatyard near where Ketch lived, and the salty dog had been the first real friend Ketch had made upon moving to Avon. Ketch had started serving as mate on his occasional fishing charters this past summer, even though he himself had never fished and had no desire to start now. He just liked driving the boat and spending time on the water.

Before he knew it, Ketch was pulling into the parking lot of the Captain's condominium complex on the outskirts of Hatteras. The old mariner was out on his covered deck, which Ketch saw had been gussied up with strings of orange lights for Halloween, along with some tiki torches for the mosquitoes. The tacky skipper's cap the man habitually wore was easy to spot. And though Ketch knew he technically wasn't in costume, the rest of the outfit he was wearing tonight made him look a lot like the Skipper from that old *Gilligan's Island* TV series.

"Ahoy there, swabbie!" he thundered at Ketch over the blaring reggae music and general hubbub. "Where the hell you been?" A couple of dogs started barking somewhere within the neighboring units. "Did you finally get some action or somethin'?"

Ketch left his jacket behind in the truck, but remembered the candy. "Hello, Captain," he replied in a normal tone of voice when he'd gotten close enough to not have to yell. There were a lot of people at this party, more than he'd expected, and even more inside than out. But he could see that most of them were costumed, like him, so he didn't feel any more out of place than he would have anyway. He didn't generally do well with crowds. "No, no action," he said. "But I did meet a woman on the way down here."

"You dawg! Do tell! But first, lemme get you a beer." The Captain put two fingers in his mouth and whistled loudly at a pirate wench standing near a keg. "Ahoy there, Kitty," he called, "three beers!"

"Kitty?" Ketch inquired.

"Yeah, you hadn't met her yet. I asked her out the other night over at the Froggy Dog."

"You just started going out with her, and you're already ordering her around?"

"She's a dang barmaid! So she's used to waitin' on me. *My girlfriend is a waitress, my girlfriend is a waitress,*" he began singing. "You remember that one? The Iguanas!"

The wench arrived promptly with three Solo cups and delivered them to the Captain in what Ketch thought was a sarcastic, though benign, manner. Then she sashayed away, looking back over her shoulder to make sure he was watching. She was shapely and attractive, but looked to be at least in her mid-forties - a bit long in the tooth for the Captain, given what Ketch knew of some of his past conquests.

The Captain passed two of the cups to Ketch. "Why three?" Ketch asked, taking them.

"'Cause you got some catchin' up to do! All right now, you set yourself and your candy on down here and tell me 'bout this lady a yours," the Captain said, directing Ketch to the only vacant seat at a nearby picnic table. "'Scuse me, darlin'," he then said to a girl sitting opposite Ketch. Taking her by the elbow, he escorted her to her feet and sat down in her place. She looked to be three sheets to the wind already, and was apparently oblivious to what the Captain had just done. Ketch watched her weave her way unsteadily toward the entrance to the condo.

"Aren't you worried someone might make a complaint about all this noise?" Ketch asked the Captain.

"Naw! And I'll tell you why. See if you can follow me here. Who's the one does the complainin' 'bout a loud party? Somebody that didn't get invited, right? So I invited everybody in the whole dang place!"

Ketch took that to mean all of the condos in this complex – but who knew, from the looks of things he might have invited some other neighbors as well. And then some others who weren't neighbors, of course, such as himself.

"Good thinking," Ketch said.

"You're lookin' spiffy. Who're you supposed to be, Blackbeard's accountant?" the Captain laughed. "I'm just kiddin', you look good. It's no wonder you got the ladies followin' you around!"

"Right. Speaking of ladies, have you seen Kari yet?" Ketch inquired.

"Nope, nor Len. But they both said they was comin'. Mario too, but he ain't here yet neither."

Ketch was ambivalent about Mario. He seemed like a jovial and friendly sort, but Ketch had heard he was somewhat of an outlaw. Len was an okay guy, though. They were both young and both staying at the boatyard, Len on a rented houseboat and Mario on his old trawler.

"How come you're askin' after Kari?" the Captain asked. "You gettin' sweet on her now? I wouldn't blame you if you was. She's a looker, all right. Say, ain't you workin' for her now?"

"Yes, I'm assisting with the pool work for her diving classes. And I'm only asking after her because that would make two people I know at this party."

Kari Gellhorn, a PADI instructor who owned and operated the Sea Dog Scuba Center in Avon, was indeed a looker, especially considering that she must be pushing forty. He being a certified divemaster (a level below instructor), Ketch was pack-muling for her classes and helping with the training exercises in exchange for free air fills and other minor perks at the shop rather than for money, because he knew she was having trouble making ends meet. But she had a boyfriend. That would be Mick, a no-good layabout in Ketch's opinion – but that was none of his business.

"Oh yeah? That's all? Then how come your face is changin' colors like one a them little lizards?" the Captain teased. "Never mind. Tell me who you met tonight."

Ketch cleared his throat and took a drink. "Well," he began, "I decided to pay a visit to the Cora Tree in Frisco on my way here. I assume you've heard of it?" The Captain nodded. "There was no particular reason, I'd just never seen it before and I happened to think of it." Ketch then proceeded to recap the incident, leaving nothing out – including his irrational panic at the end of it. The Captain didn't interrupt (much), to Ketch's surprise.

"Whoa!" the Captain exclaimed when Ketch had finished. "Sounds like it mighta been the ghost a Cora her own self!"

"No, I don't think so. I was probably just blinded by the flashlight, and that's why I didn't see her walk away. But I found it disconcerting at the time."

"There you go again, with them big words a yours. You mean you was spooked, right? Well, I don't blame you t'all. I woulda turned tail and run too, if I seen a ghost all dolled up like that and talkin' funny and all."

"I don't think she was a spirit, Captain. This is how folklore legends get started, you know. People see something they don't know how to logically explain, so they make superstitious assumptions, and then the story keeps growing with the telling. Kind of like that cobia you caught back in August, which was almost the size of a great white the last time you told that story," Ketch added with a twinkle in his eye.

"Ha! You got me there. Well, it's still a pretty good yarn, even if it don't have big fish nor bar fights nor loose women. Not as good as my own tall tales, though, a course." The Captain sat up a little straighter and looked past Ketch out into the parking lot. "What'd you say that gal looked like again?"

Ketch began reiterating how the woman was dressed. But he didn't get to finish.

"Did she look like that little lady right there?" the Captain interrupted, pointing at a new arrival to the party. "Ahoy, Len, over here!" he brayed, waving a hand in the air.

When Ketch turned to see who he was pointing at, his face turned even redder than it had when the Captain had ribbed him about Kari. He lowered his head and sipped at his beer.

"Hey, Don," Len said to the Captain. Some of the others at the picnic table had gotten up and left, so Len plopped down on the bench next to Ketch. "Hey Ketch, how you doin'?" he said. Ketch noticed that, like the Captain, Len was not costumed, though the bib overalls and straw hat he typically wore would still qualify him if there were a contest. The girl Len had brought with him sat down by the Captain.

"Guess I ought to introduce everybody," Len declared. "This here is Cap'n Don, and this here is Ketch," he said to the girl. "Storm Ketchum is his real name, but don't call him that less'n you want your head bit off," he added with a typically goofy grin. "Don and Ketch, this here is –"

"I know!" the Captain exclaimed. "The ghost a Cora the witch, right?"

"Huh?" Len responded, perplexed.

The girl laughed. "I'm Diana. Mister Ketchum, it's nice to meet you – again," she said. "Len, this is the man I told you I spoke with back at the Cora Tree, while I was waitin' on you to pick me up."

Then Len understood. “Well, how ’bout that!” he said. “Small world, ain’t it? Yeah, she’s stayin’ at a place right by that tree.” He slapped Ketch on the back, almost causing him to spill his beer. “I guess she got you pretty good back there, huh? She’s kind of a practical joker, in case y’all didn’t know.”

“Well, we know now,” the Captain said. “Ketch told me all about it. Hey Ketch, what’s the matter? You look like you seen a ghost!” he guffawed. “I’m sorry, I shouldn’t a laughed,” he apologized to Ketch.

“That’s okay,” Ketch finally said. “I can take a joke,” he added, though the brooding look on his face wasn’t yet supporting that statement.

“Did you really think I was Cora’s ghost?” Diana asked Ketch.

“Well no, not really, that is, not after I’d thought about it,” Ketch stammered.

“Mister Ketchum – Ketch – I’m truly sorry if I alarmed you,” Diana said. “But when I saw you lookin’ for the name on that tree all serious like, and lookin’ nervous and all there in the dark, I just couldn’t resist, and –”

“Where did you go at the end, when you disappeared?” Ketch interrupted.

“Oh! Well, I just ducked around the other side of the tree and hunkered down.”

“I see,” Ketch stiffly responded.

“I’m truly sorry, really,” Diana repeated. “It’s just a bad habit of mine, playin’ jokes on people. I’ve been doin’ it since I was a kid.”

Ketch exhaled loudly. “That’s all right,” he said. “Really, no hard feelings.” He finally allowed himself a smile. One should be able to laugh at oneself, right? He’d read somewhere that it was a positive character trait, and he was trying to improve himself after all, so he decided to let his embarrassment go. “What kind of accent were you using when we talked?” he pleasantly inquired. “I thought maybe it was Hoi Toider at first."

"It's supposed to be some kind of eighteenth-century Tidewater accent. I worked up at Colonial Williamsburg in Virginia over the summer, and they taught it to us there."

"Well, that explains that, then," Ketch said. He got up from the bench. "Can I get you something to drink?" he asked her. "I don't know what there is besides beer, though. Captain?"

"There's wine and margaritas and such inside, if you want that kinda thing."

"I'll walk with you," Diana said. "And we'll bring some beers back for y'all." She got up, went to Ketch, and crooked an arm inside his elbow. "That is, if you do not mind it, kind sir," she added with a chuckle.

Ketch let out a rueful chuckle in return. "You really did have me going there for a while," he admitted as they made their way to the drinks.

"I did, didn't I?" she giggled. "I'm studyin' to be an actress in my spare time, you know, so it was a confidence booster for me, at least. But meanwhile, I'm workin' at HatterasMann Realty. What do you do?"

"I retired almost three years ago. Now I mate on the Captain's charters and help teach scuba classes."

"You're retired? You must have retired young!"

"Well, I was fifty-five, but I don't think that's very young..."

After getting everyone a round of drinks, he spent some more time with the Captain, Len, and Diana. And then, as he was realizing he was hungry and considering going inside for some food, he saw Kari going in – or rather, yet another pirate wench, but he had no trouble recognizing her. He hadn't noticed her arrival, but she couldn't have been here very long. He scanned the surroundings for any sign of Mick, and didn't see him anywhere. Maybe the scoundrel had something, or more likely someone, better to do this evening.

Ketch excused himself and followed Kari into the Captain's condo. There was pizza, subs, a mountain of peel-and-eat shrimp, a couple of veggie platters, and other assorted munchies, all laid out on the dining room table and the kitchen counters. It looked like she was going for the subs, so he joined her there.

"Hello, Kari," he said from behind her.

"Oh, hey Ketch," she said, turning to face him and eyeing his costume. "My, don't you look handsome! In fact, don't we make a handsome couple!" She rotated in place and modeled her costume for him. "Do you agree, O Captain?"

How could he not? He had to admit she looked rather fetching, even more so than usual, but how should he phrase that? "Uh, sure, whatever you say," he punted. Why did he always feel like a bashful teenager when he was alone with her? "Um, would you like to join me for dinner?"

"Sure, why not? Let's load up a couple plates and find someplace to sit."

They ended up back at the picnic table with the Captain, Len, Diana, and now Kitty as well. The Captain's new squeeze had brought a large platter out with her, and they all chatted amiably while they ate. This was fine with Ketch, since he didn't have to worry about coming up with topics of conversation, though he did sit next to Kari and pay her as much attention as possible. He unfortunately had to suffer through another recap of his adventure at the Cora Tree, but it was a small price to pay.

When some of the other guests started using the open space on the deck as a dance floor, Ketch was afraid Kari might ask him to dance. But she didn't, and instead declared that she had to be at the shop early in the morning. Being the gentleman that he was, he walked her out to her car.

"That was a funny joke Diana played on you," she said.

"Kinda cruel too, but still funny, you gotta admit. Hey, don't feel bad," she said, seeing the look on his face. "That would have scared the bejesus out of me, even worse than it did you. I would have headed for the hills as fast as these ole feet would take me!"

"There aren't too many hills around here, except for the sand dunes," he said with a smile. "It's okay, I'm over it."

"You sure? Good. Hey, c'mere." She gave him a quick hug before he realized what was happening, and then got in her car. "There's an Open Water class startin' Monday, probably my last one for the year. Will you be available for the pool work?" Ketch assured her that he would. "Great! I really appreciate you helpin' out, I hope you know that. Okay then," she said, starting the engine, "goodnight!"

After she left, Ketch stuck around a little while longer to be polite. But with Kari gone, he no longer had much of an incentive to stay, and the party was starting to grow rowdier than he was comfortable with. So he made his rounds and said his goodbyes.

It was going on midnight when he finally left the party. He hadn't had that much to drink, and he'd stopped drinking a couple hours ago and eaten some food as well, so he wasn't worried about driving his truck. He'd just have to keep an eye out for the small deer that lived in Buxton Woods.

This time he allowed himself to fully enjoy the night sky, as well as the wanly illuminated subtropical scenery along the way, which tonight ranged from ocean views to sound views and maritime forest (and a few houses and other buildings, which he mostly ignored). Although the moon was still almost full, more stars were visible here on this clear night than he'd ever seen back North. There was less light pollution here than anyplace he'd ever lived, outside of the village centers anyway. Being thirty miles out to sea on a barrier island also meant no light to speak of from the mainland.

But still, as he approached Brigands' Bay in Frisco, he felt strangely compelled to revisit the Cora Tree. It was midnight. Might he see something out of the ordinary if he went back there now, on this night when the spirts of the departed were said to roam the Earth? Did he *want* to see something that was extraordinary in that way? He'd never been able to embrace any religion the way so many others did so facilely, but did he nonetheless feel a need to find something bigger than himself to believe in?

Maybe... It wouldn't be unusual to feel that way, since most people apparently did, and had throughout history. But didn't he already have that, in the form of the glorious Nature that was all around him here? He'd never before in his life felt the kind of peace and happiness that the island and the sea around it were bringing him now. Being a part, however minuscule and ephemeral, of the beautifully complex and ever-evolving ecosystems of this island and the others nearby, and the waters that surrounded them, and appreciating all of that with the reverence it so richly deserved – wasn't that believing in something? And wasn't it big enough, and extraordinary enough?

He decided that it was, for now anyway. He drove past the Buccaneer Drive turnoff without slowing, and continued on home to *Port Starbird* – where his trusty canine companion was probably missing him, and perhaps crossing his legs, by now. If Cora and her tree had any supernatural secrets to reveal, they would have to wait for another time.

INTERLUDE: Port Starbird

June 2013

This full-length novel is Storm Ketchum Adventure #1, and this is where it fits into the chronology of the Adventures and Tales. If you'd like to read it, it's available at your favorite retailer and at my Web site (www.GarrettDennis.com).

DESCRIPTION

Friends help you move; best friends help you move the body!

Storm 'Ketch' Ketchum, a damaged emigre to the coastal town of Avon on North Carolina's Outer Banks, likes to mind his own business and isn't any kind of detective - until he's forced to become one by extraordinary circumstances.

On the verge of losing his modest waterfront home to an unscrupulous developer, Ketch stumbles onto the scene of a crime that might expose the perpetrator of an unsolved murder and enable him to save not only his own home, but also the similarly threatened bohemian boatyard community he's inexorably drawn into. And in case Plan A fails, he's hard at work on a Plan B that's both laudable and pitiable.

Together with his loyal dog, a salty charter boat captain, the sketchy denizens of the boatyard, and an alluring scuba diving instructor who may or may not have a hidden agenda, Ketch struggles to make sense of his new reality, while trying to save some of the things that really matter along the way.

INTERLUDE: Port of Refuge

September 2013

This full-length novel is Storm Ketchum Adventure #2, and this is where it fits into the chronology of the Adventures and Tales. If you'd like to read it, it's available at your favorite retailer and at my Web site (www.GarrettDennis.com).

DESCRIPTION

Witchery and mayhem on the Outer Banks!

Storm 'Ketch' Ketchum, a damaged emigre to Hatteras Island on North Carolina's Outer Banks, generally prefers to stay close to home and mind his own business - but he unexpectedly finds himself entangled with a cult-like coven of modern-day Roanoke Island witches when a relative of his paramour meets an untimely end on church property.

Is the High Priestess of the Croatoan Covenant Church really in contact with the departed spirits of the Lost Colony of Roanoke Island? Are the members of her church really from both this world and the next? Or is she just a con artist preying on gullible Wiccan acolytes - and is she a killer?

A desire to provide closure for the family drives Ketch to once again call on his amateur sleuthing skills to conjure up answers to these and other questions, in the process risking the physical and spiritual well-being of both himself and the one he loves.

Join Ketch, his loyal dog Jack, and his Kinnakeet Boatyard friends as they embark on a bewitching new adventure on the picturesque Outer Banks, where intrigue continues to cast its spell on them all.

DIXIE ISLAND

DESCRIPTION

In Storm Ketchum Tale #4, a vacation on an uninhabited islet brings unexpected developments for Ketch and his paramour.

Ketch and Kari just want to get 'away from the things of Man' for a little while, after their harrowing adventure with the Roanoke Island witches in PORT OF REFUGE. But unknown to them, their island refuge may harbor a secret regarding a purported lost treasure from the Carroll A. Deering, the famous Ghost Ship whose captain and crew mysteriously disappeared when the ship ran aground on Diamond Shoals almost a hundred years earlier. Unfortunately, a shady third party is interested in uncovering the secret of the treasure, and the would-be vacationers are drawn into yet another confrontation.

Join amateur sleuth Storm 'Ketch' Ketchum as he experiences the mystery surrounding Dixie Island in the magical Outer Banks of North Carolina, where intrigue always seems to be just around the next corner.

NOTE: Dixie Island, Ted's Island, the Ghost Ship's log, the Kinnakeet Boatyard, and the Sea Dog Scuba Center are fictitious.

October 2013

The Captain had apparently noticed that Ketch and Kari were ready to depart. He disembarked from the *My Minnow* and sauntered over to Ketch's berth.

"Ahoy there, y'all takin' off now?" he bellowed into the early morning quiet of the boatyard as he approached. On a nearby piling, an indignant seagull basking in the first light of the new day squawked in alarm and flew off across the water. A yip from Jack, Ketch's faithful canine companion, sounded from the open window of the truck – and Chuck, a recent addition to the family via Kari, began to rumble in there as well. But Kari hurried over and shushed them before they could get going in earnest.

"Yes, we're all set," Ketch answered at a more reasonable volume when the Captain had gotten close enough to hear. "And everything's locked up on the *Port Starbird*. But you have your key, right? And you're sure you'll be able to keep an eye on her for us while we're gone?" He realized his anxiety was showing and stopped talking. Though he'd promised Kari an outing 'away from the things of Man', he was a little apprehensive about leaving the houseboat behind. He figured that was probably because he wasn't quite over losing the original *Port Starbird*, his soundfront bungalow, back in June.

"A course! Said I would, didn't I? I ain't goin' nowheres. I'm gonna spend the next few days here gettin' the ol' gal ready to head south for the winter. Speakin' of, I hope you packed some warmer clothes than what you got on. I saw the first sign a winter yesterday, ya know."

"Oh yeah? What, did you see a snowflake or something?" Kari called, knowing that they were being set up but playing along anyway.

"Nope, a meth head totin' a air conditioner to the pawn shop!" the Captain cackled.

Ketch, too, had figured something along those lines

would be coming. He smiled and shook his head. He imagined some folks might find the man's irrepressible exuberance, occasionally questionable sense of humor, and more-than-occasional lack of tact hard to take, but Ketch had no complaint with the semi-retired charter captain.

His salty neighbor was without a doubt the best friend Ketch had ever had. The old mariner had eminently proven that on a couple of memorable occasions over the last few months, first in their confrontation with murderous ocean polluters at the beginning of the summer, and then just recently during their nerve-rattling adventure with the Roanoke Island witches – which Ketch also wasn't quite over, though he expected to be in time.

"You're not serious, are you, Don?" Kari protested, rejoining them. "We don't have meth heads 'round these parts now, do we?"

"Well, darlin', I don't know for certain, but I wouldn't be t'all surprised. I hear there's been some a that goin' on up the beach. Seems like it's gettin' to be 'bout as common these days as no-see-ums on a sticky night, if you watch the news." The Captain removed the tacky skipper's cap he habitually wore and scratched his head. "You ask me, I don't know why they can't just stick to good ol' square grouper. But I guess that ain't wild enough no more."

"You're probably right," Ketch hastily agreed, not wanting to discuss the subject further. "Well, we'd better get going. I don't want to have to sit in line at the ferry landing."

"Oh, you probly won't have no trouble today," the Captain said. "Most of the tourons are gone now."

"True, but we have to get some more ice, and they don't run as many ferries at this time of year. And they still haven't dredged the inlet, so it's an hour's ride instead of the fifteen minutes it could be," Ketch said, referring to the ongoing problem of shoaling in the inlet that separated

Hatteras Island from Ocracoke Island. And despite the circuitous route they were currently employing to avoid shallow water, a ferry still ran aground every now and then. The barrier islands of the Outer Banks, and their inlets, had always been changeable by nature, and so were the sources of the funding needed to mitigate those changes.

"What's a touron?" Kari inquired.

"It's a clueless tourist," Ketch began to explain.

"One that's a dang moron, which is most of 'em," the Captain finished for him. "How many of 'em had to be pulled outta the sand this season, I wonder, tryin' to drive out to Cape Point and such and not knowin' what they're doin'? Remember that one that lost his fancy-pants sports car when he got stuck'n got caught by the tide? Ain't they never heard a tide tables? And then they're askin' me, are there any sharks this week? There's always sharks! Dingbatters..." he muttered.

Ketch was about to cut him short again, but the Captain let up on his own. "Speakin' a dingbatters, you tell her where you're takin' her yet?"

"Nope, it's still a surprise," Kari answered. "All I know is, must be we have to get there by boat." She motioned toward the *TBD*, Ketch's unfortunately named Whaler Montauk, trailered behind his truck.

"Well don't you worry, hot stuff, you're gonna like it. And Ketch, don't you worry neither, I know you ain't like them other dingbatters."

That was good to hear. Though Ketch was technically still a dingbatter – that is, someone who wasn't originally from here – he was glad he at least wasn't considered a touron. He'd retired (too early, some had thought) here to the town of Avon not quite four years ago, but he'd spent more than enough time on Hatteras Island in the years before that, too, to be undeserving of that stigma.

The Captain slapped him on the back. "Guess I better

let y'all git a-goin' now. You be careful out there – and pace yourself, you ol' dawg. Don't let that young wench give you a heart attack!"

"Thanks, but I'm not that young," Kari drily remarked. "Big four-oh this time, remember?"

"True, you ain't no spring chicken. But you're still a looker, and you're a lot younger'n him," the Captain retorted.

"He's not *that* old!"

"Okay, that's enough, you two," Ketch interrupted with a chuckle. "Let's go."

"All right, see ya when ya get back. Have fun!" The Captain started to head back to his boat. "Don't do nothin' I wouldn't do," he called. "On second thought, belay that – don't do nothin' I *would* do!"

"Right. Thanks again, Captain," Ketch said, using the only name he curiously ever used for his good friend. Being the chivalrous sort, he held the door for Kari and ushered her up into the cab.

And so they headed off on their latest adventure. Ketch hoped it would finally be a quiet and uneventful one, as he'd assured her it would be. Beginning when they'd first gotten together back in June (an event that continued to amaze him), it seemed like there'd been one tumult after another. They could use a real break for a change, one that was more than just a momentary trough between clusters of storm-driven waves.

~ ~ ~

"So, where *are* we goin'?" Kari demanded, putting on her best pouty face. "I've been pretty patient, you know, for someone who isn't used to bein' patient. Can't you tell me now? Is it Portsmouth?"

Ketch continued chewing instead of answering her. They'd stopped at the Gingerbread House in Frisco, the finest bakery around in Ketch's opinion, for takeout on their way from Avon to Hatteras village, and he was thoroughly enjoying the huge turnover he'd selected for himself while they killed time on the ferry. He'd picked up a little something suitable for the dogs as well, which the two of them were enjoying on the back bench of the truck. He and Kari would have been more comfortable at one of the tables in the ferryboat's cabin, but they hadn't wanted to leave the dogs here alone. But they were being kept cool by a pleasant, salty breeze blowing through the open windows, and they still had a decent view of the cerulean waters of Hatteras Inlet and Pamlico Sound, and of Ocracoke Island off in the distance.

Seeing that her mock petulance wasn't working, Kari tried another tack. "You know," she murmured in his ear as she leaned toward him and lightly ran a hand up his inner thigh, "there's somethin' to be said for givin' me whatever I want. It makes me more likely to give you what *you* want."

Ketch laughed and almost swallowed wrong. He took a drink and then answered, "Okay, okay. Well, I can tell you it isn't Portsmouth. How could we be staying there? It's a ghost town, and I would have cleared it with you first if we were rustic camping. But you're warm." Portsmouth was the only town on Portsmouth Island, the next island south from Ocracoke. It had been an important shipping and lightering port in its heyday, but it was now a historic site maintained by the National Park Service.

She sat up straight and glared at him. "Don't you go teasin' me, mister," she warned. "I'm not in the mood for guessin' games."

"All right," he acquiesced. "Have you ever heard of Dixie Island?" She shook her head. "I'm not surprised. It was called that back in the Twenties and early Thirties. Now it's called Ted's Island, after a former owner, I guess. It's a small island, about fifty acres, a mile or so on the sound side of Portsmouth Island, and there's nothing on it except for one cottage. There are some other even smaller islands along the way, like Casey Island, Beacon Island, and Shell Castle Island, but they're uninhabited. Otherwise, there's nothing else around. Anyway, that's where we're going."

She stared at him in disbelief. "Ted's? *Ted's*? Like that island with the tiki bar in the plane wreck, in that *Captain Ron* movie?" Her face darkened. "Are you still kiddin' with me? I surely hope not! And if you are, couldn't you come up with somethin' better than *Ted's*? I mean, really!"

"Yes, you've heard of Portsmouth? Well, we're going to the island next door – Ted's!" Ketch started to laugh again, but quickly stifled himself. This might not be the time for humorous movie quotes. "I'm sorry. No, I'm not kidding, I'm serious. It really is called Ted's, and we're really going there. Cross my heart."

"Huh! Really? Well, okay..." She thought for a moment. "I guess you meant it when you said we'd go somewhere away from the things of Man. But you said we're not goin' rustic, so this place must be more than just a fishin' camp, right?"

"Right, it's a real house. It has a generator, and a refrigerator, and hot and cold running water, and indoor plumbing, a septic system, and so on. There's a water cooler for drinking, though, because the tap water is just filtered rainwater from a cistern. And there's propane for heating and cooking, and there's even an air conditioner, though I doubt we'll need to use it. It was built about a hundred years ago and was originally a fishing camp, but the new owner has completely remodeled the place and added a second story. And there's a sand beach right in front of the house, from some dredging they did nearby for the Intracoastal Waterway back in the Forties and Fifties."

"Wow... It sounds terrific! But how ever did you find out about this place? Who owns it now?"

"George, the son of the guy who owns the Kinnakeet Boatyard. As you know, I got a free slip rental for the houseboat for overseeing the repairs to the boatyard after the hurricane, and then George offered to let me vacation at this house for free if I do him another favor. He just finished getting the place ready, and he wants me to tell him if I notice anything that still needs doing to make sure it's suitable for renting in the spring. Oh, and it already has bed linens and towels, which he said would come with the rental."

"Huh, how about that... Well, it sounds like this'll be exactly what we needed, a place where we can really get away from it all, just the two of us. Well, the four of us, actually," she amended as Chuck licked her ear. "I'm excited, now! So I guess we'll be sailin' the *TBD* there from Ocracoke, right?"

"Yes, and we'll be close enough to Ocracoke to go out to eat there if we want to. But I packed enough staples for us to eat in, though it won't be anything fancy."

"Sounds like you thought of everything. You're a good man, Charlie Brown!" She smiled, but then frowned. "Will our cell phones work there?"

"There's cell coverage, but George said it's kind of spotty at times," Ketch apologetically admitted. "But I have my portable marine radio, just in case. He also said there's satellite TV and Internet service. I wouldn't have bothered with that if it were me, since this is supposed to be a place to get away from it all, but it's there."

"Well, I'm not really worried about all that anyway, I guess. I wasn't plannin' on watchin' a lot of TV, and the shop's covered for the next few days. Business is droppin' off now, since we're well into October. And Mama said she'd stop by a couple times and make sure the place hadn't burned down or somethin'." That would be the Sea Dog Scuba Center in Avon, her formerly struggling dive shop. It had finally started to turn the corner this past year, with the help of Ketch's involvement.

"That's one thing I didn't pack, by the way – our scuba gear. The sound isn't worth diving in, not for pleasure anyway, so I didn't bother with it."

"Fine by me. So why was it called Dixie Island? And how do you know that? Did you research it?"

"No. I don't know why it was named Dixie Island. I'd only heard of it because Dixie Burrus Browning was named after that island. Do you know who she is?"

"She's a painter, right? An artist, I mean? I think I've seen some of her pictures."

"Yes, among other things. She paints mostly watercolor landscapes and seascapes. She's also published quite a few romance novels, some of which she's gotten awards for. I like the historical Outer Banks romances she's written. She stopped writing about ten years ago, but she still paints. She was also in a bluegrass band in her younger days, and she's fished and sailed, and she was even in a movie once. Some member or members of her family owned the island back when it was called Dixie Island, but then they lost it somehow. I don't know if it was due to the Great Depression, or a bad business deal, or what. It seemed like a touchy subject, so I didn't ask a lot of questions."

"Oh, so you know her?"

"Yes, some. I had the pleasure of meeting her when something was going on at the Graveyard of the Atlantic Museum a while back, and when I mentioned I was trying to write a book, she sat down and talked with me. Now we connect once in a while on the computer. She's a truly special lady. I should see if I could get together with her again sometime..."

"How *is* your book comin' along, by the way?"

"Well, with everything that's been going on the past few months, I haven't had much time to fool with it. So it's still a piece of crap," Ketch smiled.

"You must have a lot of new material to work with,

though, after all that's happened this year."

"Ben Franklin said, 'Either write something worth reading, or do something worth writing.' I don't seem to have much trouble lately with the latter, but the former isn't nearly as easy. Even if I had talent, it's hard to find the time to do it."

"Well, maybe if you focused on it, instead of bein' so lazy all the time..."

Ketch gave her a puzzled look. Lazy was something he was assuredly not. Despite his 'advanced' age (a year and change shy of the big six-oh), he'd been able to keep up with her pretty well, and he was still capable of defeating people half his age at tennis (though admittedly not quite as often as before). And between the dive shop, the dogs, maintaining the houseboat (and the boatyard as well, until recently), and the Captain's charters – not to mention solving the occasional mystery when one fell into his lap – it seemed like he was always doing something or other.

She laughed. "I'm kiddin' you. I know you're a busy man, and I know some of that's 'cause of me – but *you* know I'm worth it." She craned her neck out her side window. "Hey, it looks like we'll be dockin' before long, so you better quit flappin' your lips and finish your breakfast."

"Yes, ma'am," was all he could say to all that.

~ ~ ~

Their private island was coming into view now – finally, Ketch thought. It was still only mid-morning, though. It hadn't taken too long to make the transit from Ocracoke, once they'd gotten the *TBD* in the water. From the Ocracoke Island ferry landing, they'd stopped once along the thirteen-mile highway (a continuation of Highway 12 from Hatteras Island) that led to Ocracoke village to walk the dogs at the pony pens, where the descendants of the formerly wild herd of island ponies were now confined. But Ketch had stored most of their belongings in the covered boat the night before, so there hadn't been much to do in the village beyond launching the boat and parking the truck where he'd arranged to leave it.

And outfitting the dogs for their journey across the water, of course. Jack was an old hand at this sort of thing, having also accompanied Ketch on the Captain's charters, and he now calmly sat next to Ketch's chair at the console of the *TBD*, his doggy life jacket snug around his torso, with his nose in the air and his ears flapping in the wind. But this was Chuck's first time on a moving boat, so Kari was keeping a tight hold on the understandably nervous animal in the stern.

As they drew closer to the island, Ketch observed that there was a patch of maritime forest on its northern end and along its western shore, and a salt marsh on the eastern shore. So with the sandy beach on the south end, this island had it all, despite its diminutive size. They weren't that far from either Portsmouth or Ocracoke, and he figured they'd probably have views of both islands from the cottage, at least from the second floor. But they'd still be isolated enough from the clang and clatter of civilization to allow them the luxury of forgetting about it for a while.

In short, it looked like his kind of oasis, and he could feel himself relaxing already. Though he didn't have to worry too much about running aground on a shoal with the *TBD*'s nine-inch draft, he throttled down and continued to keep a watchful eye out as they cruised along the western shore of the island.

If he were a painter, he was sure he'd find plenty of inspiration for seascapes and landscapes here. He wondered if Dixie had ever painted any scenes from this island. He'd have to ask her sometime.

"It's a pretty little island," Kari commented from

behind him, now that she could be heard over the engine. "Oh, and there's the cottage! It's beautiful! I think I'm gonna like it here. You might have a hard time gettin' me back in the boat when it's time for us to leave!"

"Oh, you'll go willingly enough when we run out of food," Ketch grinned back at her. Her trim figure notwithstanding, she could eat like a horse. "There's the dock. Don't let go of Chuck until I tie her off and shut the engine down."

"Aye aye, Captain."

When the boat was secured, Ketch lifted Jack up onto the wooden dock, and then did the same with Chuck. They weighed 'only' about sixty pounds each – and see, he could still do that even at his age. Chuck was wobbly at first and looked like he didn't know where to go next when Ketch released him. Jack however was sitting on the dock patiently waiting for his life jacket to be removed, according to the protocol he'd learned. So Chuck took his cue from Jack and sat as well.

Ketch removed the dogs' life jackets and tossed them to Kari, and she began handing the coolers and duffel bags up to him. After a quizzical look at Ketch, who gave him the okay, Jack wandered off down the dock with his nose to the ground. With a hearty bark along the way at a couple of seagulls hovering nearby in hopes of a handout, Chuck followed him.

"They can't get lost here," Ketch said. "It's a small island. And there aren't any large predators, so they can pretty much go wherever they like."

"They'll love that," Kari agreed. They each slung a backpack duffel over their shoulders, grabbed a handle on a rolling cooler, and headed up to the cottage.

When they went up the steps to the front door, Ketch set his burdens down on the porch. He wiped his sweaty brow and fished the key he'd been given from a pocket of his cargo shorts. But it turned out the door was already unlocked, and unlatched as well. When he pushed it open and stepped inside, it was immediately apparent why that was.

"Looks like somebody's been here," Kari said as she followed him in.

"Yes, and it wasn't George or his workers. They were supposed to be completely finished here yesterday, and they wouldn't leave the place looking like this."

From what he could see of the interior, it looked like there was no one else here now, at least on the first floor. He could see into the bathroom. And the open living/dining/kitchen area, pleasantly if somewhat tackily appointed in colorful beach-house décor, was vacant. But the cottage looked like it had been ransacked. Drawers and cabinets were open, furniture had been moved, and area rugs rolled back. Ketch saw that a couple of planks had been pried up from the otherwise pristine wood floor around the fireplace.

"Did somebody rob the place?" Kari asked.

"I don't think so. The TV's still here. I think someone was searching for something." Ketch went to the fireplace and selected a hefty poker. "There are three bedrooms upstairs. You stay here while I check them," he whispered to Kari. She silently nodded, picked up another poker, and took up a concealed position at the bottom of the stairs.

Ketch made his way up the staircase as quietly as possible. He padded down the hallway, sticking the poker into each room before he entered. After checking the closets and the showers, he came back down.

"There's no one here now," he announced.

"I figured. The boys came in right after you went up, and they don't seem concerned. How is it up there?"

"The same as here. Drawers pulled out and so on."

"I wonder what they were lookin' for?"

"I was just wondering the same thing," Ketch said, "and I might have an idea. George told me he'd been approached by someone early on in the project who said he was a treasure hunter, but not one he'd ever heard of. He wanted permission to search the original building and dig around the property. George said the guy offered to split whatever he found with him. But George declined the offer. And then later on, George caught him sneaking around the place one time, and he had the construction guys run him off the island."

"So you think he came back once everybody else was gone?"

"Could be."

"And that would've been yesterday or today, so he might still be around. He could be spyin' on us right now..." Kari mused. "Well, so much for sex on the beach then, unless you brought the ingredients for that bar drink," she ruefully concluded. "You know, if he's watchin' the place, he probably doesn't know why we're here. Maybe he thinks we're lookin' for his treasure, too. He might think we're his competition."

"Maybe so. But I don't think he'd be bold enough to bother us during the day. I have an idea on how we can test our theory. If we're lucky, we'll know by morning if someone is still hanging around here."

"I wonder what he was lookin' for? Some kinda pirate treasure?"

"I don't think so. George said he told him some crazy story about the captain of the *Carroll A. Deering* hiding something here back in the Twenties."

"The *Deering*? Isn't that the Ghost Ship of Diamond Shoals?"

"Yes, but she wasn't carrying any cargo when she wrecked, and I've never heard anything about any treasure associated with her."

"Okay, so what's your big idea?"

Ketch let out a sigh. "Let's pick up first, set some water out for the dogs, put our things away, and make this place shipshape. Then we can relax, and I'll tell you all about it. Deal?"

"Deal. But in case you don't remember, I'm not real good at waitin'. So let's goin'!" she admonished him with a smile.

~ ~ ~

"I got everything squared away up there," Kari announced as she came down the stairs. "I made up the king bed, too. Did you get all the food put away?"

"Yes," Ketch answered from the fireplace. After they'd straightened things up on the first floor, he'd sent her upstairs while he took care of the coolers. Now he was on his knees with a hammer and a punch.

"What are you doin' now? And where are Jack and Chuck?"

"They came out back with me a few minutes ago. They're still out there nosing around. I found some tools in a storage area under the house. I'm going to nail these planks back down, and then I have something to show you."

She followed him outside when he'd completed his task, and he led her to a large flat stone resting on the ground behind the house.

"George put in that new water cistern over there," Ketch explained. "The gutters along the roof divert rain to that pipe that leads into it. But the old underground brick cistern is still here, and this slab is covering it." He pointed to a rock and a crowbar lying on the ground nearby. "I did a little experiment when I was out here before. With that lever and fulcrum, I can move that stone." A hint of an evil grin appeared on his face. "That hole's at least ten feet deep, and it's wide enough that someone could fall into it, if that stone wasn't there."

"And if it was covered with some brush so they didn't

see it," Kari concluded. "I get it – a trap!"

"Right. And don't turn around, but did you notice that boat that's anchored behind us, way out in the sound? It's hard to make out, but it's there."

"Oh, I hadn't seen that. A fisherman, do you think?"

"Maybe, but maybe not. If I gambled, I'd be willing to bet there's either a telescope or a set of good binoculars aboard that vessel. I say we come out here just before sundown, set our trap, and do a little digging nearby to make it look good. There are shovels in the storage area."

"Well yeah, but..."

"But what?"

"If that's really that treasure hunter guy out there, and if he thinks we found somethin', do you think he might try to break into the house again when we're sleepin'?"

"If he did, it wouldn't go unnoticed. We have two watchdogs, remember? And we can lock the windows and throw the deadbolts. He might be able to pick the lock on the front door, as I think he did before, but the deadbolt would stop him.

"He could break a window."

"Not without alerting the troops, and I think that crowbar is going to be my constant companion for a while." A crowbar had been the Captain's weapon of choice at that witchy church up on Roanoke Island, and it had served him well. "Besides, I'm thinking I'll probably stay up tonight. If we can draw him in, I figure the sooner this is all over, the better."

Kari sighed. "So much for gettin' away from it all. I swear, ever since you decided to be a Hardy Boy, it seems like trouble just keeps followin' you around. Even out here, in the middle of nowhere! When will it ever end, I wonder?"

"I'm sorry," Ketch said. She was right. He wasn't a detective, at least not a licensed one – but since he'd finally been bitten by the sleuthing bug this past year, it seemed there was no end to opportunities for him to live up to what his late parents had hoped he'd be. As avid fans of noir mystery, their not-so-secret desire had been that he'd become either a private investigator or a noir film star. That was why they'd saddled him with his ridiculous name, which he himself never used and which others did at great personal risk.

"Oh, it isn't your fault," Kari said, giving him a hug. "And I'm not mad at you. I like mysteries and adventures too, but I was hopin' this would be a quiet time for a change. And I know you were, too."

"Maybe it *is* my fault, though. I've heard it said that we create our own destiny. Maybe I'm looking for trouble, even if it's subconscious and I'm unaware that I'm doing it, and that makes it easier for trouble to find me."

"Well, you were lookin' for somebody like me, and I found you – and I'm definitely trouble, so you might could be onto somethin' there." She smiled up at him. "Hey, how about some lunch?" she suggested, pushing off of him. "I'll make some sandwiches, and you go play with the boys. I think they ran off to hunt ghost crabs down at the beach. Meet you on the screen porch?"

"That sounds good to me. If something's going to happen, I don't think it'll happen until tonight. And then maybe a shower and a nap after lunch, in case I'm up all night."

"Now you're talkin'! And I might be up all night too, if you are, so I guess I better join you. Don't worry, we'll sleep – after I'm through with you." She laughed then, at the look on his face. "I told you I was trouble!" she called as she made her way back inside.

Indeed she was, Ketch thought – but not the bad kind, he didn't think. But then again, those alluring green eyes could be downright hypnotic to him... He shook his head and refocused. Onward to the beach.

He picked up the dog toys, which he'd left on the front

porch earlier, and joined the dogs at the water's edge. He'd swim sometime when he got a chance, but not right now since he wasn't wearing his bathing suit. The dogs were pleased that he'd joined them, and more so when he pulled a flying disk and a ball from the bag. Jack enjoyed playing Frisbee. Chuck did not, and was less interested in toys in general than Jack, but he'd taken a shine to a particular floating ball of late. Ketch sailed the disk and threw the ball out over the water several times, to the delight of the dogs, and then Kari called them all in for lunch.

There was also a towel in the toy bag. He dried the dogs as best he could and wiped their feet before he let them into the house. They followed him in to the screened porch, where Kari had set out plates of finger sandwiches and chips on a white plastic picnic table, with a bucket of Land Shark beers as the centerpiece.

"Nice spread," Ketch complimented her.

"Thanks," she said, sitting and popping the top on a bottle. Ketch and the dogs sat opposite her, Jack on the deck at Ketch's right and Chuck on his left. The dogs knew he expected them to be separated in order to forestall conflicts over the scraps he'd soon be feeding them.

"Oh, by the way," she said, "just so you know, there's no dishwasher. Also, I hadn't seen a washin' machine nor a dryer anywhere yet."

"I know," Ketch replied as he appropriated a bottle for himself. "But are those really essential items when one is getting away from it all?"

"They are if you're a family with kids and you're stayin' here for a week or more. Just sayin'..."

"Okay, I'll mention it to George." Ketch started eating. "Another 'by the way' – did you notice the painting over the fireplace was done by Dixie Browning?"

"No! I hadn't noticed that. Is she hauntin' this place or somethin'?"

"I don't think so, since she's still with us."

"I guess it just seems like that because you've been talkin' about her."

"I wonder if she knows that painting is here. I'll ask her sometime. I took a picture of it with my phone." They chewed in silence for a bit. "Do you know how many steps there are on the staircase?" he asked.

"Nope, hadn't noticed that neither. Why, should I have done?" Then she remembered. "Oh, I get it, you're teasin' me because I didn't see that paintin'. I recall you tellin' me that Sherlock Holmes looked down on folks who weren't observant enough to notice simple things like that, when they do or see 'em every day. But you know what? It's not my job to notice every dang little thing, Storm Ketchum, and that particular joke has outlived its usefulness. So you better hush your mouth and get some new material."

When she used his given name, Ketch knew she was serious. "Sorry," he mumbled.

"Tell me more about the Ghost Ship," Kari said, and dug back into her sandwich.

"I thought you wanted me to shut up," Ketch responded. "Besides, what makes you think I'm an expert on that? I don't know everything."

"Oh come on now, you're an expert on just about anything that's historical 'round these parts. You know more about these islands than anybody I know, and you weren't even born here! Why, I bet you know just as much as that ol' David Stick did. You're sure sexier'n he was, anyway..."

"Okay, okay," Ketch said, mollified now. He scratched at his closely cropped salt-and-pepper beard and smiled at her. He'd never know as much as David Stick, the preeminent Outer Banks historian, had. But it was still a nice compliment, even if it had been a bit left-handed.

"Well," he began, "the *Carroll A. Deering* was a fairly new five-masted schooner. In the fall of 1920 she sailed from Norfolk, Virginia to Rio de Janeiro in Brazil with a cargo of coal and a crew of ten Scandinavians, plus the captain and first mate – who were not Scandinavians. The original captain, I forget his name –"

"Ha! So you're not perfect after all," Kari interjected with a grin.

"Yes, well," Ketch continued, ignoring her. "He got sick along the way, and he and his son, who was the first mate, were dropped off. The company quickly hired a retired captain named Wormell, and a mate named McLellan, to replace them. Wormell didn't much like his mate or his crew, and they didn't like him, either. After they delivered their cargo in Rio, they laid over in Barbados for supplies on the way back. McLellan was overheard in a bar saying he'd 'get' the captain before they got back to Norfolk, and he was arrested. But Wormell bailed him out, and they continued on."

"That's odd. Why did he do that?"

"We don't know. Maybe he didn't want to be bothered with trying to find a new mate, or he couldn't find one. Anyway, toward the end of January, 1921, someone on the deck of the *Deering* hailed the Cape Lookout lightship, saying they'd lost their anchors in a storm off Cape Fear. The lightship keeper said the man who hailed him had a foreign accent, and he said the crew were milling around on the foredeck of the ship. He thought that was odd because crew weren't normally allowed on the foredeck. Three days later, on January 31, the ship was sighted aground on the Diamond Shoals off Cape Hatteras, with all of her sails set."

"And there was nobody on board, right?"

"Right. Rescuers couldn't approach the ship until four days later due to bad weather. When they boarded her, they found that everyone was gone. Both of the ship's lifeboats were also gone, and so were the personal effects of the crew. The ship's log and the navigation equipment were also missing. But there was a meal laid out in the galley. So whatever happened, they must have left in a hurry."

"Or they were abducted by aliens," Kari said. "Wasn't there a theory that somethin' happened to the ship in the Bermuda Triangle?"

"Yes, that was one possibility that was raised. But the ship wasn't in the Triangle when she ran aground, nor when they hailed the lightship at Cape Lookout. There were several severe storms throughout the area, and some other ships had disappeared there at that time. Investigators also considered pirates and rum runners, and even a Communist plot, but there was no evidence to support any of those theories. There's no concrete evidence of mutiny, either, but most consider that the most likely explanation."

"What do *you* think happened?"

"Well, there could have been a mutiny, and then the ship could have run aground because the remaining crew weren't competent enough to sail her on their own. Due to what the lightship keeper reported, that seems likely to me. They probably abandoned ship when she ran aground. No survivors were ever found – so if they were unable to row the lifeboats to shore because of the weather, they were probably swept out to sea and drowned."

"Huh. And there was nothin' valuable on board the ship? No treasure?"

"Not that anyone knows of. They weren't supposed to be carrying any cargo on the return trip. The Coast Guard tried to salvage the ship, but they couldn't because of the weather and the currents. So they dynamited it and scuttled it, so it wouldn't be a danger to other ships. Part of its bow drifted off and eventually washed ashore on Ocracoke Island, and the rest of it sank."

"I remember hearin' somethin' about the Ghost Ship sailin' again after that, though," Kari mused. "But how could that be?"

"Well, over time the wreckage on Ocracoke got buried under the sand, due to storm surges and such. But in 1955 a hurricane unearthed it and set it afloat, and the bow drifted up to Hatteras village. So it wasn't the whole ship sailing again, just part of the wreckage."

"Okay then, that explains that. So where'd the bow finally end up? Probably at the Graveyard museum, right?"

"Sadly, no," Ketch informed her. "A Hatterasman named Wheeler Ballance hauled the capstan and the remaining timbers to his filling station on the newly paved Highway 12. So what was left of the Ghost Ship ended up as part of the tacky nautical décor of a gas station."

"No! That's terrible!"

"Yes, an inglorious end for what had been a glorious sailing vessel. Such is life... But the museum did eventually end up with the capstan, and they also have the ship's bell, a flask, and a winch. And Dixie Browning just recently donated a lantern from the *Deering* that had somehow ended up with her."

"Well, that's good at least. But this guy that might be watchin' us, he thinks there was somethin' worth goin' after on that ship that nobody ever found, and he thinks it might be 'round here someplace. Wonder why?"

"Beats me." Ketch yawned. "I think I'm just about ready for that nap. Let's finish up here."

"Okay. Give whatever you have left to the boys, and then lock the doors and come upstairs. We better rest up in case we see some action tonight. I'll put this stuff away." She gathered everything but Ketch's plate and current beer onto the tray she'd carried it all out on, and started to head back in to the kitchen. "Oh, and speakin' of action," she called back along the way, "I'll be in the shower when you come up, and that door won't be locked. Another 'by the way' for you...," she sneered, but with a twinkle in her eyes.

~ ~ ~

"Do you think we've done enough diggin' now? My arms are gettin' tired, and the mozzies are startin' to find me."

Ketch shaded his eyes and looked out over the sound. The mystery boat was still there. "Yes, I think so. He's had plenty of time to see what we're doing, and we're about to lose the light anyway."

He carefully stuck his shovel into the ground so that it stood upright next to the old cistern. "Didn't you use the Skeeter Beater I brought?"

"Yeah, but still..."

"Okay. You take the dogs inside with you, and I'll lever this stone to the side. Then I'll hide the hole and come in."

It was easier said than done, but Ketch managed to uncover the cistern. Then he spread the brush they'd gathered earlier across the now-gaping hole. It was just about dark now, and it was good that the dogs were inside, as he didn't want one of them to fall into the cistern.

The dogs had grown tired of helping with the digging early on, and they both looked now like they could use another nap, which didn't surprise him. They'd been more active here on the island today than they normally got to be back home, plus their bellies were full. In addition to their usual dinnertime fare, Ketch had grilled burgers for them on the gas grill when he'd prepared a quick, light supper earlier. He hadn't shared any of the baked beans with them, though. No sense asking for more trouble than they already had.

"So, what do we do now?" Kari asked when Ketch was back in the cottage. "Just sit around and wait? And what are you doin' with that thing?"

"The crowbar?" Ketch stood it up in a corner. "I told you before, I'm keeping it close for the time being, just in case."

"Okay – I guess. So now what?"

"Well... I didn't bring my guitar because I didn't want to chance getting it wet, but I did bring a few of our DVDs. I know we didn't come here to watch TV, but maybe we should watch a movie and then turn all the lights out, as if we were going to bed. Then we can watch through a window to see if anything happens. I brought *Captain Ron*."

"Ha! Well, I guess that'd be appropriate, huh, since we're on Ted's Island. But I don't know, I'm kinda nervous. Aren't you? I don't know if I could concentrate on a movie."

"Me neither. But we have to do something to pass the time."

"Do we? Why do we have to wait? Why couldn't we just be goin' to bed early? It's dark now, and we've had a busy day. I don't think that'd seem too strange. Then maybe he'd come sooner, if he's comin', and we could speed things up and get this over with. I'm gettin' tired of worryin' about it."

"You know, that's not a bad idea. Okay, let's turn the lights off."

They decided to stay on the first floor and station themselves at separate windows. Kari took one that would allow her to cover the back of the property, where the cistern was, and Ketch opted for one that provided a view of the front in case their quarry approached from the beach. They each pulled up a chair from the kitchen table and settled in to keep watch, Ketch with his crowbar at the ready near his chair. The doors were all locked. So were the windows, except for the two they were using, which were cracked so they could hear what was going on outside. It was a cool evening and it wasn't stifling inside, despite everything being closed up – which Ketch appreciated, since the noise of an air conditioner might mask other sounds.

"You thought about how we're gonna keep the boys

quiet if that guy does come sneakin' around?" Kari softly inquired.

Ketch glanced around the room. Jack was curled up on a throw rug in front of the fireplace, and Chuck was upside down with all four feet in the air between the couch and the coffee table. They were both snoring.

"We might not have to worry too much about that. They're zonked. But if they get antsy, I'll give them bones to distract them."

"Okay."

They monitored the grounds in silence for a while from their separate vantage points, and then Kari said, "Hey, Ketch? Are you scared?"

"A little," he admitted. "It would be foolish not to be. But we've been through worse times than this. I think things will turn out okay."

"You do? Good."

And then more silence. Ketch realized he was tiring again. He'd finally been allowed to take a nap earlier, but it had been a short one, and all the activity of the day, as well as the stress of the situation, were taking a toll. Nonetheless, he sat up straight in his chair and forced his eyes to rhythmically pan his field of vision. Although it was full dark now, there was enough moonlight to see by. There was nothing to see yet, though.

He started thinking about the events of this past year. It was hard for him to believe sometimes that it had all actually happened. Just a couple of years ago he'd still been pretty much a timid semi-recluse, as he'd been for most of his adult life, keeping mostly to himself and flying under the radar. And look at him now. Solving mysteries, confronting villains, engaging in activities of questionable legality – and enjoying the company of the love of his life. It didn't seem possible.

He'd started working at getting better, though, as soon as he'd moved here. He'd made himself get out more and make new friends, the first of which had been the Captain. The turning point, he thought, had been that peculiar dream he'd had about Olde Christmas, which he still remembered most of, oddly enough. He didn't usually remember his dreams. Relocating to the Outer Banks had been the best thing he'd done in a very long time, despite all the trials and tribulations. This place was good for him, and probably good for his soul, too, if there was such a thing...

The sound of an engine interrupted his thoughts. He picked up the binoculars he'd retrieved from the canvas backpack he always carried with him these days, and tried to focus through the window. Yes, there was a boat approaching the dock – and strangely, it looked familiar to him.

As the boat came closer, he saw why. It was the *My Minnow*, and there was the Captain up on the flying bridge. What was he doing here? Was this the boat he'd been watching all day? If so, that would make him feel pretty stupid, after the trouble he'd gone to with that cistern and all. But why would the Captain hang around like that – and who was that standing at the bow, almost like a figurehead? It looked like a woman...

Why, it was Dixie Burrus Browning! And what was that she was brandishing? Was that a rifle she was pointing toward the water ahead? No, it looked more like a spear, and now he could see that it was three-pronged, like Poseidon's trident. Had Dixie come to help him and Kari, or did she want the treasure of the Ghost Ship for herself? Maybe she was working with that treasure hunter – but then how was the Captain involved? He was supposed to be his best friend...

"Ketch!" Kari called to him.

He woke with a start, his chin snapping up from its resting place on his chest. Momentarily confused, he soon realized he'd nodded off. A sentry sleeping on the job –

that certainly wouldn't look good on the resume. Had Kari noticed?

"Yes, what is it?" he replied. What a peculiar dream. He must have had Dixie on the brain after talking about her earlier.

"Do you hear that?"

He strained to listen. Yes, there it was, the faint sound of a boat engine. Hadn't that sound been part of his dream? It was fading already, so he wasn't sure.

"Yes," he acknowledged. He got up and went to Kari. The sound was a little louder at her window. He raised his binoculars, which were indeed hanging on a strap around his neck, and trained them on the water through another window. "I can't see that boat anymore. It sounds like he might be approaching the other end of the island. He'll probably tie up there and make his way here on foot."

"Okay, now I'm *really* gettin' nervous!" Kari exclaimed. "But on the other hand, I'm kinda glad we didn't end up just sittin' here all night long for nothin'. I guess we still have to wait some more, though."

"Yes, and we'll have to do it as quietly as possible." She apparently hadn't noticed his little lapse – if she had, knowing her, she certainly wouldn't have let it slide without some serious ribbing first.

Both dogs were awake now, though they hadn't moved from their spots. Ketch wondered if he should get a couple of bones out for them, but before he could act on that thought, they both closed their bleary eyes and went back to sleep.

Ketch returned to his station in case the man decided to go around to the front of the cottage, and Kari continued to keep watch at her window. Among numerous other useful items, Ketch had a roll of duct tape and a fish fileting knife in his backpack. Inspired by dream-Dixie's trident, he occupied his time by duct-taping the knife to one end of his crowbar. Thanks, Dixie, he thought, that was a good idea.

They didn't have to wait too long. About twenty minutes later, Kari animatedly motioned for Ketch to rejoin her – which he did, after first picking up his crowbar spear.

"He's here," she whispered. "He just came out of the woods."

Ketch crouched next to her, and watched with her as the man advanced toward the cottage. They both kept as still as possible and didn't speak. The man looked nervous, his head rapidly turning left and right while he walked, purposefully but as stealthily as possible. He stooped to glance into the holes Ketch and Kari had dug, and then went to the shovel Ketch had left standing up next to their trap. He looked like he was considering using it.

Ketch held his breath and gripped the crowbar tightly. Would he have to go out there and do battle with this guy? Or defend the cottage if he tried to enter? It would all depend on where the man stepped next. Ketch wished he had a weapon with a longer reach than the crowbar, though the crowbar was somewhat more formidable now that he'd modified it *a la* Dixie's trident. But it wouldn't be a match for a gun, unless he could somehow take the man by surprise.

Or if he could distract the fellow. He did have two dogs that could help in that regard – but no, he didn't want to risk them getting shot. He looked around to check on them. Still sleeping, he saw, and snoring again to boot. Some watchdogs...

But not to worry – the man turned and stepped directly onto the brush covering the cistern. His arms flailing, he dropped into the hole, grunted, and cursed.

"What the hell! God damn it! Oh, man!"

"BA-RA-ROO-ROO-ROO!" Chuck's incredibly loud bark of alarm suddenly sounded. He was generally a quiet dog, but when he let loose it was amazing how much noise he could make. Both dogs were soon up and barking at the window beside Ketch and Kari.

"HELP!" the man in the cistern yelled. "JESUS CHRIST! HELP!"

Kari opened the window and yelled back. "SORRY, WE'RE DOIN' THE DISHES!" To Ketch she added, "I hate thieves. It's a good thing I don't have that crowbar in *my* hand."

"HELP!"

Ketch worked at calming the dogs, but he didn't have much luck. "Look, I need to go out there. Can you please see what you can do with them? Maybe give them those bones I set aside. Just don't let them out. I don't want them falling in that hole, too."

"What if he has a gun? I hadn't thought of that before."

"Don't worry, I'll be careful." Ketch had thought of it, most recently just a few moments ago, but he'd decided to not bring it up. Logic dictated that there probably would be one, if their visitor had intended to rob them – especially given the presence of the dogs, which he might have seen earlier from his boat.

"You better be," she said. Then she did as Ketch asked, and he slipped out the door.

The barking had mostly quieted by the time he'd reached the cistern. He hesitated for a moment short of the mark, his heart pounding. No, that was the old you, he told himself. You're over that, you've got this. He breathed deeply and tried to let anger prevail over his anxiety. For this situation, anger was better.

It worked. He took one more deep breath and said, in as menacing a tone as he could manage, "Toss your gun up here right now, or I'll blow your head off and ask questions later!"

"I ain't got no gun!"

Ketch dropped to the ground and completed his advance in a stealthy army crawl. Just short of the edge of the hole, he picked up a handful of pebbles and threw them a few feet away, as a decoy. Nothing happened, so he rose to his knees, pulled a penlight from his pocket, and shone it into the cistern.

Its skinny, mullet-haired occupant was a sorry sight in the spotlight. He was sitting with his back against the bricks, his face a rictus of pain, shielding his eyes with one hand. He didn't appear to have any kind of weapon.

"So, no gun? That's good, because I don't have one, either," Ketch said. "But I do have this, just so you know." He displayed the crowbar.

"What the hell is that, a spear? Jeez, turn that light off!" the man groaned.

"What kind of robber are you?" Ketch asked. "What were you going to do if I'd let the dogs out?"

"I don't know. Come on man, the light!"

Ketch obliged and clicked the penlight off. "So, what can I do for you this fine evening?" he asked, politely but through gritted teeth.

"What? You can help me get the hell outta here, that's what!"

"I'm sorry, but not just yet. We have some talking to do first. What's your name?"

The man glared up at Ketch. "Why was this cistern uncovered? Did you do that on purpose?"

"Yes. I saw you watching us today from your boat. You're that treasure hunter George told me about, aren't you? I figured you'd come around when you saw us digging."

"I'm gonna sue you!" the man threatened. "Get me outta here!"

His eyes looked wild and the poor guy was obviously in pain. But Ketch had zero sympathy for him after the run-ins he'd had this past year with others of his ilk.

"You aren't going to sue me," he replied. "First, I'd never admit to setting this trap in court. Second, you're trespassing on private property right now, not to mention the breaking and entering you did earlier. And third, there's no one here but us chickens. I could just move that stone back on top of this hole, shovel some dirt over it, and let the eel grass take over. Someone might uncover your bones someday, I suppose, but I doubt it."

There, that had quieted the son of a bitch, Ketch thought. Stay focused. "Now let's start over," he said. He glanced back and saw that Kari was at the open window. The dogs were quiet now, so she must have succeeded in distracting them with their treats.

"What's your name?" he asked again. "And speak up, so the lady can hear you." When the man told him his name, Ketch said, "Well, I've never heard of you, so I guess you're not too good at what you do. Are you hurt?"

"I think I have a broken ankle, and my shoulder might be dislocated," the man sullenly replied. "Come on, man, help me out here!" He grimaced in pain. "Please?" he grudgingly added.

Ketch ignored the request. "So you can't climb out of there on your own? Good, then I might not need this after all," he said, displaying the crowbar again. "Why are you here? What are you looking for?"

"You know, man! The treasure from the Ghost Ship." Despite his injuries, it appeared to Ketch the man was on the fidgety side and having trouble staying still. Was he on something? Maybe he was just nervous. "Did you find it?" the man asked. "Is it in the house?"

"No," Ketch answered honestly. "And we weren't looking for it. We only dug to lure you here, so we could have some peace. We're just here on vacation." He paused to let the irony sink in, then continued. "So what, you were hoping we'd found something and left it lying around out here for you to steal? And then what if we'd taken it inside? What would you have done then? Try to break in and steal it while we were sleeping? Even though we have the dogs?"

"I don't know. I didn't know you had dogs."

"Really? You must not be very observant. It appears you're about as good a robber as you are a treasure hunter. And speaking of, I'd never heard of any such treasure until George told me about you, and neither has anyone else, from what I've read about that ship. Why do you think there's a treasure? Tell me what you think you know."

"Aw, come on, man! Hey, tell you what, help me out and I'll split it with you, fifty-fifty, how about that?"

"You know what else this crowbar is good for, besides what would legally be considered self-defense?" Ketch mused. "It's how I moved that stone cover before."

"All right, all right! I'll tell you." Continuing to fidget and grimace throughout, the man told his tale. Ketch listened without interrupting.

"I see," he said when the interloper had finished. "Let me make sure I have this straight. There was supposedly a mutiny aboard the Ghost Ship, because the captain had stolen some kind of treasure from some – what did you call them? – portagees, when they were in Rio, and he'd refused to give the crew shares of the treasure. Brazilian gold, you said? And the captain escaped from the Ghost Ship, with his treasure, in one of her lifeboats, and someone who claimed to be a descendant of one of the mutineers told you all this. And then some old fisherman you ran into in some bar told you he heard that some even older fishermen had once found a lifeboat on this island that they thought came from the Ghost Ship. So you think the ship's captain landed here, and that's why you think there could be a treasure here somewhere."

"Yeah, that's right," the man said between groans.

"The captain and crew of the Ghost Ship were never found, and none of them ever turned up anywhere later, to anyone's knowledge," Ketch expounded. Just to be annoying? Perhaps... "There was a theory that, if they abandoned ship when she ran aground and they got swept out to sea, they could have been picked up by a passing steamship that was known to have been in the area at the same time – but that ship sank in another storm, with no survivors, before it could make port."

"Whatever, man! Now can you get me outta here?"

"My point is," Ketch continued as if he hadn't heard, "your story seems a little far-fetched. Are you sure you didn't just make it up to attract investors?"

"Investors? What're you talkin' about, man? I ain't got no investors."

"Really? That's unusual for a treasure hunter these days, isn't it? A professional one, anyway."

"Whatever! Come on, man!"

"By the way, did you know that 'portagee' is a pejorative term for someone of Portuguese descent?"

"Huh?"

"Yes, it's like using the N-word for an African-American person."

"So what? Come on man, I told you everything, now help me get outta here!"

"You're not from around here, are you? I guess that makes you a dingbatter, and probably a touron as well."

"What?"

"Never mind. Okay, I guess I've heard enough," Ketch said. "Kari," he called, "please get my marine radio from my backpack and raise the Coast Guard. Tell them we caught a pirate and we need a medevac, but not by air."

"Hey! Wait, man!" The trespasser seemed even more alarmed now. "Can't you just cut me some slack here? I didn't mean you no harm. Just help me get back to my boat, and I swear I'll never bother you again!"

"I'm sorry, but no. I don't think being complaisant would serve the lady and myself well in this case."

"Huh? What do you mean?"

"Complaisant – eager to please others and easily convinced to do what they want," Kari called from the window. "He uses big words, and I had to look that one up not long ago. Ketch, I've got the radio."

"Hey now, wait, come on! If you call the Coasties, they'll tow my boat, and I can't have them crawlin' around on my boat!"

"Oh? Why is that?" Ketch asked. He leaned forward a little and again panned his light across the disheveled figure down below. "Is that a glass pipe sticking out of your pocket? Are you what they call a tweaker? Is that why you're so jittery?" The man didn't answer. "Do you have drugs on your boat? Meth, and maybe some heroin? I hear those are the biggies these days. Are you a drug dealer?" Ketch wondered how old this man really was. He looked middle-aged, but that might be due to drug use.

"Okay, look," the man said. "Yeah, I deal, and I cook. But I told you the truth about that treasure, honest! Hey, even if there ain't no treasure, I could pay you. I've got cash on my boat. How about that, huh? Come on!"

Ketch's face hardened. "I don't think so. People like you are a scourge on society. The use of addictive drugs is becoming epidemic and ruining a lot of lives, and taking one more of your kind out of circulation means more to me than money. Kari," he called, "were you able to get the Coast Guard?"

"Yep," she called back. "They're on their way. They said about thirty minutes."

"Good. Please meet them at the dock and direct them back here." Thirty minutes – like a pizza delivery, Ketch thought. He could have had Kari ask them to bring one, but he supposed that would have been disrespectful.

"Aw, man..." came a dejected comment from below. "This really stinks, you know that? Thanks a lot, man! Damn..."

"Shut up," Ketch said. He found a stump a little farther from the cistern and settled in to wait, with the crowbar resting across his lap. He had no further interest in his prisoner and didn't care to even look at him anymore, but he'd continue to keep watch over him until the Coasties arrived.

Surprisingly, the treasure hunter obeyed Ketch's directive and fell silent. It seemed the man in the hole had nothing more to say for the time being – which was fine with Ketch, as he had nothing more to say to him, either.

~ ~ ~

"What do you think about going on a little field trip tomorrow?" Ketch called to Kari after he'd used the last of his remaining strength to move the stone cover back atop the old cistern. He was crashing now from his adrenalin rush and looking forward to hitting the hay – and preferably without having to take a roll in it first. But she looked like she was worn out as well.

The Coasties had come and gone, taking their latest tormentor with them, and Kari had just brought the dogs out. There had been some serious barking when the Coast Guard arrived, and the excited animals had been itching to get outside. After they made sure Ketch was okay, they started patrolling frantically, noses to the ground.

"Why, do you want to check out that guy's boat? I don't think that's a good idea. It's a crime scene now, you know. Plus they said they'd be back for it in the mornin' – and I don't know about you, but I won't be gettin' up at the crack of dawn."

"No, I was thinking about his story, about the treasure."

"You believe that story?"

"I'm not sure – but I think *he* did. I noticed when we came in on the *TBD* that the way the current was flowing through the inlet and around Portsmouth, it would have taken us to the northwest tip of this island if I'd cut the engine and drifted. I know it was almost a hundred years ago and things could have been different then, but if a lifeboat from the *Deering* did beach here, maybe we could find some indication of it up that way."

"Huh. Would we walk or sail?"

"Well, this is a small island, so I thought we could just hike along the shoreline. There's a mostly sandy strip between the water and the woods, and Jack and Chuck would enjoy it. It probably wouldn't take too long, and if we don't find anything, so what. It could still be fun, right?"

"Okay, I'm game." She walked over to Ketch and gave him a hug. "I know we got off to a rocky start, but now we have this island all to ourselves, don't we? And you know what that means, right?" she grinned, looking up at him. "We can do whatever we want, wherever we want! But don't worry, not tonight. I'm bushed, and I bet you are, too."

"Yes, I am."

"I guess Don was right, huh? That meth crap can turn up just about anywhere nowadays – even here, of all places!"

"The Captain is usually right, about most things anyway."

"Ha! That's what he'd like us to believe. Well, let's get the boys back inside and turn in before we run outta dark. If I don't get my seven hours, I get cranky, and you know you don't want that!"

~ ~ ~

They'd indeed slept in a little this morning, atypically for him and less so for her. But it was still the tail end of rush hour for working folks, and after a hasty breakfast the four of them were on their way up island.

This is more like it, Ketch thought, more like what he'd had in mind when he'd decided to bring Kari here – a little peace and quiet away from the things of Man with the woman he loved, even if only for a short time. It was just what the putative doctor would have ordered, had there been one and he or she'd had a clue. Jack and Chuck were enjoying running free in the relatively crisp (for this locale) morning air, exploring at the shoreline and the edge of the maritime forest, and carousing in the placid waters of Pamlico Sound now and then along the way. And he'd seen the Coast Guard launch steaming away from the island earlier with the treasure hunter's trawler-slash-floating meth lab in tow, so that was the end of that unpleasant business.

"What are we supposed to be lookin' for?" Kari asked.

"Oh, well – I guess either a lifeboat that has *Carroll A. Deering* stenciled on it somewhere, or a treasure chest," Ketch quipped.

"Very funny. I'm seein' some driftwood here and there, but nothin' that looks like it was part of a boat."

"Well, keep your eyes open."

"You do realize that if a lifeboat from the Ghost Ship did end up here, it probably rotted away or got smashed up by storms, or both. I mean, it's been a long time."

"I know. But it's my place to hope for my people."

She laughed. "*Joe Versus the Volcano*! Give it up, mister, you can't stump me. Did you bring that DVD, too?"

"Yes, I did."

They walked in silence for a while, one or the other occasionally wandering off to investigate an interesting-looking piece of flotsam and/or jetsam. Which would a marooned lifeboat be classified as, Ketch wondered, flotsam or jetsam?

The distinction was important in maritime law, he knew. The definitions he'd seen had varied, and were thus confusing (to him at least). One he'd seen said that flotsam is debris from a ship that was not deliberately thrown overboard (as in the case of a shipwreck), and jetsam is debris that was deliberately thrown overboard (as when lightening the load on a ship in distress). Flotsam could thus be reclaimed by its original owner, whereas with jetsam it was 'finders keepers' – in theory. But whether jetsam was really jetsam could also depend on whether or not the ship sank after the items were jettisoned.

And he knew marine salvage rules could get even murkier than that, being also dependent on the legality of claims of ownership, determination of abandonment, and feasibility of recovery. He figured this lifeboat should be considered jetsam, since it was deliberately put into the water and wasn't part of a sinking ship (since the Ghost Ship hadn't sunk on her own), and it wasn't aboard the ship when it had been dynamited. But would this particular lifeboat be classed as abandoned, or an unrecoverable derelict, or 'lagan', which was an item cast overboard with the intent of recovery later by its owner?

He also knew there were legal complications involved in claiming ownership of an abandoned boat of any kind – but this boat wouldn't be in the water, and would instead just be debris on a beach, so would salvage laws apply to it at all? If they did, and if the original owner filed a claim on it, then Ketch would be entitled to a finder's fee. But he'd also read that if he brought it to port, he could legally claim ownership for himself. Also, this boat was almost a hundred years old. Any insurance claims related to the Ghost Ship had been settled long ago, the ship's manufacturer was no longer in business, and the original owners were undoubtedly deceased. But what about their estates? Could they claim ownership? And could the insurance company, if it was still in business, stake a claim?

And then, if there was some kind of treasure – well, that was another legal can of worms. State and federal laws related to recovery and ownership of treasure, and tax implications, could also come into play in that event. And how would George figure in all this? He owned the island now. But Dixie's family had owned it when the lifeboat had beached here. And what would the archeologists say if he and Kari compromised what they'd probably consider a historic wreck?

What a mess! It was no wonder there were so many lawyers. If they did find something on the beach today, would they need to retain an admiralty lawyer?

Well, they hadn't found anything yet. And if they *were* to find anything, it needed to happen soon. This island wasn't quite a mile long and they'd almost reached its northern end already, and he wasn't dedicated enough to their quest to go sloshing through the salt marsh on the opposite shore. Anyone with any sense wouldn't have landed there anyway, if it could have been avoided.

But maybe the landing site for that lifeboat had been a matter of chance. Maybe the fleeing captain had been injured during the mutiny, or he'd lost his oars, and he hadn't been able to maneuver the boat to a site of his choosing. That would make sense, since he surely would have tried to reach a settlement, either Portsmouth or Ocracoke, if he'd had a choice. If that were true, and if the local currents hadn't changed too much since then, he should have been carried through the inlet between Portsmouth and Ocracoke and then made landfall somewhere in the area he and Kari were now exploring.

"Ketch, come on over here," Kari called from somewhere behind him. "I think I might've found somethin'!"

He turned around and retraced his steps. By the time he joined her, she was on her hands and knees, brushing sand away from something. The dogs, probably hoping she was digging up something of interest to them, were milling about there now as well.

"Hi, guys!" he said to them. "Are you having fun? Good boys." He gave them each a pat and said, "So, what have you got there?"

"Well, I saw part of this curvy old piece of wood stickin'

up. Now that I'm seein' more of it, I think it could be part of a gunwale. What do you think?"

Ketch examined what she'd unearthed so far. "I think you might be right," he said. He tried to dig some more, but it was hard to do by hand. "Hang on." He went a little farther into the woods and returned shortly with a couple of decent-sized flat stones that could serve as scoops. "Here you go," he said, handing one to Kari.

The dogs thought this second digging game in two days was great fun, and they again pitched in. Amusingly, it was Jack who made the next significant discovery.

"This looks like the prow of a small boat," Ketch announced upon examining Jack's work. "Good job, boy!"

"Do you think the whole boat is buried here?" Kari asked.

"Maybe, or it might just be a piece of it. Let's start here at the prow and see how far back we can go."

Jack lost interest after that, and decided to rest in a shady spot by the woods. Ketch and Kari continued to scoop earth and sand away along the gunwales of the boat, one to port and the other to starboard.

"I wonder how this boat got buried like this?" Kari asked. "I know there's been storm wash and such over the years, but still..."

"The beach is wider here than it was farther down the island," Ketch answered. "I know sand was dumped at the south end of the island, where the cottage is, during the dredging that was done for the Intracoastal Waterway. Maybe they dumped some here, too." He set his stone down. "Well, it looks like we've uncovered enough to see that this is the outline of most of the boat. It's probably intact. Maybe we should stop now."

"What? But we hadn't found the treasure! Maybe we should go back and get the shovels, and dig the sand out of this boat. Maybe there's a box or a chest or somethin' underneath this mess."

"I doubt it. Think about it – that tweaker's story has panned out so far. If some fishermen really did stumble across this boat way back when, and there was some kind of treasure aboard, I'm sure it's long gone. Besides, we may have maritime salvage laws to consider, and we're on private property – I was thinking about all that just before you called me over here – plus this could be considered a historic site, or at least a historic find. And this wood is pretty rotten. I don't think we should disturb it further."

"You're probably right," Kari wistfully agreed. "So what should we do? Report it to somebody?"

"Yes. I think we should contact the North Carolina Archeological Society in Chapel Hill. They could arrange to send some archeologists here, maybe from one of the universities. But I should probably inform George first, I suppose."

Just then Jack got up to see what Chuck was doing. Ketch had thought Chuck was through digging, like Jack, but he'd apparently still been busy a little farther down the beach. Now Ketch could see that all ears were up, both tails were swishing, and both noses were focused on the hole Chuck had dug.

"Look, Chuck must have found something," he said. "We'd better investigate."

"Maybe he found the treasure," Kari said. "Maybe that captain buried it near the boat."

She got there first. "Oh Lordy!" she exclaimed when she saw what Chuck had uncovered. "My goodness! Y'all get back now, hear? Shoo!" The dogs were reluctant to obey, but they did back off a little.

"Captain Wormell, I presume?" Ketch said when he knelt and saw what was definitely a human skull and part of a shoulder. He wondered how long the beleaguered old mariner had been marooned here before succumbing to his wounds, or the elements, or both. Not that long, he'd wager. "Rest in peace, Captain," he murmured.

"Remember when I mentioned university archeologists?" he said to Kari. "Well, now we can add forensic archeologists to the mix." He ran a hand through his hair. "So I think the Coast Guard is who we need to call. Seems to me they should know what to do and who else should be informed."

"They were just here this mornin', and last night, too. They're gonna get tired of us callin' on them."

Ketch shrugged. "That's their job. And I should still call George, too, of course. But first, I think I'll ask the Captain if he agrees with calling the Coast Guard for something like this. He was a Coastie at one time." Ketch watched as Jack snuck another sniff at the bones, then started zigzagging toward the woods with his nose to the ground. "What's he after, I wonder?" he said, and then returned his attention to the bones. "Do you have your phone handy?"

"You want to start callin' people right now?"

"No. I think we should wait until tomorrow, or maybe even the day after. We haven't gotten much of a vacation so far, and these things have been here for almost a hundred years. A couple more days won't matter. I'd like you to take a picture of these bones, and one of the boat. I'm going to find a stick and tie my bandana to it, to mark this spot."

While she got busy with her phone, Ketch walked up toward the woods. He saw that Jack was now sniffing around a sizeable old live oak, so he went that way. Chuck was still preoccupied with the bones, though he was behaving and not digging anymore.

Ketch saw that the oak had a hollow, a fairly wide elliptical slit that ran up the trunk on one side. Jack had noticed it as well, and was now nosing around the bottom of the opening.

"What are you onto there, boy?" he asked the dog. He tried to peek into the hollow without putting his face too close to it. He wasn't hearing any movement from inside at the moment, but a hollow like this would make a good home for a number of small but bitey critters. It was deep and dark inside, and he couldn't see much.

"I'll be right back," he said to Jack. He completed his original task, jamming a sturdy twig upright in the sand near the bones and tying the bandana to it that he always carried in a back pocket.

"Could you take another picture, with the flag this time?" he asked Kari as he fished his penlight from his backpack.

"Okay. But what are you up to now?"

"Jack may have found something in a hollow in that tree he's sitting in front of. I'm going back to check it out."

He was shining the light into the hollow when Kari joined him. "Do you see anything?" she asked.

"It's pretty deep, and I can't see the bottom from this angle. But I think there's some kind of bag in there."

"Well, I hope it's treasure, and not another dang skull." When Ketch pocketed the penlight, she said, "Wait, you're not gonna stick your hand in there, are you? Who knows what else could be in there with it?"

"True, it might be like that old Dean Martin song. '*See that thing in the reef with the big shiny teeth, that's a moray... put your hand in the crack and you won't get it back, from a moray...*' he sang. He hadn't thought of that parody by the Barefoot Man in many years. He and his old scuba buddies back North had thought it was pretty funny when they'd first heard it.

"Stop it, I'm serious. That's another way to ruin a vacation, you know, gettin' bit by somethin' nasty."

"I know. I'll try to hook it with a stick first." He looked around and found one that he thought might work – and it did. He inserted the stick down into the hollow and snagged what appeared to be a weather-beaten sailcloth bag. It didn't look like it was ripped, but there were a few small holes in it, and it was mildewed. Animal droppings of some kind rolled from the bag as he slowly worked it up to the level of the opening, taking care to avoid tearing it. Then he used his hands to gingerly extract it through the slit and set it down on the ground.

Jack sniffed at Ketch's find. "Did you track this, boy?" he said, giving the dog another pat and kneeling beside the bag. "Could he have done that?" he asked Kari. "I know dogs have an extraordinary sense of smell, but could that man's scent still be discernible to him after all this time?"

"I don't know, does it matter? What is it? Open it!" Kari demanded, finding it hard to control her excitement. Chuck came bounding up to them then, to see what was going on.

"Hang on." The bag was tied off with some kind of cord, which crumbled when he tried to untie it. He spread the bag open and exposed a flaking, salt-stained leather satchel. Letting it rest where it lay, he cautiously pulled its brittle flap back far enough to see what was inside.

"It's a book," he said.

"Huh? What kinda book?"

"A ledger of some kind, maybe. It has a hard cover. I don't know, and I don't know if I should handle it."

"Oh, come on, aren't you curious? We'll be careful with it, and we can put it back after, if you want to. If we aren't gonna get any treasure out of all this, I at least want to know what kind of book that is. Don't you?"

Though he had misgivings, Ketch gave in. "Okay. But I think you should keep Jack and Chuck with you and hold onto their collars. I don't want them to step on it or otherwise damage it." When she'd gathered the dogs beside her and restrained them as directed, he slid the book out, placed it atop the satchel, and carefully opened it.

He slowly leafed through several musty and crinkly pages. The handwriting was small and cramped, and the ink had faded with time. But it didn't take him too long to determine what kind of book it was.

"Well? What is it?" Kari asked.

"It's the ship's log," Ketch said. He let out a long breath and looked up at her. "From the Ghost Ship."

"No kiddin'? Wow... Can I take a look at it?"

"Okay – but be careful with it," Ketch reminded her as they traded places. "Easy, guys," he told the dogs, who weren't happy about being restrained.

"Don't worry, I will," she said. She gently turned the book over and opened it to the last page. "Dang, no treasure map tucked in the back." She flipped a few more pages, then settled on one toward the end. "It looks like the last entry was made on January 30, 1921."

"That was the day before the *Deering* was sighted aground on Diamond Shoals," Ketch observed. "What does it say?"

"The handwritin's kinda shaky here at the end, and it's pretty faded, but I think I can make it out." She read silently while Ketch patiently waited with the dogs. It was probably good, he thought, that she was the one doing the reading, given her well-known lack of patience and dislike of waiting. And he didn't mind if she wanted to summarize what she was reading. He could take a closer look at the log himself later, in more comfortable surroundings.

"Well," she finally continued, "it was written by Captain Wormell – and there *was* a mutiny! He says he heard the first mate started a rumor among the crew that the captain had come into possession of some gold in Rio and buried it in Barbados, and he'd decided not to tell the crew about it nor give 'em their fair share of it. Pretty much like that guy in our cistern said! But it says here there wasn't any gold and there was nothin' buried anywhere, it was just a story to get the crew riled. Dang!"

"And Wormell and his crew were already at odds with one another, so they were probably more than willing to swallow that story. And the first mate wasn't getting along with him, either."

"Right. Well, when Wormell heard about it, he made sure his pistol was loaded and he carried it with him at all times. And when the crew mutineed, he shot the first mate! But he got shot, too. But he was able to escape a little while later in one of the lifeboats."

"So he *was* injured when he landed here. I thought so. That would explain why he drifted here instead of sailing to Ocracoke or Portsmouth. He probably couldn't row the boat."

"That's right! He says it here, that he couldn't row. He says he drifted for a couple days before he got here."

"The mutiny must have occurred shortly before the *Deering* hailed the Cape Lookout lightship, most likely early on the twenty-eighth since he said he drifted for two days."

"He doesn't say exactly when it happened." She paused for a moment. "I guess he wrote this entry right here on the island, after he got here. But we didn't find a pen, nor an inkwell."

"Maybe he dropped them in that hollow alongside the bag."

"Right. Well, somebody else besides me'n you can stick their arm down in there later on if they want to. So," she went on, "he had no food and no water, and he was hurtin'. He says he figured he was fixin' to die, and he wanted to write down what happened before he went." She closed the book and slid it back into the satchel. "How sad," she said. "He died right here, all alone."

Now that the book was relatively safe, Ketch released the dogs. They immediately ran off toward the water, disinterested in Ketch's find. It was apparently old news to them now.

"Wow, this is a pretty historic find," Kari said while Ketch re-bagged the satchel. "Now we finally know what really happened to the Ghost Ship!"

"Well, we don't quite know everything," Ketch pointed out. "We still don't know what happened to the rest of crew. Though it seems obvious that they probably all crammed into the remaining lifeboat when she ran aground, and then got swept out to sea."

"I guess... Hey, you know what's ironic? That treasure hunter probably docked his boat right around here last night, and he had no idea all this stuff was here. Why, he might have walked right over top of those bones!"

"Yes, that *is* ironic."

"So now what? Are you really gonna put that bag back in that ol' hollow?"

Ketch thought a bit before answering. "No. I'll keep it with me for now. I don't think me keeping it will disturb the site for the archeologists. In fact, it may be better that we don't leave it here. I know it's survived this long, but what if a storm comes along and takes that old tree down before they get around to starting a dig here?"

"Sounds like a good rationalization to me," Kari said with a smile. "So, you want to start headin' back? I'm gettin' kinda hungry. We didn't eat much this mornin'."

~ ~ ~

"Now *this* is the life!" Kari declared, taking another sip. "I can't believe you snuck a bunch of my favorite wine in with all our other stuff. I'm impressed!"

"You're welcome," Ketch said, finishing the remainder of his beer. The dogs were snoozing on the floor of the screened porch beside him. They hadn't even begged when he'd eaten his sandwich. Their big outing this morning must have tuckered them out again.

"Would you like to sail to Ocracoke later on?" he asked her. "We could get something better than sandwiches or burgers for dinner. We'd just have to make sure we're back by dark."

“Nah, I don’t think so. I’d rather just relax here. Maybe we could go tomorrow for lunch, and then we wouldn’t have to rush.”

“Fine by me.”

“Besides, you probably want to read that ship’s log, don’t you? I can tell you’re thinkin’ about it.”

“I’d like to read it sometime, yes, but not right now. I’ll look at it later, or maybe tomorrow.” The logbook was safely stowed in his trusty backpack inside the cottage. Though he was indeed itching to read more of it, it could wait. He had time.

“What’re you gonna do with it after you read it?”

“Well, I was thinking I might give it to Dixie, if she’ll have it.”

“But what about George? It’s his island. He might say it belongs to him.”

“Well, I might be able to say it belongs to me, since I found it, depending on how the salvage laws are interpreted. And it wasn’t George’s island when Wormell landed here. It belonged to Dixie’s family then, so if push came to shove, she might have a legal basis for an ownership claim. And I’m not confident that George would do the right thing with it.”

“Which is?”

“I think Dixie, above all others I know, will appreciate its significance and give the log, and Wormell, the respect they deserve. I imagine she’d donate it to the Graveyard museum sooner or later. She’s donated other items to them.”

“What about the Coast Guard, and the forensic archeologists? They might want to impound it as evidence.”

“I doubt it, but I suppose it’s possible. That’s why I said ‘if she’ll have it’. Dixie, or maybe the museum, might have to scrap with them, and maybe with George as well. But she’s a feisty lady, and I’ll bet she’ll take it.” Then Ketch’s brow furrowed. “When George asked me check this place out, he also asked me if I had any ideas about what to name it. A house has to have a name around these parts, you know, and the island could also use a new name. I was thinking ‘Dixie Island’ might be good for one or the other, and maybe both. I think it’d be historic and appropriate. But he might not like that idea if I give that log to Dixie.”

“Oh, I don’t know, you might be surprised. He seemed like a decent guy that one time I met him. But what about you? You might could be on the news again! Are you sure you don’t want to keep it for yourself?”

“You mean, for fortune and glory, kid, fortune and glory?”

“*Indiana Jones and the Temple of Doom*!”

Ketch nodded. “Well, I don’t need all that.”

“No? Well, at least you’ll have a good tale to tell around the next campfire. I bet Don’ll be jealous! He’s the one likes to tell the tales.”

“Maybe. Anyway, I don’t need fortune and glory, because I have you,” Ketch said to her with a smile. “And that’s enough for me.”

She laughed. “Well, aren’t you the sappy one!” She drained her glass and set it aside. “But I’ll have you know, mister, that flattery will get you – well, pretty much everywhere with me, actually.” She stood up and gave him a salacious wink. “You up for another nap, Indy?”

Postscript

No one knows what really happened to the captain and crew of the *Carroll A. Deering*, the Ghost Ship of Diamond Shoals; there is no such place as Dixie Island (nor Ted's Island) on the Outer Banks; and Dixie Burrus Browning was not named after this fictional island.

But Dixie herself is quite real – and whether or not she wants to admit it, she's been an Outer Banks treasure for quite some time. And now she's a state treasure as well, according to the Governor of North Carolina, whose office awarded her the Order of the Long Leaf Pine in a ceremony held at the Graveyard of the Atlantic Museum in Hatteras in 2016. This prestigious award is bestowed on individuals who have a 'record of extraordinary service to the state'.

Dixie considers herself primarily an artist. A noteworthy painter of watercolor landscapes and seascapes, she taught art and co-founded the Watercolor Society of North Carolina. But she's also an award-winning writer or co-writer of over a hundred romance novels, including historical romances set on the Outer Banks – and an all-around adventurer and lover of life, from what I've heard.

I had the pleasure of meeting Dixie and spending some time with her during my last visit to the Outer Banks. I'm honored to count her as a friend now, and when I mapped out my series of short Storm Ketchum Tales, I resolved to include her somehow in one of them as a tribute. Hence *Dixie Island*, the story you just read.

If you'd like to learn more about Dixie, and you happen to be on Hatteras Island sometime in 2017 or early 2018, the Graveyard of the Atlantic Museum is hosting a special exhibit titled *Dixie's World*. The museum is worth visiting on its own merits, but this exhibit will make your experience even more memorable.

Lastly, if you ever find yourself in possession of a small Outer Banks island that needs a name – why not *Dixie Island*?

THE WAYWARD MARINER

DESCRIPTION

In Storm Ketchum Tale #5, an uninvited visitor at Ketch's houseboat on a dark and stormy night brings him more trouble than he's in the mood for.

Ketch is exhausted and simply wants to go to sleep, but a knock sounding from the cabin door as he's putting his grandson to bed changes his plans for the evening. To his dismay, a castaway blown into the boatyard by a nor'easter creates an unexpected and unnerving problem for him, one that he'll once again need some help from good old Captain Don to resolve.

Join amateur sleuth Storm 'Ketch' Ketchum as he deals with the mystery of a tragically wayward mariner on historic Hatteras Island, where intrigue always seems to be just around the next corner.

NOTE: The Kinnakeet Boatyard, the Sea Dog Scuba Center, and CSFCP (Common Sense for Cape Point) are fictitious.

February 2014

Ketch sat down on the floor and made himself as comfortable as possible alongside Bean's bunk.

"It was a dark and stormy night..." he began, as had become his custom of late. Bean had grown weary of his meager collection of children's books, and now preferred to be told a tall tale at bedtime.

"Papa," the boy protested, "you can't say that all the time!"

Ketch laughed. "But I have to say it, because you enjoy it so much. So – it was a dark and stormy night..."

"Papa!"

"But it *is* a dark and stormy night," Ketch persisted, referring to the February nor'easter they'd been enduring and which was finally winding down today.

"Ketch, you quit teasin' that poor boy now!" Kari called from the master bedroom.

When Bean continued to give him the stink-eye, Ketch decided to desist. It had been a long day for the boy, and he was probably exhausted – though of course he wouldn't admit it. Little do they know... Bean was one of those children who'd never willingly consent to nap during the day, either, whereas most adults Ketch knew might consider killing at times for an opportunity to do so.

Including himself, on this particular day. But he hadn't had time to nap. It was Saturday, Kari had been needed at the dive shop, and Bean and the dogs had all had cabin fever – understandably so, since the houseboat, though a relatively spacious one, was even more cramped than his old *Port Starbird* house had been – and they'd been pretty much cooped up here most of the time for the duration of the storm.

So despite the still blustery weather, he'd bundled the boy up and loaded both him and the dogs into his pickup. The water that had blown across Highway 12 from Pamlico

Sound at the Haulover was receding today, so he'd driven them from Avon to Buxton. It was just a few miles farther down the island, not much of a road trip, but it was somewhere to go.

He and Bean had an early lunch at the Orange Blossom Café, and then they'd all hiked partway up toward Cape Point along the windswept beach by the iconic Cape Hatteras Lighthouse – one of his favorite spots on the Outer Banks, especially at times like this when there were precious few tourists around. And for him, the sea was as soul-soothing when it was angry as it was on a sunny day, so he hadn't minded the weather. But though he usually stayed up later than this, tonight he was looking forward to hitting the hay as soon as possible.

But his day wasn't done yet, and it wouldn't be until he came up with a story. He and the boy would have to take a road trip down to Buxton Village Books, his favorite bookstore and the only one here on Hatteras Island, one day soon. They probably should have stopped by there today, since they'd been in the neighborhood. He was running out of stories to tell.

He racked his brain for one he hadn't yet told the boy, and one that would be appropriate for his six-year-old grandson – which disqualified most of his friend the Captain's salty yarns. Actually, 'almost seven' was the youngster's preferred age when asked, but that didn't make any difference. Meanwhile, the night sounds of the boatyard and the remnants of the storm, and the somnolent rocking of the houseboat beneath him, weren't helping his concentration.

"What if a monster knocked on the door?" Bean helpfully suggested. "And what if we go'd to it and opened it! What would happen after that?"

"What if we *went* to it," Ketch absently corrected him.

"Maybe Scooby Doo could save us," the boy added.

"No," Ketch said, rubbing his eyes. "I don't think I

should tell you a scary story at bedtime. Besides, it would be foolish of us to answer the door for a monster, don't you think?"

"But we wouldn't know it was a monster. We wouldn't know until we opened the door!"

"But we *would* know. Do you remember why?"

"Yes, Papa. We always look out the window to see who it is first. But we don't have to do it in the story!"

Jack wandered into the boy's bedroom. Ketch thought at first that his faithful companion was there for the story, which he often enjoyed listening to, but then he noticed the dog had a concerned look on his face. Chuck shortly followed him in, and both of them looked expectantly at Ketch and growled.

"What's the matter, guys?" Ketch asked them. "Kari," he called, "what are the dogs upset about?"

"Beats me," she said, coming to the doorway. "They've both been kinda antsy for the last little while, but not like when they want to go out. Might be they need to, though, I don't know. I could take 'em if you want."

Before Ketch could answer, a sound (not unlike that of a knock on a door) reached their ears from the stern of the houseboat (where the door in fact was), and all hell broke loose. The first knock was shortly followed by another, and both dogs turned and ran from the bedroom. Their feet scrabbling for purchase as they rounded the corner, they raced down the corridor and through the galley to the cabin door, barking all the way.

"What in the world!" Kari exclaimed. "They usually behave better than that when somebody comes to the door. Maybe it's somebody they don't know?"

"I'll check it out. You two stay here," Ketch directed.

"What if it's a monster? Look out the window first!" Bean reminded him.

"I will," Ketch assured him. "But don't worry, I'm sure it's not a monster."

He followed the dogs' path to the door and managed to mostly quiet them, though there was still some low-pitched grumbling going on. Per the directive he'd instilled in Bean, he first opened the blinds and took a look around through the window.

The outside light above the door was still on, adequately illuminating both the stern of the boat and the adjoining dock. He'd taken the gangway in earlier, he remembered – so if there was someone on deck, it would have to be someone nimble enough to make a short leap from the dock. As he scanned the area, another knock sounded and the dogs started barking again. There was no one in sight, however, and Ketch realized the sound wasn't coming from the door.

"There's no one at the door," he called back to Kari and Bean after again hushing the dogs. "Something in the water is bumping up against the boat, probably a tree branch or something like that. I'm going out to take a look."

He retrieved his rain parka from the closet and put it on. It was no longer raining, but it was still windy and chilly out there. He was stepping into his Wanchese slippers when Bean joined him and the dogs. The boy also had a pair, which he quickly started to pull on. The 'slippers' were white fishing boots like the ones traditionally worn by the commercial fishermen of Wanchese on Roanoke Island. Kari had a pair as well, which Ketch had given her on her last birthday, but hers were a stylish modern variation reminiscent of go-go boots.

"Now hold on there," Kari admonished Bean as she joined the group. "You're in your PJs, young man, and you need to stay right here."

"Aw!" Bean protested.

"She's right," Ketch said. "You're not properly dressed, and it's still a little stormy." He tousled the boy's hair.

"Besides, we don't know what's out there yet, and I want you to be safe. I don't want you to get hurt, okay?"

"Yes, Papa," Bean demurred. He took his boots off and put them back in the closet without further complaint, though it was obvious he wasn't thrilled about doing so.

"And you stay, too," Ketch added, looking down at the dogs.

Chuck snorted, retreated from the door, and flopped down on the mat in front of the sink in the galley. Ketch knew Jack would argue a bit first, but then he'd obey and follow suit. After they'd observed this little ritual and Jack was settled away from the door, Ketch stepped outside.

He was glad he'd worn his coat. The wind had died down considerably and the temperature had to be pushing fifty, but the damp chill would have soon sent him back inside for it if he hadn't put it on. Although it wasn't raining, the houseboat's deck was slick and he made sure to tread carefully as he took a look around.

It didn't take him long to find the source of the mysterious knocking sound – but it was no tree branch. Instead, what was bumping up against the stern of the boat looked to be some kind of container riding low in the water. He knelt on the deck and bent over the transom to examine it more closely in the dim light.

When he was finally able to discern what it was, and to believe what he was seeing, he let out a long sigh. Yes, that was definitely what it was, just bobbing there in the agitated water like a buoy on a crab pot. There was ordinarily not much wave action here on the sound, but tonight some small storm-generated breakers were causing the object to periodically nudge the boat.

Good grief, he thought – really, tonight? When all he wanted to do was get some sleep? Now he supposed he'd have to call someone and somehow deal with this situation, and who knew how long that would take?

Retirement wasn't all it was cracked up to be, he

reflected. Between his divemaster duties at Kari's Sea Dog Scuba Center, mating on the Captain's occasional charters, keeping an eye on the upkeep of the Kinnakeet Boatyard, caring for two dogs now instead of one, his housing conundrum, and Bean's adoption – not to mention solving the occasional odd mystery, like this new one in the water right in front of him – he figured he had to be at least as busy now as when he'd been a working stiff. And then there was his involvement with CSFCP (Common Sense for Cape Point), a local citizens' group addressing National Seashore beach access issues for surf fishermen and their ORVs, which was part of his ongoing effort to become more civic-minded and less of a hermit.

His saving grace was that he wasn't too old for it all quite yet, having retired young and being in good health – and that, all things considered, he wouldn't have it any other way. He was exactly where he wanted and needed to be, and he loved his island life and all it entailed. So he'd buck up as usual and git 'er done, as the Captain would say.

His first order of business would be to tell the others what was happening, and then he'd need to find a way to get the castaway out of the water so it wouldn't drift away and end up who knows where. So he got up and ducked back inside the cabin.

Where he was met by a regular greeting party. Kari and Bean had both been watching him through the window, and the dogs were acting like they hadn't seen him in hours.

"Down, guys, down!" he said, fending off the dogs while affectionately patting both of them in the process. He gave Bean a quick hug as well. He'd found he couldn't get seriously cross with any of his new family, regardless of how fatigued he might be.

"So, what's the verdict?" Kari asked.

"Is it a dolphin?" Bean excitedly inquired. "Or a big turtle, or a giant crab? Can I see? Can I keep it?"

Ketch thought for a moment. His first instinct was to be cautious about what he said, because Bean was still sensitive about his mother's passing. But he didn't know how to sugarcoat this particular situation – and he questioned whether he even should.

"Well, it's not a sea creature, and it's not a branch or another boat," he hedged. He paused again, and then decided he might as well just spit it out. "It's a casket."

"Seriously?" Kari asked. The look on Ketch's face answered her question. "It couldn't just be a crate or a box, now could it?" she pointedly challenged him. "You know, like somethin' washin' ashore from a shipwreck?"

He felt guilty about possibly upsetting the boy, and he was sorely tempted to take the proffered mulligan. But he decided it would be wrong to lie, even if said lie was of the white variety. It seemed to him that too many parents excessively coddled their children these days, to no good end in the long run in his opinion. Disturbing things happen now and then throughout life, and he thought children should learn to handle situations that are outside of their comfort zone. He didn't want Bean to end up like he himself had been not that long ago, always trying to avoid unpleasantness and responding to it by sleeping through it – and for a time a while back, drinking through it – all the while hoping it would simply go away.

"It could just be a box," he quietly replied, standing up a little straighter. Bean was back at the window with the dogs. "But it wouldn't be for long, if someone were to look out a window later. We've all seen caskets before, and sometimes things like this happen when there's flooding from a storm. It's just something we have to deal with."

"Huh," Kari huffed.

Ketch supposed there might be a private discussion about this in his not-too-distant future. But if so, then so be it.

"Well, how in the world did somethin' like *that* end up

here?" she exclaimed. "Where did it come from?"

"I don't know," Ketch said. "But I have an idea."

"And what are we gonna do about it? Are you gonna call somebody?"

"Yes, but first I think I should get it out of the water. If it floats away, it won't do any good to call anyone."

"Why not just tie it up?"

"I don't think I could, without going into the water. And if it's out of the water, maybe I'll be able to find some kind of identification on it."

"Well, that water *is* cold, I'll give you that, and the bottom's pretty mucky hereabouts. But you don't have to figure everything out yourself, you know. Just call the police and let them do it. That way, maybe we could get it taken care of right quick. I think that'd be the best thing, don't you?" Kari concluded, with a meaningful glance in Bean's direction.

"Yes, I agree."

"Well, okay then. So how are you gonna get it out of the water? And where are you gonna put it?"

"There's a gaff on the *TBD*. The, uh, box looks like it has handles on it. Maybe I can hook a handle or pole it to shore, and then I'll pull it up out of the water."

"You think you can do that on your own? I bet it's heavy. I might could help, but..." Kari's voice trailed off as she rested a hand on Bean's shoulder.

"No, you stay here with him, I'll manage. Maybe the Captain's around. The *My Minnow*'s back, and I saw a light on over there."

"I saw that too! Shouldn't he still be down south? What's he doin' back here so soon?"

"I don't know. We were out this afternoon and I didn't see him pull in, and he wasn't aboard when we got back."

"Is there a dead body in the box?" Bean squeaked.

The adults fell silent. The poor little guy, Ketch thought. He'd tried to avoid making up a scary bedtime story for the boy, and the unfortunate lad had gotten a real one instead.

"I don't know yet, son," Ketch answered. "But there may be, yes."

"I bet there is," Bean said, looking worried.

"You go on back out there," Kari told Ketch. "I'll take care of him." She put an arm around the boy's shoulder and steered him toward the living room. "Now don't you go worryin', hear? Everything's fine. Your Papa will take care of it. Say, how 'bout you and me find somethin' good to watch on TV? There's no school tomorrow, so you don't have to go to bed right away. You too, guys," she called back to the dogs. "Jack and Chuck – come! Hey, y'all want some popcorn?"

Ketch gratefully left the home front to her and slipped back out the door. He heard another knock from the stern and double-checked the casket's location. Good, it was still there.

The *TBD*, his mistakenly named Whaler Montauk, was tied up alongside the houseboat. He carefully pulled the cover back, boarded her, and set the gaff up on the deck of the houseboat. Then he climbed back up himself and picked it up again.

But now what? He could hook one of the casket's handles with the gaff – but with the dock to port and the *TBD* to starboard, how would he maneuver the casket to shore? He supposed he might have to move the *TBD* first and tie her up farther down the dock.

"Ahoy there, matey!" came a familiar and welcome bray. Although he hadn't heard it since late October, Ketch would recognize that endearingly abrasive voice anytime and anywhere. He turned and saw that, sure enough, his good friend Captain Don was approaching along the dock.

His best friend, actually, and probably the best one he'd ever had or ever would have. He'd sorely tested the Captain in that regard over the past year, albeit unintentionally for the most part, and the man had come through for him every time. He knew the Captain was a kindred spirit who'd always have his back, and who, like himself, was loath to permit legal impediments to stand in the way of fairness and justice. Kari was a member of this outlaw fraternity as well, and each of them was sullied accordingly in his or her own way – and that bond was as strong for them as family.

"Ahoy yourself, Captain," Ketch responded when the effusive mariner was close enough so he wouldn't have to yell. "It's good to see you." The Captain hopped down onto the deck, and Ketch shook his hand. "What are you doing back here so soon? Did you run afoul of the law down there?"

"Ha!" the Captain snorted, not unlike the way Chuck had. "Nope, not this time. I just got tired a livin' in Paradise, all them hot sunny days and such. The Keys are a genuine bother that way this time a year, y'know."

"So you decided to sail back home in a nor'easter?"

"Nah, I was behind the storm all the way up, just caught up with what's left of her today. Weren't a problem t'all." The Captain's grin faded. "Truth is, one a my great-nephews, I reckon that's what you'd call him, come back from the Middle East in a box. He was in the Army, so they're gonna do a memorial for him up in D.C. next week."

"Oh. Well, I'm sorry to hear that. My condolences."

"Yeah, damn politicians and their dumbass wars. I didn't know him, though, hadn't even see'd him since he was a knee-high runt. But it's family, y'know? But thanks."

Ketch wouldn't know, though, in truth. He was an only child, both of his parents were gone, and he didn't have much of an extended family – especially since neither his ex-wife nor his son, Bean's biological father, wanted anything to do with either of them. He knew his son was in the military and was serving somewhere overseas, but he didn't know much else. He'd care if they'd let him, but it apparently wasn't to be.

"So, whatcha got goin' on here?" the Captain asked. "And what're you fixin' to do with that gaff you're pointin' at me? I don't recall pissin' you off *that* much before I left! But y'know, they say the memory is the second thing to go, and I forget what the first thing is..."

Ketch had heard that one before, but he allowed the Captain an amused grunt anyway. "Turn around and look over the transom and see for yourself," he said.

The Captain bent over the transom and peered intently at the water. "What the Christ!" he exclaimed, standing back up. "Where in hell did *that* come from?"

"I'm thinking maybe that cemetery up in Salvo," Ketch said, "the one that's washing away. But I won't know for sure until I know who's in there."

"Yeah, I heard about that." The Captain removed the skipper's cap he habitually wore and scratched his head. "Well, I guess this is what you'd call one a them cosmic coincidences, huh? I come back for a funeral, and then there's this here starin' me in the face." He swiveled to survey the rest of the houseboat. "Where's Hot Stuff and the boy, inside? They know 'bout this?"

"Yes. Bean's a little upset about it. He heard it knocking against the boat when I was putting him to bed. Kari's distracting him with TV and popcorn while I deal with it."

"I'd say he's probly thinkin' 'bout his mama. Shame he had to be reminded a that. How come the pups ain't barkin'?"

"They like popcorn."

The Captain nodded. "Well, I won't bother 'em right now then. So I'll ask again, whatcha thinkin' 'bout doin' with that gaff? That ain't no hooked fish down there. You can't just stick it and hoist it up."

Ketch scratched at his Hemingway-esque beard, which he really should trim again soon. "I know. I just want to get it to shore so it doesn't drift off, and then I can call someone to pick it up. But I have to figure out how to get it around everything that's in the way. I thought about moving the *TBD*, but now I'm thinking I could tie a line to the end of the gaff, using a slipknot with some slack on the loose end, and thread the line through one of the handles. Your bowline is better than mine, so you could tie the knot since you're here."

"Uh-huh..." the Captain said.

"Then we could pick up the loose end of the line and yank it, pull the gaff out, and we'd have the handle lassoed, so to speak. Then we could tow it to shore. What do you think?" Before the Captain could reply, Ketch added, "Do you have a good-sized coil we could use? I may not have enough line on hand for the job."

"Well yeah, I guess we could do all that." The Captain gave Ketch a once-over. "You're lookin' beat," he said. "You been runnin' yourself ragged over somethin'?"

"Just the usual, but I am kind of tired tonight. Why do you ask?"

"Well, 'cause you ain't generally this dumb, is why," the Captain smirked.

"What? What do you mean?" Ketch sputtered.

"Lookee here. That coffin drifted into our little harbor from out there in the sound, right? So how did that happen? Well, the wind and the tide carried it here, and it's bangin' against your boat right now 'cause it wants to keep on goin'. So all we gotta do is point it in the right direction and give it a shove, and let Nature do the job for us."

Ketch stared at the Captain as what the man had said sunk in, his face reddening. "Yes, you're right," he said. "I'm sorry. I guess I really am tired."

"Hell, that's okay, we all make mistakes – even you now'n again, Doctor Ketchum!" the Captain chuckled. "Here, gimme that, ya dumb Yankee."

He wrested the gaff from Ketch's unresisting grip and

gave the casket a healthy poke. It drifted out around the stern and toward the *TBD*. The Captain went to starboard, leaned out over the gunwale, and thrust the gaff once more at the casket – which then smoothly rounded the bow of the *TBD* and lazily floated in toward the shore.

"Last one ashore's a rotten egg!" the Captain cackled. He set the gaff down and hopped back up onto the dock, but waited for Ketch to follow.

"It's not a coffin, you know," Ketch said as he stepped up to the dock. "A coffin is tapered at the ends. A rectangular container like this one is a casket."

"Oh yeah, Perfessor? Well, know what? You forgot to call me a dumb cracker, like you usually do when I call you a dumb Yankee. I guess you *are* tired!" the Captain laughed.

Ketch had to allow the man a grudging smile. As was the case with Kari and Bean, he could never stay annoyed for long with the irrepressible old sailor. He followed the Captain down the dock to the parking lot.

The casket was now trying to make landfall not far from the dock. Luckily, it appeared to be coming to rest at a patch of sand and eel grass near the southern boundary of the boatyard, just before the marsh that would begin to predominate a few yards away. The Captain was fortuitously wearing his boots as well, so he and Ketch waded into the water. They each grabbed a handle and pulled the casket to safety ashore.

But not without expending some effort in the process. "This thing's a mite heavier'n I thought it'd be," the Captain remarked between huffs and puffs.

"But it isn't as heavy as I thought it might be. Regardless, none of them are light, you know, even when they're empty," Ketch said. "That's why they need so many pallbearers."

And this one was no simple wooden box, either, Ketch saw. In fact, it wasn't wooden at all, but rather metal, and it looked to be what Ketch had learned was a sealing casket.

"How could a heavy metal box like that be floatin' around in the water?" the Captain asked. "Seems like it shoulda sunk right to the bottom a the sound."

"Come now, Captain," Ketch chastised him. "You were in the Coast Guard, and you were just standing on the deck of another big heavy box. You should know how it could float."

"Now you mention it, I do recall some old Greek guy named Archimedes from my trainin' days. But still..."

"This casket is sealed. The lid has a rubber gasket, so water can't get inside and make it sink." Ketch had also learned – unfortunately after the fact, in the case of his parents' funerals – that the cost of the gasket was only a few dollars, but funeral homes typically charged hundreds more for such caskets. He was still miffed about the unnecessarily high cost of those funerals, when he thought about it.

"So that lid must be locked too, right?"

"Yes. The lock is right here," Ketch explained, pointing to a small hole on the corner of the casket. "It's just a simple pin lock, and it locks and unlocks with an Allen wrench." And the so-called 'casket key' was simply an Allen wrench with a decorative handle attached to it, which the survivors of the deceased could keep as a memento – a morbid one, in Ketch's opinion – and again, for a price.

"Huh. Well, I guess that's good in case a vampires and such, too," the Captain chuckled. "Uh, Ketch, what's that other hole there for, and how come you're tryin' to unscrew somethin' from it?"

"This is the memory tube. It's a water-resistant receptacle that they can put a piece of paper in, to identify who's in the casket. They thread it into this hole."

"And you wanna find out who this is before you call the cops," the Captain concluded. He shook his head. "I don't know why you don't like to call yourself a detective. Seems like you're always tryin' to detect somethin' or other."

"Be that as it may," Ketch said, straining, "I can't get it to turn."

"Well hey, I got a pair a pliers here on me somewhere," the Captain said, fishing said item from a pocket of his coveralls. "I was doin' some fixin' over on my boat before. Somethin's always shakin' loose on the ol' gal these days if I make her do any amount a sailin'."

"Thanks," Ketch said, taking the pliers.

"Say, how come you know so dang much 'bout caskets anyways? Never mind, I know – you read a lot, like you always say, right?"

"Yes, there's that. But I also had to handle all the arrangements when my parents passed." Ketch finally managed to get the end of the tube to move. "There! Okay, let's see what the story is here."

He finished unscrewing the tube, pulled it from the hole, and twisted the cap off. Using his penknife, he gingerly slid a small rolled-up sheet of yellowed paper from the tube and carefully unrolled it.

"Man, what's that stink?" the Captain protested. "Did somebody run over somethin'?"

"It's gas from inside the casket," Ketch absently replied, squinting at the printing in the pale moonlight. "It's a woman," he said. "I don't recognize the family name. It isn't one of the Midgett variations, nor Farrow, so maybe she didn't come from the Salvo Cemetery after all. Most of the burials there were from those families. I recall that there are some Grays and O'Neals there too, who intermarried with the Midgetts and Farrows, but she isn't one of those, either." He thought for a moment. "I know how to tell for sure, though. I just have to go check something on my computer."

"You mean there's a list a the graves at that place on the computer?"

"Yes, there is. I found it when I was reading about the plight of that cemetery in the *Island Free Press* a while back. I saved the list on my computer," Ketch answered as he rerolled the paper and stuck it back into the tube.

"You did? What the hell for, if you don't mind me askin'?"

"Well, I thought I might want to make a donation to help save the cemetery. As you know, the shoreline there is being eroded away by storms, and it's gotten exponentially worse in just the past few years. The cemetery is washing away into the sound, graves are being exposed, and markers are being knocked down and damaged."

"Yeah, I know that – but why do they need donations from the likes a you'n me? Why don't the Park Service just fix it and put up a bulkhead or somethin'?"

"Well, it's true that the government bought up a lot of the land on this island for the National Seashore, but mostly on the ocean side – and the cemetery is on the sound side, and it's on a parcel of land they didn't take. So it actually belongs to the village of Salvo – and since it isn't National Park Service property, it's up to the citizens of the Tri-Villages to save it if they want it to be saved. The Rodanthe, Waves, and Salvo Civic Association is trying to raise money, but so far they don't even have enough to buy sandbags."

"Okay, so how much money do they need? And who exactly do you give the money to? I might could help a little, but I ain't no rich man, and neither are you."

"There are a couple of local organizations getting involved, plus some descendants of the people buried in the cemetery. I'll look it up for you if you're really interested. As for me – well, I *wasn't* rich, but now..."

"Huh? You sayin' you're rich now? What'd you do, win the lottery or somethin'?"

"No. I sort of 'inherited' some money from that crooked

witch we took down last fall. It's a long story."

"Well, do tell! And don't forget to say how come I never heard nothin' about it!"

"It was the least she could do for me, the evil bitch," Ketch darkly muttered. He made a visible effort to relax, which the Captain didn't comment on. "Anyway, it happened after you left for Florida, and I wasn't sure about it until a couple weeks ago. Really, though, it's a story for another time. But soon, I promise."

"Huh. All right then, you lemme know when you got some free time and I'll bring over a twelve-pack. So what do we do now?"

"First I'll go in and check that list," Ketch said, screwing the memory tube back in place, "and then I'll call the authorities. If you don't mind, maybe you could dig up a tarp or something in the meantime. It's been pretty quiet around the boatyard so far tonight, and I'd like to keep it that way. We don't need a bunch of rubberneckers hanging around while we deal with this."

"Right, I got just the thing on the boat! I'll go get it. Maybe I'll warm up if I work these old legs some more."

"I'm sorry for making you stay out here on a night like this."

"That's okay. At least there ain't no skeeters. Don't worry none about it."

"Thanks, Captain."

The two of them headed back along the dock, Ketch dropping off first at the *Port Starbird*. When he boarded the houseboat and went inside, Kari and the dogs were waiting for him in the galley.

"Hi, guys," he said to Jack and Chuck, squatting so they could lick his face and giving each a pat on the head. "How's Bean?" he asked Kari.

"He's okay, I think. He fell asleep on the couch before we'd even finished off the popcorn. I covered him with a blanket and left him be for now."

"Good. And thank you again," Ketch remembered to say. He saw that his laptop was on the table where he'd left it, so he went to it and booted it up.

"So what's goin' on out there? I saw you and Don got the casket ashore. You made the call yet?"

"Not yet, but I will shortly. There was identification on the casket, so I want to look something up quick. I suspect our visitor is from the Salvo Cemetery, and I want to verify that." But of course, no modern technology was quite as quick and easy as they made it look on the TV commercials, and Ketch's laptop was no exception.

"Uh huh. And why exactly do you need to know that?" Kari said, eyeballing the little spinning circle in the middle of the computer's screen. "Never mind, I know – it's a mystery. But please get this taken care of soon's you can, okay?"

"I will. Ah, I think it's almost ready," he said, sitting down at the table. "Good! Okay then." He found the site he'd bookmarked and brought up the list. Kari stood behind him and rubbed his tired shoulders while he scanned the list of names.

"There's actually a Web site called 'Find a Grave'?" she marveled. "How bizarre! And you can search by cemetery. I guess you can find just about anything you need out there these days."

"There she is," Ketch said. "The woman in the casket, that is. And it isn't that old. She died in 1978."

"I didn't know they were still buryin' folks there. Look, that one there's from 2005! But the others are mostly a lot older."

"True. It looks like the oldest one is, let's see, Watson Midgett in 1872. And that's the year the cemetery was started. But there are only thirty-four names listed here, so I guess that cemetery wasn't, and isn't, often used."

"Maybe that's a good thing, considerin'. It was supposed to be just a Midgett family cemetery anyway, right?"

"Yes. There were a lot of them up around Rodanthe back in the day, and some people still call it the Midgett Cemetery. It looks like that's who they mostly are. I see other names, but they appear to be interrelated. There are some Farrows and Grays, and a couple of O'Neals, but they're all connected with the Midgetts. There are a few Paynes on the list as well. Those are all old-time island families, and I recognize at least three of the names as surfmen with the old Lifesaving Service that predated the Coast Guard. There are also a couple of odd names I don't know – and our visitor is one of them – but they may all be related somehow or other." Ketch closed the laptop. "What's happening to that cemetery is a shame. I hope something gets done about it."

"Yeah, me too."

"Well, I'd better get back out there," Ketch said, rising somewhat laboriously from the table.

"I'm sorry you're havin' to deal with all this tonight," Kari commiserated, seeing the haggard look on his face.

Ketch shrugged. "Could be worse, could be raining," he quoted in a rather poor British accent.

"I know that one – *Young Frankenstein*!" Kari chuckled. "You can't stump *me*, mister!"

Kari and her movie quotes. She had indeed been unstumpable so far, but... "We'll see," he retorted. "There's a first time for everything, you know."

"Yeah? Well there can be a last time too, so don't you go gettin' cocky on me," she reprimanded him. "At least not 'til a little later on," she added with an evil grin.

"Yes ma'am, as you wish, at your command as always," he murmured suggestively, quickly running a hand through her auburn hair. "Okay. You guys stay here," he said to the dogs, who didn't seem to mind being left behind this time. It was getting late, they'd already been let out for the night, and they were tired as well.

Ketch himself was beyond tired now. Hopefully the police would come soon, and then he'd be able to wrap this all up and grab some shut-eye. Assuming Kari would let him, of course, which she probably wouldn't right away. Perhaps he shouldn't have encouraged her. Whatever would or wouldn't happen later, he decided to stop thinking about it in the meantime.

When he rejoined the Captain, he was surprised to see that his friend had indeed fetched a tarp. But instead of it being draped over the casket, the Captain was sitting on it on the ground and looking decidedly ill.

"Captain, is something wrong?" Ketch said as he approached. "You look a little green around the gills."

"Yeah, well..." the Captain sighed. "I did a dumb thing, and I got a faceful a that gas you mentioned."

"You opened the casket?" Ketch asked in disbelief. The Captain held up his Allen wrench kit and glumly nodded. "Why on earth did you do that?"

"Well, I just got curious, is all. You ought to be able to understand that, you're worse'n me that way. And besides, did you or did you not turn me into a dang graverobber last fall up at that ol' witch church?" the Captain tacked on with a wan smile. "Anyways, did you find out where it come from?"

"Yes, it's definitely from the Salvo Cemetery."

The Captain nodded again. "I thought I might like to see a real skeleton, y'know? And I thought maybe there might be some kinda old treasure, like folks used to be buried with sometimes. 'Course, I wouldn't filch nothin' without talkin' to you about it first. I just wanted to see."

"It wouldn't be that old, if there was anything. This woman died in 1978."

"Oh yeah? That casket looks older'n that."

Ketch agreed that it did, from the outside anyway. He could see that it wasn't constructed of what was considered a premium metal for a casket, such as bronze or copper, but rather some kind of steel. And perhaps a cheaper gauge of steel at that, since it wasn't quite as heavy as it looked like it should be, so that could be why the casket appeared as weathered as it did. If it had been exposed to saltwater and sand-laced storm winds for any length of time, that would certainly have taken a toll, especially on a lesser quality metal.

"And she sure melted down right quick in there." At Ketch's quizzical look, the Captain added, "There's mostly just a pile a brown muck in a dress in the bottom a that casket, hardly even any bones to speak of."

"Oh. Well, that doesn't surprise me. I've heard that can happen when a casket is sealed. Instead of decomposing naturally and leaving behind a skeleton, the body just dissolves. Anaerobic bacteria do it, because there's no air circulation. And she may not have been embalmed, which usually isn't required by law."

Another thing Ketch had learned was that sealed caskets don't preserve the body, whether embalmed or not, despite some manufacturers' and morticians' claims to the contrary. Furthermore, they can cause embarrassing, and sometimes downright gruesome, problems in mortuaries when the gas inside builds up, the seal degrades, and the casket leaks. There had even been rare cases of such a casket exploding.

"Am I gonna get sick from that gas?" the Captain asked.

"You might turn into a zombie," Ketch replied with a straight face. "Maybe I should keep that gaff handy just in case."

"Knock it off!" the Captain growled, but with a worried look on his face.

"I'm kidding, of course. I don't think you'll get sick. Supposedly, there's no public health risk from decomposing bodies." Which was another reason why sealed caskets were an unnecessary expense. "It's just unpleasant, is all."

"Well, that's good to hear anyways."

"Can we cover that casket now? I'll call the police while you do that, if you don't mind."

"Yeah, I guess that's who you ought to call, for sure – 'cause I hadn't told you the best part yet."

"Oh?" Ketch inquired.

"There's somethin' else in there you might want to take a gander at, if you can stand it. Me, I'm gonna step back some, myself. I seen enough for one night!" The Captain handed the appropriate wrench to Ketch and then moved away from the casket.

Ketch inserted the wrench, gave it a twist, and lifted the lid enough to see inside. This casket was of the full-couch variety, meaning the lid wasn't split, and thus meaning it was that much heavier than a split lid. But it was manageable.

Although he'd long ago become inured to unpleasant odors through his work with laboratory animals, the smell was still potent enough to almost make him gag despite the gas inside having been largely dissipated by the Captain's shenanigans. He held the lid up only as long as it took to see what needed to be seen, and then he closed it and relocked it.

"See what I mean?" the Captain said. "That lady from 1978 ain't the only one stinkin' up the joint! Who in hell is that other guy in there on top of her, and why in hell is he even there?"

"I have no idea about the former," Ketch answered. "He hasn't been there long enough to decompose much, but I don't recognize him. But I have a good idea as to the latter. Did you notice what looked to me like a big bloodstain on his shirt?"

"Why no, I didn't. But it's kinda dark out, y'know."

"And I suppose you didn't see the fish knife lying next to his body?"

"What? A knife? Do tell!"

"Indeed. I think someone stabbed that man, and then stuffed both his body and the murder weapon in that casket, thinking neither would ever be found. The casket may have already been exposed by the erosion at that cemetery, but I'd also be willing to bet the killer tried to rebury it. This nor'easter, however, probably unearthed it again and set it adrift."

"And then it ended up right here in your back yard," the Captain concluded. "You can't tell me things don't happen for a reason. If justice was to be served, it couldn't've ended up in a better place!"

"But it took a semi-retired graverobber to make the discovery," Ketch ribbed him. "I probably wouldn't have opened that casket, myself."

"Oh yeah? Well I know you, and I bet you would've done. Don't deny it! But anyways, it took a detective like you to spot the knife and the bloodstain."

"I'm no detective," Ketch modestly reiterated for the umpteenth time. He pulled his phone out and brought up his contact list. "But I'm about to call someone who is."

"You ain't callin' the police? Oh, I get it – you're gonna call your SBI friend, Dan, right? That one from that bidness with the witch, what Pauline done hooked up with?"

"Yes," Ketch said. Dan, the state investigator with whom Kari's widowed mother up in Manteo had indeed become romantically entangled, had been instrumental in helping them all get through that nasty ordeal with the witch coven, and had developed into another of Ketch's good friends in the process.

The Captain got up and threw the tarp over the casket. "Well, I think I'll mosey on back to the *Minnow* and pick up that twelve-pack right now. Or at least a couple bottles. I feel like I could use a beer. How 'bout you?"

"Yes, thank you." A beer or two wouldn't make him any warmer or any less tired, but what the hell. "Hello, Dan?"

he said into the phone. "Ketch here. I'm glad I was able to reach you. Yes, it must be my lucky night. Actually, it isn't, really. I have a situation here that I thought you might want to look into..."

The conversation was over when the Captain returned with a bucket of beers. He opened one for Ketch, then one for himself, and they both sat down on an edge of the tarp with their backs against the covered casket.

"You're sure you didn't touch anything inside the casket, right?" Ketch said after he'd taken a welcome swig.

"Hell yeah, I'm sure! I was too busy gaggin'! I swear, I didn't touch nothin', honest," the Captain insisted. "I dropped that lid right quick and locked it up again, soon's I got that snootful a whatever."

"Good. It's okay that our fingerprints and DNA are on the outside – I'm sure numerous others have touched it over the years – but we certainly don't want to confuse things on the inside. This casket is now a crime scene, and I assured Dan it would be intact when he arrived – which he said would be in an hour or so. He's rousting a couple of CSI types, and then they have to drive down from Manteo."

"Well then, I guess we got some time now for that tale you been meanin' to tell me, 'bout that money you got from that witch. If you ain't too tired, a course."

Ketch decided to oblige his friend. Why not? He couldn't go to bed yet anyway. By the time he'd gotten through it, including an abortive attempt to explain to the less-than-technologically-savvy Captain how bitcoins worked, he'd gotten through two beers (and the Captain three) and Dan's crew was arriving.

While his lab guys examined the casket, Dan interviewed Ketch and the Captain. Ketch filled in details to support the summary he'd given to Dan over the phone, and the Captain corroborated from time to time as needed.

"Well, I guess this can serve as your statements," Dan

finally concluded. "You know, this *is* your lucky night. My people wanted to cordon off the whole boatyard and designate it a crime scene and interview everyone in it – and that would for sure have happened if y'all had called the Dare County Sheriff's office – but I convinced them it wasn't necessary in this case. We'll just transport the casket back to the lab and work things from there."

"Thank you, Dan," Ketch said. "You've been a big help, as usual, and I appreciate it."

"Well, I appreciate what you've done, too. I figure I owe you for going undercover and helping me nab that assassin everybody was itchin' to get their hands on. That was a real feather in my cap."

"It needed to be done, and I was happy to help." Ketch shook Dan's hand. "Have a safe trip back, and give Pauline our regards."

"Yeah, what he said," the Captain chimed in. "See ya, Dan!"

He and Ketch watched the investigators pull out of the parking lot, and then he said, "Well now, I'm bushed too! I'm gonna go on home and turn in. And then tomorrow I might go see what they got to pick from, up at that Ford place. Thanks, Ketch!"

"You're quite welcome," Ketch said. He'd promised to share some of his recent windfall with the Captain in the form of a new F-150, plus whatever repairs the aging *Minnow* might need that the Captain couldn't handle himself. The man deserved a reward for what he'd done to help take down that witch, not to mention helping save Ketch's life in the process. And for once in his life, he could afford to give such rewards.

Alone and obligation-free at last, Ketch trudged back to the houseboat – only to be greeted at the cabin door by Bean and both dogs.

"What are you doing up, son?" Ketch gently asked the boy. "And why do you have your coat and boots on?

Where's Kari?"

"She's sleepin' on your chair." That would be the recliner that was ostensibly Ketch's but had turned out to be community property. "I think Jack and Chuck want to go out."

They'd been out just before what he'd thought was going to be bedtime, and they'd seemed tired earlier, but Ketch figured they were probably restless due to tonight's unscheduled activities. "You weren't going to take them out yourself, were you?" he asked Bean.

"No, Papa, I was waitin' on you. I saw the policemen drive away out the window. Can I go out with you?"

Bean still wasn't dressed properly for tonight's weather, but they'd only be out there for a few minutes. "Okay, why not. Come on, guys," he told the dogs, ruffling their fur. He'd have to set out the gangway again, and then take it in again, for his entourage, but what was that in the Grand Scheme? "We'll bring the leashes just in case, but there's no one around, so we'll just let them go on their own this time."

They followed the dogs down the dock and around the perimeter of the parking lot as the dogs did their sniffing and whatnot, particularly where the casket and the investigators had been.

"Who was it?" Bean asked as they walked.

"In the casket? Oh, a lady who died a long time ago," Ketch answered, deciding to leave it at that. He didn't think the boy needed to know all the gory details, not tonight anyway.

"Why did she come'd here?"

Ketch also decided to forgo the grammar lessons for the day. "The storm washed some sand away from a cemetery by the water, and the casket got loose and floated here."

"So it was a accident?"

"Yes. Well, I don't know how she died, but she floated here by accident."

"My mama died," Bean said after what Ketch knew had been a pregnant pause.

"Yes, she did."

"And she's never gonna come back," the boy matter-of-factly stated.

"No, she isn't." Ketch put his arm around the boy's shoulders, thinking he might need some comforting.

"I like this place," Bean said. "I like your boat."

"You do? I'm happy to hear that," Ketch said. "But it's your boat now, too. And it's your home. And you know Kari and I love you, right?"

"Yes, Papa." They walked in silence for a bit, and then Bean said, "You're my papa now. Can Kari be my mama now?"

"Why, yes, I think she can," Ketch answered, trying not to sound too surprised. "I think she'd like it if you called her Mama sometimes. Do you want to do that?" Bean nodded. "Good."

He stopped, gave Bean a pat on the back, and called the dogs. "Jack! Chuck! Time to go in!"

The dogs dutifully followed them back to the houseboat. Kari was up when they got inside.

"I wondered where everybody went!" she exclaimed. "Benjamin Ketchum! What on earth were you doin' out there this time of night in this weather, young man?"

"He woke up and wanted to help with the dogs, so I let him come with me," Ketch explained as he put away their gear. "And now I think you should give them each a treat," he said to Bean, "and then back to bed."

"Yes, Papa."

While the boy went to the treat jar, closely trailed of course by the dogs, Kari said, "So everything's all taken care of now?"

"Yes. I'll tell you all about it later."

"Not *too* much later, I hope," she pouted. "You know I'm not real good at waitin'."

"I know," Ketch smiled. "Don't worry, I'm not going to pass out right away. I'm past that point now, I think."

Bean was finished with the dogs. He rubbed his eyes, gave Ketch a hug, and blearily said, "Goodnight, Papa." Then he hugged Kari as well and said, "Goodnight, Mama."

As the boy trundled off to his bunk, Kari cocked her head queryingly at Ketch. He thought she looked pleased, though.

"Like I said, I'll tell you all about it," Ketch smiled.

~ ~ ~

A bell tinkled overhead when Ketch opened the door and entered the dive shop. Kari left off what she'd been doing in the back and came up front. There were no customers, but that wasn't unusual at this time of year.

"Well hey, look what the cat done drug in!" she said. "What's the occasion? Were you missin' me? Fess up! You just couldn't go another minute without seein' me, right?"

"Yes. As usual, you have me all figured out," he smiled. "Actually, I'm on my way to pick Bean up from the bus."

"Well, you're a mite off-course." She glanced at the wall clock. "And you're early. Wanna fool around?"

Ketch let that one pass. "I stopped by to tell you I got a call from Dan a little while ago."

"Yeah? What about?"

"He wanted to update me on our wayward mariner. He said they were able to identify the extra body that was in that casket. They also got the DNA results back, and they arrested someone for the murder. And he confessed. He also claimed he had an accomplice, and they rounded up that guy, too."

"Huh. Sounds like he's been earnin' his pay. Anybody we know?"

"I don't know any of them." He recited the surnames he recalled from his conversation with Dan.

"Nope, I don't know 'em neither," she said. "They were probably from up the beach. So what's the rest of the story?"

"Well, there was an altercation at the Old Christmas celebration in Rodanthe last month. I know it doesn't happen much nowadays, but that party used to be famous for brawls between the fishermen. They'd get to drinking when they all got together, and then they'd settle their disputes the old-fashioned way."

"Yeah, I know."

"Apparently the victim was accused of poaching crab pots, and he and the killer got into a fistfight. They were both drunk, and they were both told to leave the party, which they did. The day after, the victim was reported missing. There were witnesses to the fight, and the police questioned everyone, but nothing came of it."

"But now they have DNA evidence?"

"Yes, and fingerprints. The blood on the knife that was in the casket matched the victim's blood, and the handle of the knife matched up with the killer. The killer also left fingerprints elsewhere in and around the casket, and so did his accomplice."

"Good thing you and Don had sense enough to not touch anything in the casket and mess all that up."

Ketch chuckled. "We're lucky the Captain didn't throw up in it when he opened it."

"I'll say!" Kari rolled her eyes. "It's just a hop, skip, and jump from the community center in Rodanthe to the Salvo Day Use Area, where that cemetery is. Pretty handy, I'd say, plus there'd likely be nobody hangin' around there in the cold and dark."

"Yes, my theory was correct. According to the killer's confession, he and his friend ambushed the victim in Rodanthe that evening and stabbed him – by accident, supposedly. Then they drove the body down the road to Salvo, took it to the cemetery, put it in an exposed casket, and tried to rebury the casket."

"Which the nor'easter dug up and dropped right in the lap of Avon's greatest detective!"

"Thank you, but I'm not a detective – and if I were, I'd be the only one in town, so that wouldn't be much of a compliment."

"Well, you're still my hero anyway," Kari concluded. "Hey, you had a chance yet to look into those cabins we were talkin' about, down around Portsmouth?"

She was referring to Portsmouth Island, which was below Ocracoke, and was where the Cape Hatteras National Seashore left off and the Cape Lookout National Seashore began. The town of Portsmouth, the only one on the island, had once been an important seaport and was now a historic ghost town. The Park Service operated a campground on the south end of the island, including several rustic rental cabins. Neither Ketch nor Kari had camped there before, and they thought it would be a fun end-of-school excursion for Bean.

True, there'd be no boardwalks there, nor the modern-day amusements that often came with them. But there'd be beaches, and they could hike the island and tour the ghost town. Ketch knew these activities would appeal to Bean, who, perhaps not entirely coincidentally, seemed to be developing the same interests in the sea and local history as Ketch.

"Yes, I went to the NPS Web site this morning. It looks like I can reserve two adjoining cabins, one for us and one for Suzanne and her kids, and I can get them for right after school lets out for the summer."

"Bean and Sally are gettin' to be real good friends, and I'm sure Henry will have a good time there too. Especially if he gets some attention from you, which could happen if Bean has Sally to do things with."

"I know, I haven't been spending as much time with Henry since Bean came to live with us. I'll do something about that soon, and I'll make sure he gets some quality time with me on Portsmouth."

Ketch had met Henry when his mother had moved the family to Avon and the boy had offered to do yard work around Ketch's old house. Despite his youth, the enterprising lad was now also Second Mate aboard the *My Minnow*, and occasionally First Mate in Ketch's place when he backed away from his duties on a charter to allow Henry to gain more experience.

"Okay then," Ketch said. "If you're sure you want to do it, I'll go ahead and make the reservations."

"Silly man! You should know by now, I always want to," Kari laughed. "But we've wasted too much time chatterin', so you'd best just go on and get our boy."

"Yes, 'our' boy." And our family, he thought. *My* family. "See you back at the ranch."

"Yah, you betcha!" Kari said, giving him a quick hug and kiss.

Ketch chuckled. "Even I know that one."

"Well, I'd hope so! That one's for sure a classic."

"As are you, my dear," Ketch mock-bowed. Continuing to smile inwardly, he took his leave.

Postscript

The Salvo Day Use Area Cemetery, aka the Midgett Cemetery, is real. It was begun in 1872, and its modern-day plight is real as well. Due to storm erosion, it's currently situated smack dab on the water of Pamlico Sound. Its shoreline buffer has been completely washed away over the years, and some of the graves along with it. Most of the damage has been inflicted since 2011, by increasingly destructive hurricanes and nor'easters. A small offshore island that once provided some protection is gone now due to rising sea level. And the government can't just step in and save the day, since it isn't government property.

Efforts are underway to mitigate the damage, under the umbrella of the non-profit Rodanthe, Waves, and Salvo Civic Association. The Hatteras Island Genealogical and Preservation Society is also involved, as are descendants of those buried in the cemetery. Many of the graves have historical as well as sentimental value, for example those of several legendary surfmen of the U.S. Lifesaving Service and Coast Guard, who routinely risked their lives to rescue shipwreck survivors in the bad old days of the Graveyard of the Atlantic.

Applications for grants have been made, and there's a GoFundMe campaign in progress to help raise the funds needed for a permanent solution in the form of a bulkhead and rock wall. Enough money has been raised to finally install a temporary sandbag barrier, but the GoFundMe has to date raised only a small fraction of the estimated total cost of the project.

If you're interested in helping, a good place to start would be the SAVE THE SALVO DAY USE CEMETERY campaign at www.gofundme.com . They could also use more volunteers to help with the work, if you happen to be in the area and are looking for something meaningful to do. See the campaign page for more details.

INTERLUDE: The Port Fee

June 2014

This full-length novel is Storm Ketchum Adventure #3, and this is where it fits into the chronology of the Adventures and Tales. If you'd like to read it, it's available at your favorite retailer and at my Web site (www.GarrettDennis.com).

DESCRIPTION

Underwater, everybody can hear you scream, but they can't tell where you are...

Ketch is at it again in the magical Outer Banks of North Carolina!

It's a picture-perfect summer afternoon on a pristine beach near a ghost seaport on an uninhabited island. What could go wrong?

But things do, when two bodies wash ashore and Ketch stumbles upon clues that lead to the sunken treasure of an old-time buccaneer off Portsmouth Island. Ketch isn't the only one who has an interest in the treasure, and it exposes both him and his adversaries to unexpected obligations and consequences. It seems everyone has to pay the port fee...

Good guys and bad guys, boating and diving, a dash of romance, and a mysterious otherworldly presence all come together in THE PORT FEE, Ketch's most challenging adventure to date.

PHARAOH'S TREASURE

DESCRIPTION

In Storm Ketchum Tale #6, a Saturday morning chore turns into a treasure hunt.

While Ketch and the kids work at clearing a space for a new boathouse, they stumble upon an artifact that may or may not be related to an arcane bit of island lore. Did an eighteenth-century windmill operator really amass a legendary treasure? Did he bury it in Ketch's back yard? And will Ketch be able to hang on to his find despite an unhealthy interest from some unsavory neighbors?

Join amateur sleuth Storm 'Ketch' Ketchum as he exposes the mystery of Pharaoh's treasure on historic Hatteras Island, where intrigue always seems to be just around the next corner.

NOTE: The Kinnakeet Boatyard and Sea Dog Scuba Center settings in this story are fictitious.

August 2014

Ketch reached into his ever-present backpack and passed the safety goggles and work gloves he'd picked up at Ace Hardware to Bean and Henry. While they tore the tags off the new items, he also fished his own gloves and safety glasses from the backpack, and wiped some sweat from beneath his tarp hat with his bandanna. It was already getting hot. Maybe keeping the beard this summer, though it was trimmed short, hadn't been such a good idea.

He'd stopped at Ace after a quick visit to the Avon post office to check his box earlier this morning. He wasn't overly anxious about it, but he was anticipating the arrival of a particular piece of mail that would give him a great deal of satisfaction. Although the envelope would contain a check, that wasn't what was important about it.

He no longer desperately needed the money, but he'd nonetheless finally decided to retain a lawyer to not-so-gently persuade the insurance company to offer an acceptable out-of-court settlement for the loss of his old *Port Starbird* house. Dealings of this nature were ordinarily anathema to him, but in this case it was a matter of principle. The fact that the settlement would cover only part of the cost of the new house after legal fees wasn't optimal, but that was immaterial. He'd made them pay something when they'd wanted to welsh on their obligations and pay nothing, and that had been the point.

He'd thought the check might arrive today, but the post office had been a bust in that regard. So he'd moved on to the hardware store, where he'd also purchased the lightest sledgehammer he could find – which Bean was now hefting and attempting to wield.

"Benjamin, set that hammer down and put on those goggles like I asked you to," he admonished his seven-year-old grandson. "Please," he added, remembering his resolution to be as calm and polite as possible with the boy, while being firm and consistent at the same time.

Bean had been living with Ketch for just a few months now, and he wanted the youngster to feel secure and loved in his new home. The poor kid had already experienced enough trauma in his short life. He didn't need any more of that, but Ketch didn't want him to become a spoiled brat, either. So it was a balancing act.

"But it's too dang hot!" Bean protested.

The boy had resided in Virginia early on, so he'd gotten a head start on his accent, but he'd recently begun peppering his speech with ever more Southern vernacular, particularly of the Banker variety. This wasn't really all that unusual given his current environment, Ketch knew, but he still wondered who might be influencing the boy the most. Maybe not the Captain, as nothing too colorful had yet come out of his mouth, at least not in Ketch's hearing. So Kari, then? But Bean hadn't been around her much since her accident. And he of course hadn't been in school all summer, and Ketch himself was a Yankee dingbatter.

But he did have some contact with other native islanders, and there was their neighbor Henry and his younger sister Sally. Bean spent a considerable amount of time with them, especially with Sally, both at their house and at Ketch's *Port Starbird* houseboat. Although their mother, Suzanne, was originally from Michigan, the kids had been brought up in Charlotte before their move to Hatteras Island. So they were probably a factor as well.

Regardless, it was indeed hot, as Bean had said. It was the middle of August, and somewhat muggy as well since they were soundside – but, safety first.

"Henry and I are wearing ours, see?" Ketch patiently responded, tapping his own goggles. "When we start breaking up this cistern, a piece of brick could hit you in the eye. That would hurt you, and I don't want you to get hurt. Do you understand?"

"Yeah, you don't want to go to the clinic," Henry said in

support of Ketch. "They'd make you wait all dang day, and then they'd stick a funny-lookin' bandage on your face. Probably give you a big ol' shot in the butt too," he added with a straight face.

"Henry's right, that wouldn't be much fun for you. So if you want to stay here and help, you have to wear your goggles. Otherwise, I'll take you back and you can play with Sally."

"All right, Papa." Bean, with a slightly worried look on his face, donned his goggles without further complaint.

Henry, as usual acting older and wiser than his thirteen years, had known exactly what to say to persuade Bean to toe the line. Being 'funny-looking' was possibly enough of a deterrent for a child Bean's age, but Ketch thought the part about the shot was a nice touch and was probably what had done the trick.

"And don't forget your gloves," Ketch reminded the boy.

"Yes, Papa."

The probability of flying shards of brick and mortar was also why they were all dressed in long-sleeved shirts, jeans, and boots even though the heat of the day was already bordering on oppressive despite it only being midmorning. And it was why Ketch had taken the dogs for a sunrise run on the beach and then dropped them back at the houseboat. He didn't want them to get injured hanging around here, either. His precautions notwithstanding, he imagined he might still catch flak from Kari about allowing Bean to take part in this. But he thought it would be a good experience for the boy, and she wasn't here.

The cistern resting in a hole at the water's edge wasn't the largest Ketch had ever seen, but it was made entirely of brick, including its rounded top. It was a circular structure, which Ketch had been relieved to see when his friend Len, who'd found it, had shown it to him. Since it had been buried under the sand, he'd been afraid when he'd first heard about it that it might be a burial vault, which could lead to complications and delay the project.

But he was now belatedly noticing that there were no openings on it anywhere, which was odd. If this were truly a cistern meant to collect rainwater, there should be both a way for the water to get in, and a way to get it out. Furthermore, the top looked like it was mortared onto the body, and it didn't appear to be movable. He supposed the cistern might have been retired from use and sealed, but walking around the hole, as he now was, he couldn't discern any obviously patched spots.

He also now recalled Len remarking that there'd been nothing protruding above the surface to indicate the presence of the cistern. He'd only found it when he and his buddies had started digging. This made Ketch wonder why it had been buried, though he knew that could have occurred naturally. The sands were perpetually shifting on the barrier islands of the Outer Banks as they migrated inexorably westward, and if the cistern had been here long enough, it could have become buried by the wind and the tides over time.

Len, a fellow denizen of the Kinnakeet Boatyard who'd been summering on one of the derelict rental houseboats there for the past couple years, had helped Ketch refurbish the docks at the boatyard after the previous season's big blow. He was good at building, and he'd offered to rebuild the dock on the site of Ketch's old house. Ketch had done him one better and hired him to build not only the dock, but also the boathouse he'd decided to indulge himself with, and which wasn't included in the contract for the construction of the new house.

When the boathouse was finished, Ketch's trusty Whaler Montauk, the *TBD*, would no longer have to be perennially exposed to the elements. Plus he'd be able to dry-dock her and repaint her hull. She was old and he could afford to buy a new boat now if he wanted to, but she ran well and they'd been through a lot together.

"Is everything okay, sir?" Henry asked Ketch, watching him.

"Yes. I was just taking a closer look." If this cistern in fact had some purpose other than collecting rainwater, Ketch hoped he wouldn't end up regretting involving the kids in this endeavor. "I want to take a couple of pictures before we start hammering. Please step back, you two." The kids cooperated while Ketch snapped a shot of each hemisphere of the cistern with his smartphone. "Okay, let's get to work."

Ketch lowered the stepladder into the hole and leaned it up against the side, and laid out the shovels and crowbar he'd also brought along so they'd be reachable from the hole. And his backpack, of course. Then he dropped his sledgehammer into the hole and climbed down the ladder. Henry passed his and Bean's hammers to Ketch and made sure Bean made it down the ladder as well before joining them.

"Len said this thing was smack dab in the way for your new boathouse, didn't he?" Henry commented. "Won't he be surprised when it's gone come Monday!"

"Maybe," Ketch qualified, while verifying that the mucky substrate their feet had sunk into wouldn't be reaching the tops of Bean's boots.

Since they were on the shore of Pamlico Sound, there was some standing water in the hole. And that was another reason for the jeans and boots. Ketch hadn't ever seen any venomous snakes on his property, but an unlucky cottonmouth, or water moccasin, could have gotten stranded in the hole if there were any around.

"Why do you say 'maybe', sir?" Henry inquired.

"Well, this might not turn out to be an easy job, for one thing – though since today's Saturday, we'll still have tomorrow if we need it. But at least they've dug enough around it so we shouldn't have to, and we won't have to haul away any rubble if we break it up enough. Len said he'd just leave it here and use it for fill."

"So all we have to do is just bust it up good, right? Doesn't seem like that should be too hard."

"Maybe, but it also depends on what, if anything, we find inside. Some old cisterns have been found to contain important historical artifacts, and this one looks pretty old. If there's anything like that in there, we might have to stop working and call in an archeologist."

Which would most certainly delay the project, but Ketch wouldn't begrudge that kind of delay. Being essentially in love with his island and its history as he was, he knew he'd be as patient as necessary if an archeological dig became warranted – especially if it had anything to do with the history of the pre-European inhabitants of Hatteras Island, Chief Manteo's Croatan Indians, and their link to the Lost Colonists of Roanoke Island, a topic that was of special interest to him. That had been the case with the shell middens that had been unearthed in the neighboring town of Buxton. Or there could perhaps be Civil War artifacts. Anything was possible – including it being just an empty old cistern.

A thought occurred to Henry. "Mister Ketchum, is this gonna cost Len money? I mean, if we do it instead of him, and he doesn't get paid for it?"

"No, not at all. I'm not paying him by the hour. We agreed on a set fee for the whole job. He wasn't expecting to find an old cistern here when he started digging, so I think he'll be glad we took care of it. It'll be a pleasant surprise for him, don't worry."

"Well, okay then. Should we start now, sir?"

"Are you payin' *us*?" Bean chimed in. "How much money do *we-all* get?"

"We'll see. It'll depend on how good a job you do," Ketch retorted.

A solid *clunk* sounded from Bean's position by way of

reply. He grinned at Ketch and pointed at the piece of brick he'd chipped from the top of the cistern. Ketch smiled back at him, but then held up a hand.

"Hang on there, son," he said. "First we need to take some measurements."

"Aw!" Bean squawked.

"It'll just take a minute," Ketch promised, pulling a tape measure out of his pocket, "and you can help. Here," he said, handing the end of the tape to Bean, "you hold onto this – and Henry, you come around here and take the other end. That's right, pull it tight. Now hold still while I take a picture." Ketch leaned back as far as possible and managed to capture both kids in the picture.

"Are we dang done now?" Bean impatiently asked.

"One more picture. Bean, you squat down – don't sit in the water! – and hold your end at the bottom of the cistern. Henry, hold your end at the highest point of the lid. Good, now hold still." Ketch snapped another photo. "So, about eight feet in diameter, and four-and-a-half feet from top to bottom." Which seemed on the short side for a cistern. "Now we're ready."

"Yay!" Bean exclaimed.

"Where should we start, sir?" Henry asked.

"Let's break through the top first, so we can see if there's anything in there," Ketch directed them, refraining from asking Henry yet again to stop calling him 'sir' and 'mister'. Maybe the respectful lad would stop doing that someday, but it didn't seem like it would happen anytime soon – and it certainly wasn't something worthy of complaint, especially in these rude modern times. "No hammering on the sides just yet."

"Yes, sir," Henry said. Both kids started swinging their hammers, Henry of course with more tangible results than Bean. But Bean was pounding away as best he could. Ketch just watched them for a long minute, appreciating their determination and the sheer joy of being allowed to break something without recrimination that was evident on both of their young faces. He remembered that feeling.

He finally decided to join in the fun. As it turned out, he was the first to break through the lid, and to his surprise he did it with one great swing after a couple of initial taps. He must have lucked onto an especially weathered spot, as a sizeable portion of the lid simply crumbled and collapsed inward.

"Whoa! Good one, Mister Ketchum!" Henry exclaimed. "Your papa's pretty strong, huh?" he said to Bean.

Not that strong, Ketch thought, but sometimes that lucky. He was still nervous about what they might find, so it was another stroke of good fortune that he'd now be the first one to get a peek inside the cistern. He called a halt to the hammering and pulled a penlight from his pocket – yet another of the useful items he kept in the ubiquitous backpack, and which he'd remembered to carry on his person this particular morning.

He leaned over the lid, switched the light on, and shone the beam down into the cistern. Though it was one of those new super-bright LED lights, he couldn't make out much in the interior due to the cloud of particulates he'd raised. He hadn't thought about the dust when he'd planned out this little foray, and he wondered now if he should go buy some painter's masks. But he had a couple of extra bandannas in his backpack, and maybe that would be good enough.

"See anything in there, sir?" Henry called from the other side of the cistern.

"No, I can't see a thing. We'll have to wait for the dust to settle." Ketch switched off the light and put it back in his pocket. "And speaking of dust, we should each tie a bandanna around our nose and mouth. I forgot to get masks." He went partway back up the ladder, far enough to reach the backpack. He stuffed the extra bandannas in his back pocket, and then passed two liter bottles of water down to Henry and Bean, who'd congregated at the base of the ladder.

"Let's take a water break while the dust clears," he suggested, opening a third bottle. "Drink at least half of your water, and then we'll put the bandannas on and take another look." Bean obeyed, but grimaced on his first swig. "I know, it isn't cold," Ketch told him. "But it's important to stay hydrated in this weather."

When they'd finished with their water, Ketch tied Bean's bandanna on for him, and then did his own. He took his penlight out again, switched it on, and peered down into the opening in the lid of the cistern.

"Pick me up, Papa!" came a muffled entreaty from Bean. "I can't see a dang thing!"

Before Ketch could answer, Henry again handled the situation for him. "There's not room enough for us all to look at the same time," he told the boy. "Let your papa go first, and then I'll pick you up so you can have a look."

Ketch glanced back and gave a nod to Henry, who winked back at him. Although he considered it unlikely, there could conceivably be something unsuitable for young eyes down in there, and Henry had apparently thought of this as well. That was one smart and sensible young man, Ketch thought. He hoped Bean would grow up to be like Henry.

It was still somewhat hazy inside the cistern, but now Ketch could make out the floor and interior walls – and yes, there was something else there. He squinted as he slowly panned the light over the object.

Beneath the scattering of rubble, he could see that it was a trunk – not a coffin or casket this time, thank goodness – of the kind one might have packed for an extended journey back in the old days. It appeared to be more simply built than old steamer trunks he'd seen, and looked like it could be made of hide-covered wood. Thus, very old, perhaps early eighteen hundreds. But it was definitely a trunk. And if that's really what it was, what on earth could be in it, he wondered?

Though his excitement was mounting, he tried to tamp it. He passed the penlight to Henry and indicated that it was now okay to let Bean have a look. While Henry hoisted Bean so he could see inside, Ketch tried to imagine what could be in the trunk. Personal belongings, maybe, and perhaps valuables, of someone's from the nineteenth century? This cistern, too, could easily be that old, by the look and condition of it.

Or might it be some kind of treasure? He harbored few illusions about that, though. Blackbeard's legendary pirate treasure had supposedly never been found, but he would have buried that down around Ocracoke or Beaufort, or maybe inland in Bath, if he'd had any. And he knew that the old-time pirates, despite modern-day people's romanticized view of them, had as a rule seldom acquired nor accumulated significant amounts of what folks typically thought of as treasure. They'd mostly plundered merchant ships, not Spanish treasure galleons and such as the fables all went, after which they'd sell or trade the confiscated cargoes and spend most of their shares on drink and loose women. And he wasn't aware of any Golden Age pirates sheltering this far north on the Banks.

But then again, if the trunk wasn't precious in some way, why seal it in a cistern? And, too, there was the inconvenient fact that he had indeed uncovered a small cache of pirate treasure just a couple months ago down around Portsmouth, an exception to the rule. He still had the coordinates of that shipwreck, but he'd never go back there again after what had happened. The point, though, was that he supposed he shouldn't arbitrarily rule anything out.

"What's in that box, Papa? Is it a treasure chest?" Bean called down to him. Ketch was glad to see that Henry had a good grip on the boy as Bean leaned out over the opening.

He decided he'd better clear his mind and pay attention.

"Well, anything's possible, but I don't think so," he answered. "We'll find out soon. Come down now and let Henry take a look."

"I can see from here, sir. And I think you're right, it doesn't look like a treasure chest to me neither. It has a flat top."

"Yes," Ketch said, "it looks more like a footlocker, doesn't it? Not like what people picture when they think of treasure chests."

"How do *you-all* know?" Bean challenged them. "It might could be pirate treasure! Let's go in there and open it!"

"We're not crawling around in there with all those bricks hanging over our heads," Ketch said. "The rest of that lid could cave in on us. If you want to see what's in that trunk, you need to get back to work with your hammer. We're going to finish breaking up the top before anyone goes in there."

Ketch stationed Bean at the opening he'd created with his one mighty blow, figuring it would be easier for him to make progress there. He and Henry took up positions on the opposite side of the lid, and they all resumed hammering, Bean with an especial vengeance. That boy seriously wanted to get at what he believed was going to be a pirate treasure.

It was nearing midday when they finally finished demolishing the lid. Most of the bricks that made up the wall of the cistern had also come loose in the process, so this wouldn't be as big a job as Ketch had feared. There'd just be a few big chunks to be broken up further later. Ketch mandated another water break, and then they dragged the shovels down into the hole with them.

"We'll need to move some of the rubble away from the trunk before we try to open it," Ketch announced, stating the obvious for Bean's benefit.

There was adequate room around the trunk to clear away enough rubble to make it accessible. Again, Bean labored determinedly, with the short-handled spade Ketch had brought for his use. He'd be paying Henry, of course – and generously – as he always did whenever he enlisted Henry's help. And he'd definitely pay Bean as well, Ketch thought, if money was what he wanted.

He'd certainly worked hard enough, and Ketch was impressed by the simple fact that he'd stuck with the task this long. He'd thought Bean might tire or grow bored early on – which he wouldn't have faulted him for, given his age. He'd just have taken him back to Suzanne's place.

Now that they were finally ready, he decided to let the sweaty little mess be the one to open the trunk. The boy deserved that, after his commendable effort, and Ketch was less nervous now about what they might find. There was nothing in the cistern other than the trunk, and it wasn't large enough to hold, say, a dead body, so he was willing to take the chance.

Ketch crouched and rapped on the top of it with his knuckles. "Yes, it's wood, as I thought," he mused aloud, "as you can see here and there in the spots where the covering has rotted away. Metal handles and clasp, though, probably iron, since they're pretty rusty..." He stood up. "Well, I guess it's time to find out what we have here. But first, guess what?" he teasingly added. "More pictures!"

Both boys were too tired to object this time. They docilely followed Ketch's instructions, again holding either end of the tape measure to document the dimensions of the trunk. When they were finished, they sat down on rubble piles and stared expectantly at Ketch.

"Okay," Ketch said. "Let's see if we can get it open. Bean, would you like to do the honors?"

If the boy was unsure of what Ketch meant by that, it didn't show. He sprang up immediately, squatted before the trunk, and began working at the clasp. Ketch was surprised that he hadn't forgotten himself and knelt in the standing water, and grateful as well since he'd forgotten to warn the boy not to do that.

"Dang, I think it's locked!" Bean exclaimed in frustration.

Ketch went over and bent to take a closer look at the clasp. "Yes, it has a keyhole," he said. "And we don't have a key, of course. But that clasp is old and rusty, so the engineer's solution might work," he added with a twinkle in his eye.

"Huh?"

Bean wasn't familiar with that derogatory expression, but Henry was. He picked up Bean's hammer, because it was the lightest one, and told the boy to move back. He could have easily staved in the top or side of the trunk with it, but Ketch knew he wouldn't do that. Instead he tapped on the clasp a couple of times, as gently as one could with a sledgehammer. After a slightly more forceful third whack, the clasp fell off and dropped into the muck.

"There you go, little buddy," Henry said, and stepped away to stand by Ketch.

Bean couldn't lift the lid of the trunk at first, despite some impressive grunting on his part. But instead of complaining again, he walked around the trunk and banged along the seam with his fist, similar to what one might do with a stuck lid on a jar. Clever boy, thought Ketch, who'd been thinking of lending a helping hand with his crowbar. This time when Bean tried to open the trunk, the lid lifted easily, albeit somewhat noisily due to its creaky old hinges.

He stared for a moment at the contents of the trunk. Ketch could see disbelief, confusion, and finally elation, cross the boy's face. He couldn't see what was inside the trunk from his current vantage point, but he soon found out what it was.

"Holy moly!" Bean finally yelled. Throwing the lid fully back, he stuck both hands into the trunk and grabbed as many gold coins in each as he could hold. Then he stood up and let the coins dribble from his hands back into the trunk. Looking triumphantly at Ketch and Henry, he proudly declared, "I told y'all!"

Ketch and Henry both rushed over to investigate Bean's find. The trunk appeared to be filled to the brim with gold coins. It looked like they varied in size, but they all looked to be gold. Ketch reached in, removed a handful of the coins, and began examining them.

"These are old," Ketch said. "This particular one is stamped 1795, and this one is from 1804."

"Pirate gold!" Bean joyfully proclaimed.

"No," Ketch said. "And please lower your voice. There doesn't seem to be anyone around at the moment, but we do have neighbors. We don't want to start a gold rush."

And get knocked over the head and robbed in the process, he didn't say. Though at this time of the year, most of said neighbors were vacation rentals, and most of them would be out at the beach or sightseeing. Saturday was a check-in/check-out day for some of them – but he knew that those who were coming couldn't check in yet, and those who were going had already checked out. So there might just be a housecleaning crew here and there, for the most part. But it still didn't pay to be careless.

"Yes, Papa. Sorry, Papa."

"That's okay," Ketch said, patting the boy on the back. "And while we're on the subject, you're not to tell anyone other than our family what we found here. That goes for you too, Henry."

"Understood, sir," Henry said.

"Good. Anyway, Bean, the pirates you're thinking of were all out of business by the time these coins were made. The Golden Age of Piracy was completely over by 1730, and these aren't Spanish or other foreign coins. The ones I'm looking at are American Eagles, Half-Eagles, and Quarter-Eagles. Here," he said, showing them to Bean, "do you see the eagles? And it says 'United States of America' on them."

"I think they all have eagles," Bean corroborated, sifting through some more of the coins. "But why can't it still be pirate treasure? Maybe there were still some pirates, and they stealed the dang gold and buried it here! Like in *Treasure Island*!"

" 'Stole' the gold," Ketch corrected him. "No, there were no more pirates when these coins were made. And books like *Treasure Island* are fiction. Do you remember we talked about that when we read it?" An abridged version for young readers, of course, but he knew the boy had found it exciting. "Very few pirates ever really buried anything, and they never made treasure maps. That's just a myth, a story made up by writers like Stevenson, Poe, and Irving."

"How come most of these coins are still so shiny, if they're so old?" Henry asked.

"Gold is one of the least chemically reactive elements," Ketch explained. "Pure gold doesn't react easily with oxygen, so it doesn't rust or tarnish. Some more modern coins are pure 24-karat gold, but these early coins aren't. They're close, though. I remember reading that they had to be at least 22-karat, or about 92% pure, to be used as money. So there's also probably a little silver and a little copper in them, both of which can tarnish. But they've been shut up in this trunk, and I imagine that helped preserve them."

"We're rich!" Bean squealed, though at the lower volume Ketch had requested.

"If this isn't pirate treasure, then I wonder who-all put it here?" Henry asked.

"I have an idea about that," Ketch answered, "but I need some more evidence. Henry, I noticed some scraps of wood sticking out of those piles of sand and dirt that Len and his friend dug out of this hole. Would you mind taking a shovel and seeing if you can uncover any interesting pieces?"

"What are we looking for, sir?"

"Anything that looks like something other than a splinter. Oh, and please dump out my backpack and toss it down here, and yours too." Henry had begun toting a backpack similar to Ketch's everywhere he went as well. "While you're digging, Bean and I will fill them with as many of these coins as they can hold."

"Sure thing, Mister Ketchum." Henry climbed over the wall of the cistern and up out of the hole, and a couple of empty backpacks soon flew through the air and were caught by Ketch.

"Okay," Ketch said to Bean. "Let's start packing. And then we'll close up the trunk and shovel some rubble over it so no one else can see it."

"But somebody could steal the dang treasure! We should bring it in the house," Bean suggested.

"I don't think we'd be able to do that, son. Gold is heavy. We probably wouldn't be able to even lift this trunk. And it's very old, and it's wet on the bottom. The wood there has probably rotted, so the bottom would blow out if we did manage to pick it up."

"Okay, Papa." Bean picked up Henry's backpack while Ketch fetched the boy's shovel from where he'd left it.

"You hold the backpack open, up against the lid there," Ketch said, "and I'll shovel the coins into it."

"You forgot somethin', Papa," Bean said with a mischievous look on his face. "Take a dang picture!"

Ketch couldn't suppress a grin. "You're absolutely right, I did forget," he said, and quickly took a shot of the open trunk. "Now let's get to work."

It didn't take them long to fill Henry's backpack. When Ketch was about halfway through the trunk and beginning to wonder how much more they could squeeze into the backpack, they switched and filled Ketch's backpack almost to bursting as well. There was only a small amount of gold remaining when they were done. Henry rejoined them at that point.

"Stuff your pockets, boys," Ketch told them. "Then we can take it all in one trip." While they all did that, he asked Henry, "Did you find anything unusual out there?"

"Maybe, but I left it topside."

"Well then, let's go take a look. We'll leave the tools here for now." Ketch shouldered his backpack. "Henry, can you manage yours?"

"I think so. Sure is heavy, though."

"So that's all the treasure we get, two bags?" Bean dourly observed. "Dang it!"

"Better'n nothin'," Henry said.

"Bean, is that your new favorite word? 'Dang'?" Ketch chuckled. "Boys, let me tell you something about these two bags. The face value of these coins wouldn't add up to that much nowadays, though two hundred years ago it was a small fortune. But I think each of these packs must weigh between thirty and forty pounds. At the price of gold today, that's about a million dollars' worth of gold." The youngsters both stopped and stared at him.

"And that's if you melted the coins and sold the bullion on the gold market," he went on. "But these are antique coins, and collectors will pay even more than that for them. I've heard of auctions where a single rare coin has sold for millions of dollars."

"For one coin? Wow!" Henry said.

Bean was speechless. Ketch figured the numbers were beyond his experience and comprehension. They were almost beyond his own as well.

A windfall like this one might end up dwarfing the bitcoin harvest he'd reaped from that corrupt witch he'd thwarted up on Roanoke Island last fall, which itself had been substantial enough to ease most of his financial worries. This new find could finance the rest of his new house, college educations down the road, and – well, pretty much anything that sensible folks like himself, and what he thought of as his family, might ever need. Providing of course that these were genuine antique gold coins, and not a part of some kind of game or scam.

"Hey y'all!" A familiarly flat but sonorous female voice sounded from the new house. Ketch looked up and saw that Kelsey was out on the back deck. "I thought you might be gettin' hungry, so I carried some lunch over."

Ketch had met Kelsey at the historic old ghost town on Portsmouth Island, where she worked part-time as a naturalist and tour guide. An Ocracoke resident, she'd been instrumental in helping him resolve some rather dire problems that had arisen earlier this summer in connection with a shipwreck off that island, and she'd become another trusted friend in the process. Since she was a fellow diver as well, Ketch had hired her to help out at the Sea Dog Scuba Center, Kari's dive shop, while Kari recuperated from her injuries up the beach. She stayed at the houseboat with Ketch and Bean when she was in town, and she'd taken to helping in other ways in her spare time – and today she was apparently providing lunch for the demolition crew.

"Thank you, Kelsey. We'll be up soon," Ketch called back. "So, Henry, what did you find?"

"Well," Henry said, a little breathless after climbing the ladder with his pack of gold, "there's this over here." He pointed at a sizable fragment of rock he'd exposed in his digging. Its edges were irregular, except for one which was rounded, and the face that Ketch could see was flat and smooth. "Think that might be an Indian artifact, sir?"

"Possibly, but this looks like it was part of a larger piece of rock. And our coastline isn't a rocky one, so I don't know where they would've gotten it." Ketch bent and ran a hand over the stone. “I think this is probably sandstone. Interesting...” He stood up. “Did you find anything else?”

“Yes, sir, there’s one more thing. I leaned it up over behind this pile. It’s just two pieces of rotten ol’ wood, but they’re connected and they have some kind of ratty cloth hangin’ off ’em.”

Ketch followed Henry’s lead. “I see it,” he said when he spotted it. He picked it up and felt the texture of the ragged and discolored piece of cloth. “I think this is sailcloth. This could be –”

“Yo, kid, how you doin’?” said a new voice from behind the pile. “Whatcha got there in the backpack, kid?” a second voice chimed in from behind Henry. “Some kinda buried treasure or sump’n’?”

Now what, Ketch thought. He turned and saw that Bean had run around the pile and joined Henry. Good, he was safe then. Just past Henry and Bean stood two dark-haired, fortyish men in tee shirts, shorts, and flipflops, each holding a bottle of beer. Ketch guessed that not quite all of the neighbors had gone to the beach today.

“Just some gear, sir, and some shells we found,” Henry disseminated.

Bean didn’t say anything. Ketch thought he looked a little scared – which was understandable, given his experience back in June – so he motioned the boy over and had him stand behind him.

“Hello,” Ketch said, casually tossing aside the pieces of wood as though they were unimportant. “Are we neighbors? If so, I don’t believe we’ve met. I’m Ketch – and you are?” He was speaking in a pleasant and relaxed manner, for the moment. But there would be no handshaking.

“Nice-lookin’ place you got here,” the shorter of the two men said. He was tapping a foot as he spoke and he’d almost lost his balance at one point, and Ketch thought he looked nervous. “We saw youse diggin’, see, and we was wonderin' what you found there when you busted into that, what, is that a old well or sump'n?"

When Ketch didn't immediately reply, instead fixing a stony gaze on the interloper, his taller buddy said with an ingratiating smile, "Hey, I'm Ray, and this is Joe. Nice to meet ya. We're from New York, y'know, da Big Apple. Us and our lady friends are rentin' that old place a couple doors up from youse. We come out on our deck and saw you guys workin', and we wondered what you was up to, that's all. Hot day to be workin' outdoors, huh? Bet you guys are tired!" he finished, still smiling.

Smooth, Ketch thought, a good-guy-slash-bad-guy routine. He was doing some wondering himself now, such as about how many bar fights Ray might have had to extricate Joe from, or assist him with, more likely – and if there would be some kind of trouble here today. He glanced off to the side and saw that his crowbar wasn't too far away.

The old Ketch might have turned tail if a confrontation developed, but the new Ketch might not. Yes, it would be two against one, and they were younger – but the two were already drunk even though it was barely midday, and the one would be a crazy man with a crowbar. He figured that combination would greatly improve his odds, and he was finally through with being intimidated, as his actions in June had demonstrated. Whether that was for better or worse remained to be seen, but the only way he'd back down now would be if he thought the kids would be endangered otherwise.

"Well, I hope you're enjoying your vacation on our beautiful island," Ketch disingenuously said. "How long are you staying?"

"Oh, we already been here all week," Ray said. "We gotta check out tomorrow mornin'."

"That's a shame. Well, what we're doing here is breaking up an old cistern, to make room for a boathouse

I'm putting up on this spot."

"What's all that down in there?" said Joe, who'd wandered over to the edge of the hole. "Is that some kinda treasure chest? Did youse find some treasure in there? Get a load a this, Ray!"

When Ray went over to join Joe, Henry moved closer to Ketch. "Sir?" he nervously whispered. "You want me to do somethin'?"

"Get that crowbar for me," Ketch answered under his breath, "and take Bean up to the house."

Henry quickly fetched the crowbar and handed it to Ketch, then took the boy's arm and began hustling him up the slope as expeditiously as possible given the weight of the pack on his back.

"What's that box doin' in there?" Ray called. "What's it for?"

"And what the hell's a cistern?" Joe asked.

Good, Ketch thought, they hadn't noticed the boys making their exit. And they don't know about cisterns. "A cistern is used to collect rainwater," he slowly explained, holding his ground and leaning on the crowbar. "As you may have noticed, there aren't any freshwater reservoirs around here. The island's fresh water comes from reverse osmosis water plants nowadays, but in the old days they used cisterns. The box held cloth and stones that filtered the water." Not bad, just one little lie there at the end.

"Reverse what?" Joe called.

"They take the salt outta the saltwater," Ray said.

"Oh, is that right? Well how about that! So that's all that was in that box, just some rocks and whatnot, huh?" Joe asked, suspicion evident in his voice.

"Yes," Ketch answered.

"You sure about that?" Joe asked, squinting at Ketch in the bright sunlight.

"Yes," Ketch repeated, trying to stay calm but tightening his grip on the crowbar. "You know, the old-time pirates never came this far up the islands. Blackbeard came the closest that I know of. He spent some time down around Ocracoke, but that's quite a ways off. So there wouldn't be any pirate treasure around here."

"Uh huh. Well, okay, if you say so," Joe acquiesced, though he still looked doubtful.

Ketch saw that the boys had made it up to the deck of the house. He wondered how much longer it might be before the men noticed his bulging pockets, and decided he should make his move now.

"You'll have to excuse me, as I've been summoned for lunch," he said. "It was nice meeting you. Enjoy the rest of your stay."

He turned and began slowly heading back up the yard, ostensibly using the crowbar as a walking stick and continuing to watch the men from the corner of his eye. He saw that he'd managed to stall enough for the boys to now be inside. They were watching him from behind the sliding glass doors.

"Yeah, okay," Ray waved. "See ya later, neighbor. Let's go, Joe. Joe!"

"What?"

"Come on now, let's go."

"Awright, awright!"

Ketch kept an eye on both of them as they wove an erratic path back toward their vacation rental, muttering to each other along the way. He suspected he might not have heard the last of those two.

He climbed the steps up to the deck and went inside, using the kitchen door – which he hoped Bean and Henry had as well, since they were dirty. At least they'd taken off their boots outside, he saw, which he'd done as well. He brought the crowbar in with him.

"It feels good in here," he said to Kelsey, setting his heavy pack and the crowbar down in a corner of the kitchen next to Henry's backpack. "So I guess the air conditioning is working."

Although the house wasn't quite ready for habitation, it was close. He knew the utilities and appliances were all hooked up now, but there was no furniture to speak of, so he wondered where they'd be eating their lunch.

"Yep, I turned it on when I got here," Kelsey said. "I sent Bean and Henry to wash up," she added in answer to Ketch's unspoken question.

"Wash up, you say? With what?"

"I brought a few things over with me from the boat. Some of the extra bath towels and washcloths, your card table, your foldin' chairs, and some other odds and ends. Stuart came in early to the shop, so I had some extra time. I figured you're gonna be startin' to use this place even if you hadn't moved in yet, like today. I set the table and chairs up in the dinin' room. I hope you don't mind."

"Why would I mind? Thank you, Kelsey. You've once again gone above and beyond."

The extraordinarily even-keeled young woman didn't react, either positively or negatively. As usual, she simply took whatever happened in stride and continued onward.

"Who were those guys out there, and what did they want?" she asked. "The kids seemed worried."

"Oh, a couple of drunken tourons from up the road. They thought we might have found buried treasure in the cistern. I told them we didn't."

Kelsey's eyebrows lifted, one of the few signs of emotion she exhibited. "But you did find a treasure, didn't you? I heard Bean and Henry talkin' about it."

"Yes, as a matter of fact we did. Here, I'll show you." Ketch unzipped his backpack just a little for her, not enough so the coins would come spilling out. "Henry's backpack is full of these, too. And so are our pockets."

"Huh," was all she said. No inquiries regarding the details – she'd patiently wait until Ketch filled her in, or didn't. Either way would be okay with her.

"Have you seen any kind of bag or container around here, so I could empty my pockets?" he asked her.

"I brought trash bags," she said, pointing them out to him. "Do you think those guys believed you?"

"Sadly, I think maybe not."

"So we might have to deal with them. Do you think it's okay for us to stay here for lunch?"

"Well, I don't know for sure, but I doubt they'd be foolish enough to try to break in here in broad daylight with us here, if that's what you're thinking."

"Okay. But how about I call some friends over while you wash up, just to be safe? I saw Len and Don at the boatyard."

"I think that might be a good idea." Captain Don, whom Ketch simply called 'Captain', was his best friend and a tough old mariner, and Len was also no stranger to adversity. It would be good to have them backing him in case there was any trouble.

She nodded. "I'll make sure all the doors and windows are locked, and then I'll call Don. There's cold drinks in the fridge if you're thirsty. I brought some over in a cooler."

"Thanks again, Kelsey."

And again, no acknowledgement. But this didn't concern Ketch. It was just the way she was. Although she was intelligent and attractive, she was single and she didn't have any close friends in Ocracoke that he knew of. He didn't know why that was, and he didn't need to. What he did know was, she appreciated his friendship and being accepted by the boatyard community here, and she was agreeable, competent, brave, and loyal. That was good enough for him.

So she went on about her business, and Ketch joined the kids in the bathroom.

"Well, you two are looking considerably better. This room, less so," he chuckled. "But don't worry about that, I'll clean up when I'm done. Are you guys okay?"

"Yes, sir," Henry said.

Bean threw his arms around Ketch, and a couple of his coins clinked onto the floor. "Are the bad guys gone, Papa?" he tremulously asked.

"I don't know how bad they are – but yes, they're gone. Now why don't you go get something to drink and relax, and pretty soon we'll have lunch. You can empty your pockets into that bag I left on the countertop."

"Okay, Papa," Bean said, and he and Henry went off – both wearing clean, dry tee shirts, Ketch finally noticed. Henry's was an old one of Ketch's from Key West, and looked a bit large on him. He saw that there was another folded shirt resting atop the toilet tank, and he shook his head. That Kelsey was something else. He'd add his own sweaty shirt to the ones he now saw were hanging over the shower bar – which was no longer *sans* curtain. Okay, so she was downright spooky, but he'd take it.

He decided against a shower right now, though, as he didn't want to be incommunicado in case anything happened. Instead, he just made use of the soap – and deodorant and aftershave! – that he found on the shelf over the sink.

"Don said he'd pick Len up and be right over," Kelsey told him when he returned to the kitchen. "He said not to worry because he'd have things covered. I also called for a pizza, because I only brought enough Subway for the four of us. He's pickin' that up too."

"I want pizza!" Bean announced from the dining room, where Ketch could see paper plates and a roll of paper towels on the table. There were still only four chairs, but he and someone else could eat at the breakfast counter that separated the kitchen from the dining room. There were a couple of old stools there, which the workmen must have brought in.

"You can have whatever you want when everyone gets here," Ketch said. "What did the Captain mean when he said he'd have things covered?" he asked Kelsey. She just shrugged in answer.

"I hope you're using the credit card I gave you for expenses, and not paying for things yourself," he reminded her. He'd also given her a complete set of keys to everything – the houseboat, the dive shop, and the new house – which was another thing he ordinarily wouldn't do. But her assistance was invaluable at the moment, and she'd given him no reason to distrust her.

"Of course," she said, busying herself with the subs and some of the plates. She also had a knife, which she must have brought along with everything else.

Ketch saw that Henry was keeping Bean entertained with some sort of improvised table hockey game. He'd made a couple of goals and goalies from a paper plate, and the two of them were busy shooting little wads of paper towel at each other. Bean looked like he was having fun.

It wasn't long before two quick knocks sounded at the front door, and then a single one, and then two more. Since there was no 'ahoy' booming out from behind the door, Ketch decided to pick up the crowbar before answering it. But in the meantime, Kelsey strode straight to the door and opened it.

And there stood an atypically silent Captain Don with some kind of gear bag slung over one shoulder. Len came up behind him carrying a pizza box. Neither one spoke until they were inside and the door was closed and locked.

The Captain eyeballed Ketch and his crowbar. "Well lookee there! Good thing I got that knockin' bidness right!" the Captain said to Kelsey. "I left the truck down the street like you told me. *And*, I kept my big mouth shut, like you said."

"I didn't say that. I asked you to be quiet," she objected with the slightest hint of a smile.

"Ahoy there!" the Captain at last brayed, which started a general hubbub that went on until Ketch called for order.

"What's in the bag?" Ketch asked the Captain.

"Just a little bit a in-shurance. That there's my new friend Daisy. Say hello to my little friend! I decided to replace the one you done lost on me with somethin' a mite bigger'n scarier. Don't worry, she's empty," he added. "But I can load both barrels in a heartbeat if I have to."

So, a shotgun – and a movie reference that Kari would have appreciated. Ketch decided not to comment and draw the kids' attention to the Captain's new toy. "It appears Kelsey told you something about our situation," was all he said.

"That she did," Len said, shaking his head. "I thought you said you was retirin' from this kinda thing from here on out."

"Seems like you just can't stay outta trouble, though, don't it?" the Captain said. "Now how 'bout you fill us in on what exactly's goin' on 'round here?"

"I sure do hope there ain't gonna be more dang witches this time," Len said, and the Captain added, "Nor sea hags'n such," to which Len retorted, "And no graverobbin'!"

Though they were touching some nerves with their ribbing, Ketch knew they were doing it good-naturedly. And, undoubtedly out of consideration since they were two of the truest friends Ketch had ever had, they weren't zeroing in on the touchiest ones. So he let it go.

"I'll explain everything while we eat. The kids are hungry, and so am I."

Ketch and Kelsey took the breakfast counter and the others sat at the card table. In between quick bites, he told them everything that had happened that morning. Questions arose almost immediately, of course, but he forestalled most of them until he'd gotten through his explanation.

Bean and Henry helped by demonstrating some of their loot to the newcomers, thereby allowing Ketch to get through half of his sub as well – a Subway Club with deluxe meat, Swiss cheese, lettuce, tomato, pickle, mayo, and salt and pepper. Dang, as Bean would say, she was good.

It occurred to Ketch that Kari, Bean's new mother figure and the biggest film buff he'd ever known, would also have appreciated the irony of those 'goodfellas' from New York speaking the way they had, and being named Ray and Joe to boot. She probably wouldn't have been able to keep a straight face, he thought to himself with a smile. It was hard being away from her, but she needed to stay with her mother closer to the hospital until the doctors were sure she was out of the woods. She'd certainly get a kick out of hearing what had happened here today.

"So I guess we need a plan for gettin' that gold to a safe place, and for dealin' with those guys up the street if they come back around here," Len summarized.

"Where d'ya think all them gold coins come from?" the Captain asked. "You got any idea who buried 'em there in that cistern?"

"Yes," Ketch said, "thanks to some help from Henry. It's just a theory, though."

"Well, do tell!" the Captain demanded.

"I don't know if you're familiar with the story, but back in the late seventeen hundreds, a man named Pharaoh Farrow lived here on Hatteras Island."

"I've heard a the Farrows," the Captain remarked. "I believe there's still some a them 'round these parts."

"That's funny," Bean said. "His first name was the same as his last name!"

"Not quite," Ketch continued. "His last name was spelled F-A-R-R-O-W, but his first name was spelled P-H-A-R-A-O-H, like the ancient Egyptian pharaohs. That's because he was supposedly of Arabic descent, and was shipwrecked on this island when he was just a boy. So he got called 'Pharaoh' as a nickname, and that later became the other 'Farrow'. In that story, there was another Arabic youth from the same shipwreck who was simply called 'A-rab', and he was the founder of the Wahab family of Ocracoke. Of course, that's just one story. Other people say he was an English squire."

"Anyway..." Kelsey said. Ketch knew she was trying to dissuade him from getting bogged down in arcane details, which he knew he had a tendency to do, and he took the hint.

"Who knows?" he went on. "Anyway, from what I've read, when he was older, Pharaoh somehow came to own a great deal of land and many slaves. His land was mostly wooded, and he made a lot of money cutting down most of the trees and selling the lumber to the New England shipbuilders."

"So that's where all the trees went," Henry commented.

"Yes. He also built several windmills on some of the landings, the small peninsulas along the sound. Of course, many of those are changed now or gone altogether, due to our shifting sands. The fishermen from here traded with the mainland farmers, getting corn and wheat in exchange for some of their catch, and the windmills were used to grind the grains into meal and flour. He held back some of that as his fee, and that was how he fed his slaves. The windmills were post mills – that is, they could be rotated on a metal post so their sails could catch the wind, whichever way it happened to be blowing. They each had two large millstones made of sandstone, which was imported from Barbados in the Caribbean..."

"Really? How interesting," Kelsey said, clearing her throat and casting a meaningful glance Ketch's way.

"Yes, well," he went on, "when Pharaoh got even older and the trees were gone, he sold most of his slaves, which supposedly netted him another fortune, and he sold at least a couple of his windmills. And then the legend goes that sometime in the early eighteen hundreds, when he knew his days were numbered, he commanded his remaining slaves to load all of his gold into two trunks and bury them in a brick cistern. The trunks were said to be so heavy that a couple of neighbors who visited him on his deathbed couldn't together lift an end of either trunk off the floor. And last I knew, that cistern and those trunks have never been found."

"That's a brick cistern out back," Henry observed.

"Yes – and I don't think it was meant to collect rainwater, since there were no openings on it anywhere."

"But we only found one dang trunk!" Bean exclaimed. "Where's the other one? Are you sure Pharaoh wasn't a pirate, Papa?"

"Right. As I explained earlier, the age of piracy was over by that time, and anyway most pirates didn't bury treasure. They spent most of their money in taverns and, er..."

"Houses of ill repute," Kelsey finished for him.

"And the rest of it, they wasted!" the Captain chortled.

"What happened to all the windmills?" Henry asked, thankfully changing the subject before Bean could make further inquiries.

"Well, the big hurricane of 1899, which was later named San Ciriaco, destroyed most of them. There were only two left by the early nineteen hundreds, and they were both here in Avon. One was in the southern part of the village, and the other was at Farrow Scarborough's landing, which was somewhere here in the northern part of town."

"So the Scarboroughs must be related to the Farrows," the Captain said.

"Yes, and I'm wondering if that landing was in my backyard," Ketch said. "Though now that I think of it, I remember reading that the windmill was north of the village, up from Scarborough's landing. That would be farther north from here. However," he went on, "I think there might have been a windmill here at one time."

"You mean right here, on your lot?" Len asked.

"Yes, or nearby. Henry found a piece of wood near the cistern that I think could have been part of a vane of a windmill. It had an old scrap of sailcloth attached to it, which is what was used for the sails of the windmills. He also found a large, rounded fragment of stone that could have come from a millstone."

"So," Kelsey concluded, "you think this might be Pharaoh's treasure? But why's there only the one trunk?"

"Who knows?" Ketch said. "Maybe his slaves made off with the other one, or someone else stole it. Or maybe there were never two to begin with. Stories do often grow with repeated tellings, after all," he concluded with a glance in the Captain's direction. Len and Kelsey also looked his way.

"How come y'all are lookin' at me?" the Captain blustered.

Len laughed. "Are you kiddin'? With the tall tales you tell?"

"Are you gonna keep it this time?" Kelsey asked, making a veiled reference to the gold he'd given up at Portsmouth for Kari's sake back in June. When Ketch nodded assent, she said, "Do you think there'll be any legal problems if you do that?"

"Not necessarily. I researched this topic a couple months ago, when we found that other gold. Franklin Roosevelt issued an executive order that empowered the government to confiscate as much gold as possible back in the Thirties, to shore up the Federal Reserve during the Great Depression, and made it illegal for private citizens to own gold – unconstitutionally, many said. But that order was rescinded when Nixon took the U.S. off the gold standard. In this country nowadays, since I found the gold on my land, it's basically 'finders keepers' unless someone else can stake a claim to it that would stand up in court."

"Like maybe the Farrows or the Scarboroughs?" the

Captain thoughtfully mused.

"Possibly," Ketch admitted. "But to pull it off, they'd have to produce evidence that it was mislaid, rather than lost or abandoned. Those are legal terms with specific meanings. There's no identification anywhere in or around that cistern to prove who the owner was, or even to definitively date the find. The dates on the coins are circumstantial, as someone could have hidden them later than that. They'd also have to prove that Pharaoh owned this land when that cistern was built. And as you pointed out," he concluded, looking at Bean, "there was only one trunk, so the reality doesn't exactly match the legend. And finally, the legend is just that – a legend. It may be entirely untrue."

"So you're just gonna keep it and keep your mouth shut about it?" Len inquired.

"Yes, I think so. Everything I've told you is really just a theory – and I think we should keep it to ourselves. I don't see any sense in starting rumors that could hang us up in court for years, for no good reason."

Len raised his arms. "Okay by me, I was just askin'. But hey, I guess that makes y'all a bunch a pirates, don't it?" He poked Bean's arm. "Hey, little man, you're a pirate now, how 'bout that!"

"Well, I guess we're all pirates, then," Ketch said.

"Oh yeah? What's that mean?" the Captain asked.

"It means I intend to share my good fortune with you, all of you," Ketch explained, "the way a pirate captain would share with his crew."

"Oh, like the old-time pirate ship's 'articles' used to spell out, huh? And the captain gets the most shares, and I guess you think you're the captain? But the crew a the ship voted on that back in the day, ya know, it weren't automatic," the Captain teased. "But hey, don't worry, I think we can all agree you're the captain a this particular crew. How much you think that haul's worth?"

"At least a million dollars," Henry spoke up. "And maybe a lot more, if collectors want the coins." When Len and the Captain looked surprised, he added, "Mister Ketchum figured it out before."

"That's if they're really solid gold coins, of course," Ketch said. "I think they are, but I know some ways to test them. I'll do that later when I get a chance."

"If they're fake, maybe they'd still work in vendin' machines. Then they could keep us in Nabs'n Tabs, at least," Len joked.

"Do they still make Tab?" the Captain asked. "I hadn't seen any in a long time. Not that I'd ever drink it, mind you. I heard it ain't healthy."

"Says the guy that drinks beer like it was water," Len said.

Ketch smiled. "Assuming they're real, what I'll do is have my lawyer contact one of the big auction houses." Why not? Since he had a lawyer now, he might as well make use of him. "If they think it's worth pursuing, then we'll see what we can get. I'll have them set up some kind of trust to handle everything, and then we can withdraw money from it."

"That's very generous of you, Ketch. Thank you," Kelsey said in her typically even tone. The others echoed her sentiment, with more enthusiasm of course. "But what about the historical record?" she continued. "If this really is Pharaoh's treasure, no one will ever know it was found. Do you think maybe you should donate the trunk and some of the coins to someplace like the Graveyard of the Atlantic Museum, and tell them what you think it is?"

"I know history is important to you. It's important to me too, you know that," Ketch replied. "But there are a lot of things in history that no one will ever know. And that trunk's in poor condition, and there are already trunks like it, and coins like these, in museums. And there's not much historical context here, since we don't know for sure that this is Pharaoh's treasure. We don't really know anything about where it really came from."

"Nobody knows 'bout them shipwrecks we found down off Portsmouth," Len remarked. "We didn't tell nobody 'bout those."

"That was different," Kelsey argued, though of course without raising her voice. "There were extenuating circumstances. And they weren't part of the popular folklore of the islands, like Pharaoh's treasure is."

"Yeah, but if we tell the museum folks about your theory and they make a big deal out of it, that could open up your can a legal worms," the Captain pointed out. "Best to leave our well-enoughs alone, is what I say."

Yes, and that made Ketch wonder if he really believed that what he'd said was a morally valid response to Kelsey's concerns, or if it had been just a rationalization driven by greed. Would he be responding in the same way if they'd found Indian or Civil War artifacts instead of spendable ones? He might have to think some more on that. Meanwhile, he thought of a possible solution.

"I took pictures and measurements at each step of our excavation," he told Kelsey. "I'll create a computer file that documents our find, for posterity, and I'll print a copy for you."

"And then folks can read all about it after you're dead'n gone. Sounds good to me," the Captain said.

That appeared to satisfy Kelsey for now, though it would be hard for anyone but Ketch to tell. But he could, and he knew she wouldn't bring up the subject again.

"Okay, so that's that," Len concluded. "Now we need a plan for today," he reminded them, getting back to business.

"Well, accordin' to Kelsey, those guys that were hangin' around can't see the front of this house from where they're stayin', so they don't know me'n you's here," the Captain said. "So I say Ketch and Kelsey and the kids take off and stash the gold, and we stay here in case somethin' happens. If they're watchin' and they see the vehicles pull out, they might think everybody's gone and get brave. And then we can put a good scare into 'em for ya."

"Thank you, Captain," Ketch said. "All right then. Kelsey, you take the kids. There's a safe at the dive shop, so I'll go there and lock up the coins. Then I'll come back here. Bean and Henry, finish up and we'll get going."

"What about the tools, sir?" Henry interjected. "And the stuff we dumped out of our packs? And we hadn't finished the job yet neither."

"Y'all done enough," Len reassured him. "You saved me some time, and it sounds like I might end up gettin' paid enough to bust up about a thousand a them old cisterns!"

"Someone will go out later and pick everything up, and I'll return your gear to you when I get a chance," Ketch said. "Except for your backpack. I'll have to keep that until I find something else to put the coins in. Oh, and you and Bean should each take a few coins with you, as souvenirs. The rest of you, too, if you want to. Don't open the backpacks again, just take some from the bag."

Everyone did as they'd been directed. Henry then helped Ketch load the backpacks into his truck, again using the front door of the house and keeping to the leeward side of the building, as it were. The dive shop would still be open, so when Ketch arrived there he'd go in the back way. Kelsey herded the children into the Outback that Ketch had given her as part of her reward after the Portsmouth affair. Then both vehicles backed out of the driveway, taking their time and revving their engines a bit, and left Len and the Captain – and Daisy – behind to hold the fort.

Ketch secured the coins in the safe at the dive shop without any complications. Stuart was busy up front with some customers, so he didn't have to say anything beyond 'Hey, Stuart'. This was fine with him, as he still wasn't fully accustomed to talking as much as he'd had to back at the house. He figured his lunchtime monologue would probably have been several days' worth of jawing for him back in the bad times.

He tested the coins he'd pocketed while he was at the shop, first with the strongest magnet he could find on the refrigerator in the kitchenette and then with some white vinegar he found in the closet among the cleaning products. He also made a small divot in one of the coins with his penknife, and scraped a coin across a plate he found in the cupboard. He stayed only as long as all this took, then waved to Stuart and headed back out the way he'd come.

Everything seemed calm and quiet when he arrived back at his new house – which, by design, looked a lot like the old one. Ketch had insisted on the same dark brown cedar shake siding and wraparound porch, among other less obvious features. Of course, it couldn't be exactly the same, since the old house had been essentially a four-room bungalow on stilts, whereas this one was a two-story structure – also on stilts, but with more than double the living space of the original.

But it was close enough for him, and looking at it made him feel good. There was enough freeboard beneath the house to park four vehicles, two on either side of a central storage area, so that was where he left his truck.

As he mounted the front steps, the fact that there were no sounds at all emanating from within began to worry him a little. It seemed odd, especially since the Captain was in there, but maybe both he and Len were maintaining 'radio silence' as part of their mission. Or maybe they'd fallen asleep. He wouldn't put that past the Captain, he thought, but then Len was there, too.

He found that the front door was unlocked, which further worried him. Pulling his hand away from the doorknob he'd begun turning as though it were red-hot, he wondered if he should first go find himself something he could use as a weapon if necessary. And then the door was flung open.

"Ahoy there!" the Captain thundered in his face, making his heart skip a beat, maybe two. "Saw ya pull in. Say, what-all's the matter with *you*?" he asked, noticing the look on Ketch's face. "Aw, did I scare ya?" he laughed.

"Hey, Ketch," Len called with his mouth full from the kitchen, where it appeared he was helping dispose of the leftovers.

"I got worried when I realized the door wasn't locked," Ketch said.

"Oh! Well, we decided to unlock the doors after you left," the Captain explained. "That way if somebody wanted to come in, they wouldn't have to break nothin'."

"Well, I guess that was a good idea. So, did anyone come around?"

"Not a soul! So maybe you got nothin' to worry about after all."

"Unless they're planning on waiting until it's dark," Ketch mused.

"Don't know why they'd do that, though, 'lessen they're stupid. They should know you wouldn't just leave a bunch a treasure layin' around in here, you'd go lock it up somewheres like you just did."

"Yes, unless they're stupid – or drunk, like they were earlier."

"When did you get to be such a worrywart? Never mind, I guess I don't blame ya. Who knows what folks like that'll do, and you don't want your new place messed up. Hey, you want us to stay here overnight? We could set watches."

"On a Saturday night? Don't you have anything better to do? And what about Len? He's younger than we are, and he's probably made plans."

"Well I don't know 'bout him, but I got nothin' better to do besides help out a friend that's cuttin' me in on a dang treasure!"

"We can stay with him," Kelsey said from behind Ketch, giving him another palpitation.

Some watchdogs *they* were, he thought – no one had shut the door, no one was even looking, and she'd walked right in. He was about to close the door himself when Jack and Chuck came bounding in, big doggy grins on both their faces.

"Well lookee who's here, my two best buddies!" The Captain bent to pet both of them. "A couple a *real* watchdogs! Now we won't need to set watches. Them two'll wake up the whole house if anybody comes skulkin' around! Why didn't we think a that?"

"I guess we're not the sharpest tools in this particular shed," Ketch said, closing and locking the door this time and then hugging each animal in turn. "She is. What about Bean?" he asked her.

"I asked Suzanne if she might could keep him overnight when I was droppin' Henry off," Kelsey replied. "Bean was happy about it, and so was Suzanne after I gave her a few gold coins." Though that last part was obviously a joke, she delivered it straight-faced as usual.

"Ha! You're right, Ketch, she *is* the smart one in this bunch!" the Captain chuckled. Getting serious, he asked Ketch if he'd ever handled a shotgun.

"You're willing to trust me with another one of your guns?" Ketch joked. "Actually, no, I've never fired a gun." Other than a spear gun, of course, which he didn't mention.

"I can show him," Kelsey said. "I used to go duck huntin' with my dad before he got sick," she matter-of-factly added by way of explanation.

"Well, she's got a kick to her, so shoot low," the Captain told her. "If you want to blow somebody's head off, you might want to aim for their bellybutton."

"Got it," she said, and both Ketch and the Captain took

her at her word. Despite her perennial look of innocence and the blond ponytail sticking out of the back of her ball cap, they knew from experience that she was a tough cookie.

"Well," the Captain said, scratching his head under his tacky mariner's cap, "if you think you got things covered, then I guess me'n Len'll just mosey along. We might could stay longer anyways, but y'all got no beer!"

"I'm sorry, Ketch, I didn't think of that," Kelsey apologized. "I can go get some if you want."

"I'll be fine, please don't bother," he answered. He knew she never drank alcohol, and he no longer required it himself.

"But I did bring sleepin' bags, clean clothes, more towels, our travel kits, and stuff for the dogs. It's all out in my car. We can have takeaway delivered tonight when we get hungry."

"Dang!" the Captain exclaimed. "Where did you say you found her again? Wherever it was, I should go on down there! But hey, did you bring a TV?"

"We won't need a TV," Ketch said.

"Oh, is that so? You dawg!" the Captain leered. Before Ketch's face could redden too much, he grinned and backtracked. "Hey, I'm just teasin', you know that." Then he winked at Kelsey. "Sorry, darlin'," he said. "I can't quite fit my whole foot in my mouth, but that don't stop me from tryin'!"

That got another little half-smile out of her. The Captain didn't know this, but she had in fact once extended an invitation to Ketch when Kari was still in a coma and the prognosis was grim, in case he was 'feeling low' and might 'need a body to keep him company' during that difficult time. But the offer had been pragmatic rather than romantic or salacious, and was simply an act of kindness in keeping with the girl's bohemian nature. When he'd politely declined, she'd nonchalantly accepted that and said no more about it.

"What's goin' on," asked Len, returning from a bathroom. "What'd I miss? Hey, guys!" he said to the dogs.

The Captain did the explaining this time, and both he and Len shortly took their leave. When they were gone, Kelsey showed Ketch how to hold and prepare to fire the shotgun, and how to load it. Then she kept watch while he took a couple of bags, and the dogs, out back and gathered up the tools and other flotsam he and the boys had left behind earlier. Finally, he brought everything in from her car and, after tossing the dogs each a bone, collapsed onto one of the folding chairs in the dining room.

"You look like you're worn out, Ketch," Kelsey said, coming up behind him. She began kneading his neck and his shoulders with both hands, as she occasionally did for him when she knew he was stressed. She was very good at it, and he couldn't help but selfishly let her do it when she was so inclined. "Why don't you shower, and then roll out a sleepin' bag in one of the bedrooms and take a little rest?"

Sleeping bag? He could fall asleep right here, if she kept massaging him like that. "I just might do that," he said, and relaxed and closed his eyes. A couple of delicious minutes later, though, he reluctantly disengaged. "Thank you, that was nice," he said, getting up and going to the refrigerator for a drink. "But what about you? Aren't you tired?"

"I'm okay. I'll just hang with Jack and Chuck 'til you wake up. I have a book."

"All right then, if you say so. Thanks again. Oh, by the way," he said, sitting back down again, "I tested some of the coins when I was at the shop. They weren't attracted to a magnet, they didn't change color when I exposed them to acid, and they didn't make a dark mark when I scraped them across a plate. I also dug a small hole in one of them. It looks like they're gold, all right."

"That's good," she said, settling onto another chair. "Guess what, I have some interesting news too."

"Oh?"

"I told you I started doin' some genealogical research online, right? To learn more about my ancestors, since nobody ever told me much about them. Well, I found an unexpected connection. Have you ever heard of a guy named Black Jack Ketchum?"

"Yes, I have. He was an outlaw in the old West, as I recall."

"Right. He and his gang were train robbers, like Butch Cassidy. Matter of fact, his gang hid out sometimes at the Hole-In-The-Wall, with Butch's Wild Bunch gang. Well, I found out I might be related to him."

"Really? That *is* interesting. I've never heard that I'm related to him, though, even though our surnames are the same."

"Well, that's why I'm tellin' you about it. I'd like to look into that, if you don't mind. Who knows, we could be distant cousins or somethin'. Wouldn't that be a hoot," she drily concluded.

"Indeed it would," Ketch agreed. "And it would be quite a coincidence. But go ahead, I don't mind."

"Thanks, I will." She got up and checked the back doors to make sure they were locked. "Okay, you can go on and do whatever you want to do. I'll keep an eye on things."

Ketch appreciated this particular offer, as he was both dirty and tired. A hot shower and the clean clothes she'd brought him solved the former problem, and the sleeping bag took care of the latter one. He gratefully dropped off to sleep as soon as he lay down on it.

When he woke, he was surprised to see through the bedroom window that it was dusk. That was strange, he thought. He hardly napped at all these days, and when he did it was never for this long. But he supposed it had been an arduous and stressful day – and like it or not, he *was* getting older. Still, he felt ashamed that he'd left Kelsey alone all that time, and that they'd be having such a late supper. He got up immediately and exited the bedroom.

He found her sitting on the living room rug, reading her book. She'd placed the other rolled-up sleeping bag against the wall and was using it as a backrest. The dogs were both snoozing nearby. Jack woke up and wagged when he saw Ketch, but Chuck kept snoring.

"Well hey, sleepyhead," Kelsey said, closing the book.

"Kelsey, I'm sorry," Ketch apologized. "I didn't mean to sleep for that long."

"That's okay. You must have needed it," she said, shrugging off his apology. "Your timing's good, anyway. I called out for some seafood. The delivery person should be here soon. I also fed the dogs, but I didn't take them out."

"I'll do that right now, if they want to go." It looked like they did, as all ears were now up. "And then, after we eat and I take them out again, I think we should leave most of the lights off, as if we're turning in early – even though I just got up," he ruefully added.

"In case anybody wants to try to break in here tonight, so we can get that over with," Kelsey said, completing his train of thought. "Do you think we should leave the doors unlocked again?"

"No. I think the dogs will alert us before they have a chance to break a window or whatever."

"Okay," she said.

Their food was delivered shortly, and without incident. After they'd eaten and the chores were done, she took a turn in the shower, and then they talked for a while at the table in the dark. Kelsey was finally tired out at that point, and Ketch was surprised to realize that he was again as well, so they both turned in – but in separate rooms, contrary to the Captain's bawdy suggestion. Since they now had the dogs to keep watch, they figured they could afford the luxury of sleeping. And sleep they did, though not right away for Ketch.

As he lay alone in the cool, peaceful dark, he found

himself starting to fantasize about what might happen if Kelsey were to silently enter his room and join him in his sleeping bag. But he stomped that ember out in the next heartbeat, chastising himself for even fleetingly thinking about it. Kari didn't deserve that, especially after what she'd already been through on his account. Maybe he was indeed a 'dawg', as the Captain liked to call him. Or maybe he was just human, he thought, cutting himself some slack.

Anyway, he didn't have to worry about what he might actually do if push came to shove, because he knew Kelsey wouldn't do something like that if he didn't ask her to. However, he also knew, or thought he did, that she would if he did ask, and there was the rub. But he dismissed that fact as irrelevant and finally just went back to sleep.

The next time he woke, the morning sun was peeking through the blinds. He squinted against the glare and stayed put for the moment, groggily appreciating the warmth of the body that was snuggled up against his back. Rolling over, he came face-to-face with Jack. His faithful friend woke as well, languorously stretched, and gave him a lick. Chuck must be with Kelsey, he thought.

"Good morning, buddy," he said, and stroked the dog's flank.

Kelsey did enter his room then, but she was fully dressed and remained standing. "Good, you're up," she said.

"Did I miss something?" he asked.

"Didn't you hear the dogs barkin' and the gun goin' off?" she deadpanned.

"*What?*" he spluttered.

"Just kiddin'. Nothin' happened all night long. There's somethin' I thought you might like to see, is all."

He was still wearing his shorts, thankfully. He got up, pulled his shirt on, and followed her out onto the back deck. The dogs came along as well, and went out with them.

"See there? They're checkin' out early," she said, pointing to the rental a couple doors up. "They've been loadin' their stuff for the last little while."

And now they were leaving. Ketch watched as Ray and Joe, and their 'lady friends', got in their SUV and pulled away from the house.

"How about that," he said. "False alarm, I guess. Now I feel foolish for taking up so much of your time, and Len's and the Captain's as well."

"Well, you shouldn't ought to," she told him, resting a hand on his arm. "You never know what-all people might do. Maybe they would have come back here, but their girlfriends talked them out of it. Who knows? Anyway, I was happy to help, so don't feel bad." Then she surprised him with a quick kiss on the cheek. "Come on, let's go wash up and pack our own stuff, and then maybe I'll take you out to breakfast. If you're good," she finished with another of her half-smiles.

Ketch flashed her a brief smile back. Yes, who knew what people might do, he thought. For example, she didn't usually take liberties like the one she'd just taken. Maybe certain of his assumptions were flawed and he'd gotten lucky last night, though not in the way folks usually meant when they said that.

He mutely followed her back inside, shaking his head. He got a trash bag from the box in the kitchen and started collecting the clothes he and the kids had left lying around. The last item he picked up was his jeans from yesterday. He paused before adding them to the bag.

He'd thought he'd emptied his pockets before he'd showered, but he realized now that there was still something in one of them. Ah yes, the clasp from the trunk, he saw as he fished it from the pocket. He'd snatched it up out of the muck and pocketed it on a whim just before he and the kids had left the cistern.

It hadn't been noticeable yesterday, or maybe he

simply hadn't looked at it closely enough, but he saw now that there appeared to be some kind of pattern on it beneath the rust and crusted sand. He took it to the kitchen sink and thoroughly rinsed it, then started scraping away some of the rust with his penknife. Yes, there was definitely a symbol of some sort. A monogram or seal, perhaps?

When he thought he'd loosened enough of the rust, he rinsed the clasp again and vigorously rubbed it with an old workman's rag from under the sink. Then he got his penlight out and shone it on the clasp. He found he could now make out what was etched on it. It appeared to be just a single letter, after all that – but a potentially significant one. Though he had misgivings, he dutifully got out his smartphone and took one final picture, this one of a rust-laden but discernible letter 'P'.

He stood at the sink and stared unseeing out the kitchen window. His misgivings stemmed from his uncertainty about how Kelsey would react to this new development. He was sure the others wouldn't object to him going ahead as planned and anonymously auctioning off the coins to collectors with money to burn, but she might. Hell, he might now, too.

The question was, was this an important enough find after all, historically speaking, to be made public and exhibited in a museum? They could still keep and auction off most of the coins in that case, though, he supposed. But then what about the possibility – nay, the probability in these litigious times – of becoming entangled in court with Pharaoh's descendants? Or was the evidence honestly too circumstantial to justify subjecting themselves to all that?

Honesty... That would have to figure in the answer to that question, and he wondered if he could make an unbiased evaluation on his own at this point. He'd already considered simply omitting this last bit of information, and the photo of the 'P', from the document he'd promised to create, or perhaps just from the copy he'd give to Kelsey. But he'd immediately dismissed both thoughts, so maybe he still had some honesty left in him. Neither she, nor history, deserved to be deceived or lied to. It might help to discuss the matter in confidence with his lawyer, he thought then, and also with someone at the Graveyard of the Atlantic Museum, which was just down the road in Hatteras village. He could look into that before proceeding further.

In the meantime, maybe he wouldn't call Kelsey's attention to his discovery just yet. Or maybe he would, perhaps over breakfast. Yes, he should do that, he decided. He didn't want her to think he was trying to hide something from her. She trusted him at least as much as he trusted her, and trust was a hard thing to find again once it had been lost.

With a sigh, he wrapped the clasp in a paper towel and zipped it into a cargo pocket of his shorts. He'd come back later and put the trunk in the storage area under the house, in case the museum wanted it. For now, he'd just finish helping with the packing and wash up for breakfast.

ROUTE 101

DESCRIPTION

In Storm Ketchum Tale #7, a shipwreck nearly a hundred years ago strands a Ketchum ancestor on the Outer Banks.

In her present-day genealogical research, Ketch's friend and assistant Kelsey has uncovered a link between her Ocracoke Island family and the notorious Wild West outlaw Black Jack Ketchum. Is Black Jack indeed a member of her family tree? And is there also a connection to Ketch's Northern branch of the Ketchum family?

The answers will depend on whether young Laura Ketchum of Virginia can survive her packet steamer running aground on the treacherous shoals off Ocracoke Island, as well as the violent storm that caused the shipwreck.

Join Laura and the citizens of Ocracoke in an old-time adventure on the historic Outer Banks, where intrigue always seems to be just around the next corner.

NOTE: Laura, Hazel, and Marshall, the main characters in this story, are fictitious.

September 1925

Laura was going to drown this night. She was almost sure of it. But why would her Maker subject her to such a terrible fate? She could understand being tested, but how could He expect a normal human being to survive in this horrific maelstrom? And then, if one were *not* normal – that is to say, in her present condition, for example – well, there was simply little hope.

She was most definitely a sinner, according to her family and the Church, so perhaps it was His will. But although her faith remained intact, she couldn't help questioning yet again how true love could be considered sinful. It was just Nature, was all, and it was ignorant of the self-righteous to deny that, in her defiant opinion. She realized that her predicament stemmed as much from her family's perceived aristocratic status as from their religious beliefs, but that was also wrong. True love knew no social bounds, nor should it be required to know any.

So, God damn her if He must – but to her way of thinking, she was *not* a bad person, this was *not* fair, and she was *not* sorry and never would be! And where was her husband-to-be? He didn't deserve this fate any more than she did. Had he also been pitched into this wildness from the suddenly canting decks? Would they be able to find each other? Was he still alive?

Such were her thoughts as she floundered in the darkly roiling sea, spitting out the salty water that seemed bent on invading her body and struggling to keep her head above its surface. She knew she was more buoyant in the seawater than she would be in fresh water, but simply floating wasn't an option, not with these waves breaking over her. So first things first, she decided, temporarily exorcising her concerns about her beau. Her sense of self-preservation was strong and there was more anger in her than fear, and she wouldn't give in without putting up as good a fight as possible. If she prevailed, she'd think of him then.

She began by kicking off her shoes and wriggling out of her plain ankle-length dress, a loose-fitting muslin affair that was more like a nightgown, in between the wind-driven waves breaking over the shoals. The unnecessary clothing would only weigh her down, and embarrassment at being seen in her undergarments was the least of her worries. Though it was late September and it was raining hard, neither the rain nor the seawater were unbearably cold here off the coast of – what island was this? Someone on deck had mentioned its odd-sounding name before the packet had begun to break up, but she couldn't remember now what it was.

She could only see a distance of a few feet in the blackness of this forsaken night, and there was nothing but a growing field of flotsam around her, none of it of any obvious use to her so far. She thought she could make out some distant-sounding shouts from some of the men over the howling wind, but she couldn't see them and she had no idea who or where they were. She thought she might have heard her name at one point, but she wasn't sure.

She tried to call out once herself, and got nothing but a mouthful of seawater in return halfway through. She didn't try again after that, as she didn't want to waste any more of her precious stolen breaths. She doubted anyone would be able to hear her diminutive voice in this gale anyway.

Fortunately, she'd learned to swim in her youth. Trying to stroke to any particular location in all this confusion was probably out of the question, and she had no clue what direction to go in anyway, but now that she was less encumbered she was at least capable of treading water until some sort of opportunity presented itself. She began casting a more discerning eye on the various pieces of flotsam that were randomly passing through her field of view. She couldn't see the ship and she didn't know how far she might have already drifted away from it – and maybe it had already sunk, who knew? – so the debris in the water might be her only chance at salvation.

If there were to be any sort of chance, she hoped it would come soon. She was holding her own so far, but her legs were already tiring. Her kicking wasn't quite as efficient as it would normally have been, so she was focusing on her sculling. Palms out and arms out, palms in and arms in, repeat... It was helping take some of the burden off of her legs, but she wouldn't be able to keep it up forever.

What was that? She'd caught just a glimpse of something larger than usual floating in the water nearby, but it was enough. She dog-paddled with as much energy as she could muster until she'd caught up with it, and grabbed onto it with one hand.

It was a rectangular slab of wood that looked like it might have been the lid of a storage locker in its former life aboard the ship. She didn't see any hinges on it, though. Regardless, whatever it had been, it floated – and it was big, big enough for her to grasp its far edge with both hands and pull herself halfway up onto it. It sank under her weight, but only a little. She noticed that it had a rope handle with space enough to put her hand through. So maybe it was a locker lid after all. She slid her hand, and her arm as well, under the handle and crooked her elbow around it.

Now an errant wave wouldn't be able to separate her from what she guessed could be considered her surfboard. She'd read about the new sport of wave surfing somewhere a while back. She knew she wasn't actually 'surfing' in what she'd read was the prescribed manner, but she certainly wouldn't be attempting to stand erect on it anytime soon, not on this wild night. No, she was happy right where she was.

More than happy – this was a certifiably blessed relief

compared to her previous situation. Now she could just ride out the waves, which logic told her must eventually take her to the shore of the nearby island, whatever its name was. She knew they'd managed to get closer to the island before the ship had grounded on the shoals, and she'd heard the men say that the Gulf Stream was at least ten miles east of where they'd been sailing before the storm, so she wasn't worried about getting caught in that powerful current and ending up God knows where. She just hoped the island wasn't uninhabited.

Though one end of her board was tipped up, the waves were still high enough to make breathing difficult when they broke over the top of it, sometimes briefly submerging both her and the board in the process. As if someone had read her mind, a piece of rigid rubber tubing floated by her free hand just as she was wondering what she might be able to do about that. She snagged it before it could drift away.

She also knew something about snorkeling. She and her sisters had played at it along the river shore with hollow reeds on occasion in younger and happier days, and she realized the roughly two-foot-long tube had just about the right diameter for that purpose. She didn't know what this tubing had originally been used for, but it didn't smell bad. So she carefully turned herself onto her back on the board, never relinquishing her hold on the rope handle even as she switched hands. Then she reestablished her elbow grip on the handle, held the tube straight up from her mouth with her free hand, and relaxed.

Now *this* was living, she giddily thought. Not only could she breathe at will, she no longer had to lie on her somewhat bloated belly. The Lord helps those who help themselves, isn't that what they say? Maybe she wasn't in His bad graces after all and He'd caused these useful items to be brought to her. Or maybe she was just smart and lucky, always a winning combination. She supposed many would consider that a heretical thought, but she no longer cared. In fact, after what she'd been through in the past couple of weeks, she honestly didn't much care what anyone might think about anything she did from here on.

Things were considerably improved now thanks to her recent acquisitions, but her lower legs were still dangling in the water. The possibility of sharks occurred to her. She tried scooting a little higher on the board and bending her knees so that her feet could rest atop it, but that made her unstable and more likely to capsize. She reasoned that since her legs didn't appear to be bleeding from any cuts or scrapes, it would probably be all right to leave them in the water. Whether or not that turned out to be true, it was the best she could do, so she dismissed further thoughts of hungry marine life from her mind. She'd always told herself to worry only about things she could change, and she'd take that good advice now.

All told, she was as comfortable as she could reasonably expect to be right now. She hoped her intended had been similarly fortunate, and she resolved to keep her eyes and ears open in case she should come across him and he needed her help. Well, her ears anyway, as the rain was now beating down on her exposed face.

She still couldn't see very well through the gloom in any case, so she closed her eyes against the rain. She'd be more vigilant once it let up some, if that ever happened. At the moment it seemed like maybe it never would, but she figured the storm would blow itself out or move away sooner or later. For now, she'd just hold on and try to rest up for whatever would come next on this hellacious night.

~ ~ ~

"She's alive!" Hazel announced, crouching next to the girl lying in the wash. "Albert Styron!" she called, accosting a man she'd recognized among the growing crowd of onlookers. "Get back in your truck and find the doc and bring him here quick as you can. And you, and you," she added, pointing, "you each take her under a shoulder and drag her up some so she's outta the water. Slow and careful, now, and not by the arms! She could be hurt. That's right, get her up onto this board here, and lay her on her side. Tide's runnin' out now, so that should be far enough. Now gimme your coats! Don't worry, you'll get 'em back. Come on now, you ain't gonna freeze to death this day." Everyone obeyed her without question or comment, as they always did when Hazel decided to take charge.

After the girl's upper body was settled on the piece of wreckage Hazel had found partially wedged in the sand nearby, she wadded up the shawl she'd thrown over her shoulders on her way out earlier and gingerly inserted it beneath the girl's head and neck for a makeshift pillow. Then she draped the coats over the girl's torso and legs and gently tucked them to her sides as best she could.

"All right then! She's probly cold from bein' in the water, but she's covered up and off the wet sand. And it ain't rainin' no more and the doc's on his way, so I guess we're set for now. You crowd can go on about your business," Hazel said, curtly dismissing her helpers and the few lingering onlookers as was her way.

The others left her to it and commenced their inevitable beachcombing, and Hazel sat down on the sand next to the girl and let out a long breath. Though it was less reliable as a source of income now than in the past, wrecking had always been a way of life in these parts and was still economically important to some of these folks. She herself figured she already had everything a sensible person might ever need, so she wasn't tempted to join the scavengers.

It looked like this girl, however, might have nothing but what she was wearing, which was scandalously little. She noted that none of the men had made any off-color remarks about that. But then, they all ought to know better by now than to do that in her presence, and they apparently did.

Though the castaway was unconscious, she didn't appear to be seriously injured beyond a good-sized bump on the noggin, and she was breathing fine on her own. Probably got herself knocked out somehow in the surf when she washed up, Hazel figured. Still, she thought she'd best hold off on doing anything else until the doctor arrived.

While she waited, she gazed out across the still-turbulent water to see what she could see. The visibility during the night had been next to nothing, but things were better now. The sea had calmed down some since the height of the storm, and the sun just coming up over the horizon was doing its best to cast its healing rays, but it was still cloudy and blustery out this dawn. Those uplander sports that came here to hunt and fish would probably think the morning a warm one, but Hazel was feeling a little chilled now without her shawl. She hugged her arms around herself and tried to shrug it off.

Though she'd spent a restless night, she'd been one of the first ones on the scene when the cry of 'shipwreck' had rung out across the village, thanks to her faithful pony. She turned her head and saw that he was still here, grazing on some sea oats a respectful distance away. Just in case she might need him again, she guessed, even though he was free to roam anywhere he wanted to on the island like all the others.

He'd started coming around her place now and then as a yearling, and when he did she'd always given him something to eat. Nowadays he still cavorted with some of the other wild ponies on occasion, but most of the time he stayed in whistling distance of her, and he always came when called if he was within earshot. She didn't know why he'd gotten so attached to her, but she was glad he had, as he was handy to have around – and a good companion as well, she had to grudgingly admit.

She could make out the wreck offshore now in the growing light. Whatever kind of ship it had been, she could tell it was pretty well busted up. It didn't happen as much these days as it once had, but she knew that ships that ran aground on the shoals in these waters generally stayed put while the relentless waves pummeled them to pieces, unless somebody towed them off. Sometimes it took days or weeks for that to happen and sometimes only hours, which looked to be the case here. Maybe this one had been damaged even before it had hit the shoals.

It didn't take too long for the truck to return, so she guessed old Albert hadn't gotten it stuck in the sand along the way. She didn't see how these newfangled automobiles could ever amount to much on this island, and she'd surely take her horse and a wagon over one of them most any day. But today it had admittedly made the round trip faster than she could have done it with her Boy.

The truck backed as close to the beach as it safely could, and the driver and the doctor got out and walked over to where Hazel sat with the girl.

"I hear we've got us a shipwreck survivor here," Doctor Angle said by way of greeting. "I also hear she might be the only one."

"That so?" Hazel said.

"Yep," he affirmed while he got his stethoscope from his bag. "One of the surfmen from up to the lifesaving station got himself a nasty gash and they brought him down to me a couple hours ago. They said they sent a surfboat out to the wreck and they're patrolling the shoreline, but they hadn't found anybody anywhere."

Actually, it was now a Coast Guard station, and had been for the past few years. The old Lifesaving Service had merged with the Revenue Cutter Service to become the Coast Guard, and it was now Coasties and rescue boats in place of surfmen and surfboats. But old habits die hard, Hazel knew, and she guessed that could be true for even a dingbatter like the doc.

"I thought you looked a mite peeked," she simply remarked.

"Yep. They also said they'd coordinate with the other nearby stations and see if anybody turns up on Hatteras or Portsmouth." The doctor stopped talking then while he checked the girl's pulse and listened with his stethoscope. Then he began gently palpating her head, neck, limbs, and torso. "Well, she's alive and breathing, her head's not bleeding, and nothing seems to be broken," he commented. "Got herself a good knock there somehow, though."

"Well, I didn't need *you* to tell me all that," Hazel chided.

The doctor chuckled. "I guess that's true. Something you maybe didn't know, though, is there's not enough water in her lungs to be a worry."

"That's good."

"Yep. I'd say she got knocked out right before she made landfall. Maybe by that big hunk of wood she's resting on, if she was trying to ride it in and she got tumbled by the waves. Lucky for her the tide's going out. Look here," he went on, "see where her skin's chafed here inside the elbow? That looks like a rope burn to me, and that piece of wood's got a rope handle on it. I bet she put her arm through there to hang on to it, and it swung around and conked her on the head in the surf."

"Sounds like a good story." A darn good one, in fact, but Hazel tried not to show that she was impressed. This dingbatter was already cocky enough as it was. "Think she'll come around?"

"I imagine so. That's a serious bump there, but I don't think there's much swelling on the brain, nor any major internal injuries far as I can tell."

"So she can be moved?"

The doctor nodded. "I believe so. The thing that most worries me right now is she shouldn't be sleeping a lot if she has a concussion. But she might just be physically exhausted. Albert, let's put her in the back of the truck and drive her down to my office. I can examine her more thoroughly there, and then we can take her to the station. They have temporary quarters for shipwreck survivors."

"You can examine her, but then she'll be goin' to my house," Hazel stated. "That station's no place for a girl that's been through what she's been through. She's gonna need some motherly care and some peace and quiet when she wakes up."

"But Hazel, she might be able to give them information they'll be needing at the station, like what ship it was, what happened to it, who's still missing, and so on," the doctor began to protest, though he knew it would probably be a futile effort.

"And what cargo they were carryin'," Albert chimed in.

That would be *his* main concern, Hazel uncharitably thought. Even if he couldn't go out there himself, he could profit from whatever there was to be salvaged from the wreck. He'd buy it at auction if there was one and then mark it up for sale at the general store he ran in town.

"The families and the ship's owner and such will have to be contacted," the doctor concluded.

"Uh huh. And we'll get all that information to 'em when she feels up to givin' it," Hazel retorted. "Meantime, she's stayin' with me, and that's that." She stood and brushed the sand from her dress, went to the pony, and gave him a pat. "You can go on now, Boy," she told him. "I'll ride along with these folks, the doc will do his exam, and then we'll bring her back home." Then she turned to the men and said, "All right now, let's get a-goin'!"

~ ~ ~

Hazel left off the stew she was working at in the kitchen when she heard the moaning. She picked up the tray she'd prepared in anticipation of this moment and hustled to the back bedroom.

The girl was trying to sit up in the bed Hazel had laid her down on. "Ooh, my head!" she hoarsely complained. "What happened? Where am I? Who are you?"

"Now don't you go thrussin' about," Hazel admonished her, setting the tray on a nightstand. "You mommucked your ride in on the surf when you washed up on the beach, is what happened to your head, and now you have to rest. Here, take this aspirin and sip some on this, and then we can talk. It's cool lemon water."

She handed the girl a tall glass and sat down on the only chair in the room. After the girl had drunk the water halfway down, she said, "One thing at a time, now. My name's Hazel. What's yours?"

"Laura. Laura Ketchum." Her voice was still hoarse, but it no longer hurt quite as much to talk, thanks to the water. She drained the glass and Hazel immediately refilled it from the pitcher on the tray. "Thank you. I feel like I could drink that whole pitcher."

"That's not surprisin', since you're all dried out. Saltwater will do that to you. So go on ahead, but do it slow."

"Thank you," Laura repeated. She looked around at the bedroom and then out the open window, through which a refreshing breeze was wafting in. "What is this place? Is this your house?"

"It is," Hazel nodded. "The doc wanted to take you up to the Coast Guard station, but I thought you should stay at a nicer place than that 'til you can get back on your feet. We don't have a hospital here. There used to be one over on Portsmouth, but it burned down and most folks there have moved inland anyways. We're lucky we even have a doctor here, sometimes we don't..." She laughed. "Sorry, I'm babblin'. I guess I'm just pleased you're all right."

"So I made it to the island? I couldn't remember the name of it, but I knew we'd got near an island."

"That you did. This here's Ocracoke Island, and you're in the town of Ocracoke, the only one on the island."

"Ocracoke, Ocracoke..." Laura repeated, rolling the unfamiliar name around on her tongue. "How long was I out?"

"Pretty much the whole time I've knowed you!" Hazel quipped. "You slept for twelve hours or so, that I know of."

"Were you the one who found me on the beach?" Hazel nodded again. "Well, thank you again for taking care of me." Laura paused for another sip of water before asking, "Um, did you find anyone else? Do you know if a man named Marshall has turned up anywhere?"

"I'm afraid you're the only one we know about so far," Hazel replied. "Nobody else has been found yet, neither dead nor alive. But Coasties from three stations are still out lookin'." Then she somberly inquired, "Is he your husband?"

A lost look came over Laura's face. "There was a lifeboat on the packet," she mumbled, "so maybe he's in it somewhere. Please God, let him be! But I got pitched into the water when the ship started to break up. It got swamped in the storm and the pumps failed and the Captain was trying to run in to the beach, but then we hit that sandbar..." She suddenly winced and held a hand to her head. "I think I'd better lie back now." When she'd gotten more comfortable, she said, "I'm sorry... Marshall – well, we're engaged to be married, I guess. Yes, I guess you could say that."

"You guess? In my experience folks usually know if they're engaged or not," Hazel teased, trying to lighten the girl's mood.

Laura rubbed at her sore head again. "I hope that

aspirin starts working soon," she said. "Is there anything else wrong with me?" she then asked, with some trepidation.

"Doc Angle says you might have got a concussion, but that's about all – except..."

"Except what?"

"Did you know you're expectin', dear?" Hazel kindly asked.

"Yes," Laura sighed.

"I wondered if you knew, since you ain't showin' much. Well, the doc said you're lucky you hadn't lost the baby in all that commotion. That's another reason why I wanted you to have some peace at this particular time. But don't you worry, we've got two good midwives here on the island, and I had one of 'em stop by to check up on you while you were sleepin'. She says you're doin' fine. She also helped me get you cleaned up and dressed proper."

"Oh. So where did this housedress come from? Is it yours? And what happened to my clothes?"

"Yep, that's an old one of mine. But it's clean. As for yours, well, you weren't wearin' much of nothin' when I found you and they was all begombed. They're dryin' on a rack by the stove now."

"That's right, I took my dress and my shoes off so I could swim. And all my other clothes were still aboard the ship, and everything else..." Laura's eyes widened and she sat up again. "Hazel, I have nothing now! How will I be able to repay you, and pay the doctor, and –"

"Now don't you fret about none of that. Folks hereabouts take care of one another. It'll all sort itself out after a while."

"Well, if you say so. Thank you so much again, Hazel..."

"And quit thankin' me, you've done enough of that already." Hazel went to the window. "Sun's goin' down now, so the moskies'll be comin' out. I better latch this screen. Then I'll bring you some dinner."

"I can get up and go to the kitchen – I think," Laura said, wincing again.

"Nonsense, you stay right here and enjoy this flaw of wind we're havin'. Most nights it ain't this airish 'round here, so this is a treat."

"You talk funny," Laura giggled. "I'm sorry, that's rude," she quickly apologized. "I don't know what came over me."

"Gettin' conked on the head might have somethin' to do with it," Hazel drily remarked. "Or maybe you're just dizzy from hunger."

"I *am* hungry! I think you're right. Whatever you're cooking smells wonderful, and I think it's getting to me."

"Well then, you just set tight and I'll be right on back. Or do you need to use the commode first? You don't have to go outside, you know. I've got an indoor one, and my house was one of the first on the island to get a septic system," Hazel proudly explained. Laura declined for now and Hazel headed to the kitchen.

When she returned, she set another tray atop the dresser and went off again for a stand that was about the right height for Laura to eat at while sitting on the bed.

"I hope you like fish," Hazel said, helping Laura rise to a sitting position. "We eat a lot of it around here. You ain't too woozy now, are you?"

"No, I'm fine. And yes, I do like fish, very much. Is this a fish stew?"

"Yep. It's drum. This kind of stew's called a muddle." Hazel set a bowl of it on the stand in front of Laura and laid out a napkin and utensils for her. "I thought it might be good to drink you a dope after you're done eatin', so I brought you one. It might could keep you from gettin' quamished."

Hazel sat on the chair again and held her own bowl on a cutting board in her lap. They both dug in for a short while, especially Laura who was famished. Then Laura stopped eating and laughed aloud. Hazel stared at her in puzzlement.

"I'm sorry," Laura said. "I don't mean to be rude again, but I'm not understanding half of what you're saying. Oh, and this is delicious, by the way."

"The vegetables come from my own garden, and I always add some pie-bread in to it," Hazel said, unsure of what the girl was getting at.

"I'm from Alexandria, up in Virginia. That's just below Washington D.C." Laura explained, turning serious. "Your accent isn't too foreign to my ear, but I have no idea what some of the words you use mean. To begin with, if you don't mind, what's a dope? And what would happen if I got quamished?"

"Oh, I see now," Hazel said with a smile. "Yep, some folks do get confused when they first come here, even if they're just from across the sound. Don't have to be far off as D.C. Well, a dope is a Coca-Cola, and quamished means you're feelin' sick. What else do you want to know?"

"Well, I take it airish means breezy, right? And, what was that you said before, mommucked? I guess that means I did something wrong?"

"Right and right," Hazel corroborated.

"And what else... Oh, what does begombed mean?

"That means soiled, or dirty."

"All right, *now* I understand. Thank you!" Laura resumed eating then, but more slowly now. "I'm a schoolteacher – or I was for a while, anyway – and I know about regional dialects and accents and such. I might just need a vocabulary lesson now and then is all."

It was Hazel's turn to laugh this time. "Oh, you might find you'll need more'n that!" she said. "If you think I talk funny, you should hear some of our old-timers. *Droime, Oi reckin that're one 'spacially hoi toide on t'saoundsoide tanoight!*" she parodied. "My folks weren't born here on the island, so I'm not near as bad as that."

"How interesting! But I guess this place is pretty isolated, right? So it's not surprising that a dialect like that could develop."

"I reckon. I was told it's kinda like the way some folks from England used to talk."

"I guess that makes sense, since they were mostly the ones who colonized these islands," Laura said, picking up her bottle of Coca-Cola.

"I got some cake to go with that," Hazel offered. "I could cut you a fladget if you want."

"Fladget – a slice?" Before Hazel could elaborate, Laura quickly amended her guess. "A skinny one?" Hazel nodded. "See? I'll get the hang of it. But no thank you, I'm quite full enough for now. Hazel," she hesitantly asked, "do you have a husband?"

"I did. He was the Keeper at the old lifesavin' station 'til he retired. He passed a few years back."

"Oh, I'm sorry. So how do you make out now? I mean..."

"What do I do for a livin'? Well, I've got part of his government pension, and he made a good wage at that job and we never spent more'n we had to. Him and some of his friends mostly built this house, and I come by most of my furniture from hand-me-downs and wreckin'. And I got my garden and my chickens and I go fishin' sometimes, so I got food to eat and goods to trade or sell. It's enough to get by on."

"That's good. Marshall can build furniture, you know." Laura took a swig of her Coca-Cola. "I'm sorry if I'm being too nosy, but, well, what about children? Do you have any?"

"I do, two of 'em. They both moved inland. I don't get to see 'em, nor the grandkids, but once or twice a year. Always around Christmas time, though, always at Christmas..." Hazel paused to dab at one of her eyes with her napkin, and then stoically resumed her narrative. "There ain't a lot of work here no more other than what comes from fishin' and huntin', so I can't blame 'em. This town used to be a shippin' and tradin' port at one time, but them other inlets opened, Hatt'ras and Oregon, up the beach, and then our inlet started shoalin' in, and – well, there you go. I hear there's some that's been tryin' their hand at bootleggin' licker, but that kinda work ain't respectable, and it's dangerous. At least my young'uns didn't get into somethin' like that, so I got that to be thankful for."

"Oh," was all Laura could think to say at first. She guessed she'd been intrusive enough for now, so maybe it was time to move on to another topic. "Are those flowers from your garden?" she asked, pointing to the large bouquet of striking red and yellow blossoms in a vase on a low table under the window. None of the furniture in this room matched, she noticed now that Hazel had mentioned it, but it didn't seem to matter. Even without the flowers, the room had a certain old-timey charm to it. "What are they? They're beautiful!"

"They grow all over nowadays. I just picked some from out in the yard. Their proper name is gaillardia, if I recall right. They're a kind of sunflower. But folks here have started takin' to callin' 'em Joe Bells of late."

"Why is that?"

"Well, there's a fella moved here by the name of Joe Bell a while back. He mostly keeps to himself, and I hadn't actually met him, but I hear he come here on account of a broken heart. Seems he was sweet on a girl back home, but her family didn't like him and they talked her into marryin' another. He brought these flowers here with him, and folks say he scatters their seeds around to remember her by."

"How sad!"

"Yep." Hazel took a deep breath. "Well now, one good tale deserves another, so it's your turn. What's the rest of *your* story, young lady, if you don't mind me askin'?"

"Well," Laura began, "I guess it's kind of like your Joe

Bell..." She hesitated, wondering how Hazel would react to what she was about to say. Despite her personal beliefs regarding her situation, she supposed she still felt somewhat ashamed and guilty – but things were the way they were and there was no changing them, so she guessed she'd better get over that. And so could other people.

"You could say I'm the black sheep of the family right about now. My family's pretty well-off, but instead of getting married right away – to somebody important that they approved of, of course – I wanted to get an education so I could be a schoolteacher. So that was one strike against me right there."

"Sounds like two strikes to me. And then along come your Marshall?" Hazel guessed.

"Yes. And he's smart and very handy, but he's a commoner – but he's the best and kindest man you could ever want to meet! And the handsomest too," she added with a quick smile. "But my family didn't approve of him, and they forbade me from seeing him."

"I guess that didn't work out too well," Hazel observed.

"No, it didn't. And I did some things I probably shouldn't have done..."

"Because you were in love."

"Yes. And then I became a real problem. They sent me to a relative in Baltimore, so I'd be out of sight of all their important friends. But then they decided that wasn't far enough after all, and they booked me on a southbound steam packet. I'm supposed to stay with some people they made arrangements with down around Wilmington, let them adopt the baby, and then come home."

"And act like nothin' ever happened."

"Right. And I don't even know those people! Well, Marshall and I changed the plan. They didn't know Marshall up in Baltimore, so he traveled there and booked passage on the same boat. He gave them a made-up name and we spent the whole time aboard ship pretending we didn't know each other, just in case. And I brought extra money with me so we could travel on to Charleston."

"So you were gonna skip Wilmington and elope to Charleston," Hazel concluded.

"Yes – and stay there for good. I don't want to ever go back to Alexandria."

"You don't want to see your family again?"

"Maybe someday, I suppose, but certainly not the way things are right now. We're not a very close family, and they don't really care about me. I'm just an embarrassment to them. I have two older sisters, and they treat me the same way. And they all act so high and mighty... I guess I'm not cut out to be like that."

"But they must love you. They probly just don't know how to show it."

Laura shook her head. "All they care about is their social standing and keeping up appearances. But at the same time, I've got an uncle who I found out visits houses of ill repute, and he's a drunkard too, and his wife – my aunt – is having a love affair with another married man. And I've heard my own father's made a lot of his money by cheating people in shady business deals and I'm pretty sure he's been fooling around with one of our Negro servant girls, and a couple of my cousins once tortured a stray cat to death... They're not nice people. But so long as they can keep all that on the down-low, and throw big fancy parties and such, everything's all right in their world. Have you ever heard of an outlaw named Black Jack Ketchum?"

"Why, I believe I did read somethin' about him one time," Hazel said, "in some magazine or other."

"Well, my great-grandfather's brother, Peter Ketchum – I guess he'd be some kind of great-uncle or something to me, though I always get confused about those kinship relationships – left Virginia and moved his family out West, and Black Jack Ketchum was one of his grandsons.

He robbed trains and killed people, and he got himself hanged for it about twenty-five years ago. There was another Ketchum that moved his family somewhere up North before the Civil War, but I don't know anything about that except that they were on the wrong side in the war, according to my family. Anyway, nobody in *my* family ever talks about *those* branches of the family, of course."

Hazel's eyebrows lifted. "That's sure some family you got there, all right," she conceded. "But the Coast Guard has to report on this shipwreck, so they're gonna find out where you are. Matter of fact, I ought to tell you, the Coasties will be wantin' to talk with you soon's they find out you're awake. We should probably ride on up to the station tomorrow if you feel up to it."

"So, I guess you're not kicking me out, then?" Laura asked with a wan smile.

"What?!" Hazel exclaimed. "Now why on earth would I do that?"

"Because of my awful family? Because I'm a sinner like them, in my own way? And a fallen woman? Because I'm being deceitful and running away? Because I have no money? There are lots of reasons. You'd only have to pick one of them."

"It's not my place to judge you," Hazel stated, "so I won't. Nor will most other folks 'round these parts. You ain't the first one's made a mistake and landed in a spot like this. At least your puck's tryin' to do right by you. Nope, you're stayin' here 'til you got someplace else to go, and that's that."

"Really? Are you sure? That's such a relief!" Laura said, and she meant it. It was bad enough that she'd been ostracized by her own family, and then if it had happened again here... "Thank you, Hazel. You're a good person, and I want you to know I'll pay you back someday when I'm able."

"Well, it's my Christian duty and a pleasure to boot. I

don't get much company these days. So don't you worry about it. And by the way, a puck is a sweetheart."

Laura laughed again at that. "All right, then. I'll go to the station in the morning. I feel a lot better already, though my head still hurts some." She sighed. "I suppose it doesn't matter if they find out where I am. It might even be a good thing. They don't know about the plan I made, so they'll hire another boat to come get me and take me to Wilmington. I lost all my money when we wrecked, and if Marshall's gone..." A hiccup interrupted her and she angrily wiped away a stray tear. "Well then, I guess I'll have no choice but to do what they want me to do."

"You had money on the ship? Tell the Coasties about it, and if they find it on the wreck they'll give it back to you."

"They could do that? Find it? And they wouldn't just keep it?"

"The water ain't that deep around them shoals. Too deep to stand up in, but not too deep to recover lost property. And I guarantee they'd return it to you. They're honest folks."

"All right then, I'll do that."

"Well," Hazel said, "That's probly enough jawin' for now. I don't want to wear you out. You lie back down and rest, and I'll go put these dishes away."

"Lie down and rest?" Laura chuckled. "I slept the whole day! I'm not tired right now. I'll help you." Hazel moved quickly to her side when the girl stood up. "Don't worry, I'm all right. A little weak, maybe, but I'm not dizzy."

"Well all right," Hazel said, "but you ain't doin' dishes this day. You go on out to the pizer and set if you want some more air, and I'll come join you when I'm done. It's got a screen on it, and it's a right pleasant spot of an evenin'."

"And a pizer is what?"

"That'd be the porch to a dingbatter such as yourself."

Laura laughed yet again. Somehow this island woman

had managed to put her in good spirits despite everything that had happened, and she realized that she appreciated this at least as much as the food and shelter, not to mention Hazel's selfless acceptance of her and all her baggage.

"Thank you," she said. "I'll do that, I'll go out and set on the pizer! And you can tell me what that other word means when you come out."

~ ~ ~

"You go on ahead and get dressed," Hazel said while she finished cleaning up after breakfast, "and I'll call my Boy to the flat cart. I'll take you on a scud around town before we head on up to the station."

"Whatever you say," Laura acknowledged from her bedroom. "You have a boy that works for you?"

"Nope. Boy's my pony."

"You have a horse? But I thought you said the horses got here from shipwrecks long ago and they're all wild."

"They are, but this one likes me."

"And you named him Boy?"

"I didn't name him. I just call him that."

The horse came trotting up to the house soon after Hazel whistled for him. She fed him a carrot, and he allowed her to hitch him to her pony cart, a light two-wheeler with a high-backed bench seat and a small cargo space behind it.

Laura went up to the horse and introduced herself when she came out. "I've always liked horses," she said.

"I think he likes you too," Hazel said, helping Laura up onto the seat. "We'll just mosey around town for a spell, and then we'll stop at Albert's store and have him or somebody pick us up back at the house and drive us to the station in his truck. This pony's strong, but I don't want to ask him to pull us that far. Let's go, Boy!"

The obedient horse set off at a walk on the mostly hard-packed sandy path that led away from Hazel's house, then eased into a slow trot when they came out onto a similar trail that led down into town.

"Don't worry, he knows this is as fast as I like to go," Hazel said. "And he'll try to keep us in the ruts, so it shouldn't be too rough a ride."

"I'm all right," Laura assured her.

"Good. So, we're goin' round Creek right now. That's the part of town that's north of the Ditch. Later on we'll go down Point, which is below the Ditch. Them woods back behind us is up Trent. Hardly anybody lives in there. So we're Creekers, if you ever need to know that."

"And the other people are Pointers?" Hazel nodded. "What's the Ditch?" Laura inquired.

"That's what we call our little bay that's in the middle of town. It's got a proper name, Cockle Creek, but folks call it the Ditch. That's where most things are, the bidnesses and fishin' boats and such."

Their riding tour took them by the waterfront, where a channel at the far shore of the Ditch led out into Pamlico Sound. Hazel showed Laura some landmarks, and the Post Office and Albert's store, and then they continued south into the Point section of town.

"It didn't seem like there was much activity by the bay – excuse me, the Ditch," Laura observed. "Except for at the fish houses, and a couple people at the store."

"Oh, there was plenty goin' on before, and there will be again later on when the fishin' boats come in. They were all out already by the time you got up this mornin'. Maybe we'll stop back at the end of the day and watch the pelicans grub for handouts. They're a right funny gang of beggars."

"All right, if we don't get hung up at the Coast Guard station."

"Now that up ahead there's our lighthouse," Hazel said. "It's the oldest one in the state. It was built more'n a hundred years ago, back in 1823. And down past there is the Point, and Ocracoke Inlet is a ways past that. We won't go there today, 'cause we'd have to leave this cart behind and do some hikin' on foot. But just past the Point there is Teach's Hole. That's where Blackbeard the pirate lost his head back in 1718. His real name was Edward Teach, you know."

"Really? How fascinating! History is a special interest of mine, and Marshall's too. He loved – *loves* – history."

"Well, there's a lot of it around here," Hazel said with a sidelong glance at Laura. "Out on Beacon Island in the inlet, there's the ruins of a Confederate fort, and there was a fort there in the War of 1812 too. And there were some German U-boats right offshore durin' the Great War, and some ships were torpedoed by them."

"You're right, that's a lot of history!"

"And there's a lot of legends and flat-out tall tales too," Hazel continued. "There's some as say they've seen a light along the shoreline by Teach's Hole sometimes at night, Teach's Light they call it. It's supposed to be Blackbeard's ghost. And when he was beheaded in his battle with the British Navy, they say his headless body swam around the ship three times. And some folks say you can see his body still swimmin' around out there lookin' for his head now and again."

"There's a lot I'd like to see someday, but I hope I never see anything like that!" Laura chuckled. "You know, speaking of history, one thing I haven't seen yet is the school. Is there one here?"

"Yep, they finally put up a schoolhouse down off the Back Road a few years back. But it's closed now due to lack of funds."

"Oh no!" Laura exclaimed. "How do the children here get educated then?"

"Well, those that want it have to go somewhere else, the mainland or up to Hatt'ras Island. There ain't as many kids here now as there used to be."

Laura mulled that over some. "This is such a beautiful place," she finally said. "The sand, the water, this big blue sky... And those gnarly-looking trees. What are they?"

"Live oaks. They grow twisted on account of the salt," Hazel explained. "There's a lot of cedars too."

"I see. And it's so peaceful here, and it's a pretty little town..." Many would instead call it dilapidated, Laura knew, but to her the buildings looked quaint, especially the ones along the waterfront. Weathered, to be sure – but nautically picturesque and charming to her. "It's a shame people have to go elsewhere to find work and schooling."

"Yep," was all Hazel had to say to that. They turned and headed back into town, taking some different paths this time along the way. Their destination now was Albert's store, in hopes of being able to arrange a ride in his truck to the Coast Guard station up island.

"How many automobiles are there here?" Laura asked.

"Exactly two," Hazel answered. "Albert Styron's got one of them Model T trucks, and Captain Bill Gaskill's got another one like it."

"Well, you shouldn't have to worry too much about collisions then. There are a lot of automobiles now where I'm from, and it seems like they're forever running into one another. They're going to need better rules and regulations."

"Rules of the road, so to speak?"

"Yes. But there are no real roads here, are there? Just these paths in the sand. It must be hard for those trucks to get around. I bet they get stuck sometimes, don't they?"

"They do, 'specially when it rains. But even on dry days, they have to carry shovels and watch where they're goin'. I don't know as they'll ever amount to much around here, though. There's plenty of ponies, and most of 'em are friendly enough. Folks can just borrow one or two when they have a need, like I do." Hazel laughed. "I'll take my

Boy and good old Route 101 anytime over them newfangled contraptions, and all that comes with 'em!"

"Route 101?"

"Yep. You say there's no roads here, but we've got lots of roads – about a hundred and one of 'em, and they suit us just fine."

"You mean these sandy tracks? That's what people here call Route 101?"

"Yep."

Laura thought for a moment. "I suppose there's probably about a hundred and one currents out there in the ocean too, huh?" she finally commented.

"You might be right about that," Hazel carefully replied. "There's some main ones, but there's lots of smaller ones at any given time, dependin' on the tides and the weather."

"So Marshall could be anywhere," Laura flatly stated. "Wherever he is, I hope he's safe and he gets rescued. I hope the ocean's Route 101 brings him back to me."

"Well, we'll soon see if they've had any news up to the station. We'll be comin' up on Albert's store before too long." Hazel was silent for a moment, and then she decided to verbalize an idea that had come to her earlier on their sightseeing tour. "You know, whether Marshall turns up or not, you don't have to leave here if you don't want to."

"I don't?" Laura responded in surprise. "What do you mean?"

"Well, you're a schoolteacher, right? You could school the children right here. The main reason the schoolhouse closed was they couldn't pay enough money to get a real teacher to stay on. But you could keep stayin' with me, so they wouldn't have to pay you much. And they'd probly let you use the schoolhouse. I know there's still books and whatnot in there."

Laura didn't say anything right away, and Hazel's face reddened in embarrassment. She hoped the girl wasn't thinking she was just a lonely old woman trying to hang onto her for selfish reasons. She did miss her own children and grandchildren, of course, almost constantly in fact, but that wasn't her only motivation. At least, she didn't think it was.

"That's an interesting idea, Hazel," Laura said. "And it's very generous of you. But what about the baby? What would you want with a crying newborn around your house all the time?"

"It were long ago, but I'm no stranger to all that," Hazel smiled. "It wouldn't be a bad thing to have some new life in that old house. I could watch it for you while you're at the school, or you could take it with you if it'd behave well enough. And if your Marshall's around, he could help some too."

"Well, I don't know... I'll have to see what Marshall thinks about it. I bet he'd like it here too, though. And he could find some kind of work, maybe at a fish house or on a boat to begin with. Maybe he could do handyman work here and there, at the lighthouse or up at the station. It wouldn't be any less certain than what we might find around Charleston, though I imagine there'd be more possibility of work for him there..." Laura paused in thought again. "I know I can't go on to Charleston on my own, if I don't have Marshall, and I guess I might have to learn to face up to that. So realistically, it'll probably just be up to me to decide between here and Wilmington, though I'd certainly rather stay here in that case..."

"Now don't you go thinkin' like that," Hazel scolded her. "Think positive. Look here, there's the store. Let's go see what's what, and then we can take things from there."

~ ~ ~

"Ooh, look at that, Hazel! What a gorgeous view!" Laura exclaimed, gazing past her in Albert's truck at the sunlit water, calmer today, and the pristine sandy beach that seemed to go on forever up the Atlantic shore of the island. It was a tight squeeze, but all three of them were riding up front. "And look over there – more ponies! Aren't they beautiful?"

Hazel just nodded and smiled. The poor girl had been bubbling over ever since Albert had told them at the store that he'd heard the Coasties had rescued the occupants of a lifeboat off Portsmouth Island yesterday evening. He didn't know any more details than that, though, so she hoped Laura wouldn't be disappointed when they reached the Ocracoke station. And though he was doing a good job so far even though they weren't driving the bank of the beach today, she hoped to God he didn't get them stuck somewhere on the way. That girl needed to get to the station soon as possible if there was to be any peace for her today.

"Is that where the ship wrecked?" Laura asked, squinting. "Way out there? It looks like there are a couple of other boats there too."

"Yep," Albert corroborated. "They're salvagin' the wreck."

"And what's all that washing up all along the beach there?"

"Well, it seems most of their cargo was lumber, and most of that's been comin' ashore with the tides. Me'n Captain Bill's been hired to gather it up and haul it to town with our trucks. I'm supposed to start doin' that after I drop you two back off at Hazel's place."

They made it in good time, thankfully without running aground in the sand. Hazel had to practically put a bridle on the girl to keep her from jumping from the not-quite-stopped truck and running full-tilt through the front door of the station.

"Slow down there, girl!" she demanded, restraining Laura by one arm. "I'm old, and you're in no condition to be runnin' around like you're offshore crazy!"

"I'm sorry, Hazel," Laura apologized. She stopped for a moment and tried to straighten out her hair, which had been blowing in the wind through the truck's open cab despite its windscreen. "All right, I'm ready. Let's go in."

And they did, at a fairly leisurely pace this time. One of the Coasties met them at the door and escorted them in to see the Chief. After fidgeting through greetings and introductions and explanations, Laura came to her point.

"I heard the Portsmouth surfmen rescued a lifeboat," she said. "Was it from the ship I was on?"

"Yes, it was, miss," the Chief answered. "And the message we got said everybody from that ship was accounted for, passengers and crew. Except for yourself, of course."

"Accounted for? What does that mean?" Laura demanded, her nerves on edge.

"Well, in this case, it means everybody was alive. We were also told there were no serious injuries."

But Laura wasn't fully satisfied quite yet. "Do you know their names? Was there a Marshall Boyd – er, Sheppard, I mean – on board?"

The Chief consulted a piece of paper that sat atop his desk. "There's an M.B. Sheppard on the list," he said, with a quizzical look her way. "You know him, I take it?"

Laura ignored the Chief's question. "And he's all right?"

"They're to be married," Hazel answered for her.

"Oh. Well, there were some minor injuries, and they were all sunburned and mighty parched, but that's about the extent of it. They're pretty much all fine otherwise."

"Oh, Hazel!" Laura cried, tears in her eyes. "I have to sit down!" The Coasties scurried to get a chair under her, and she collapsed onto it. "I'm sorry. I thought I was about to faint! Hazel, this is the best news ever! Thank you so much, sir! What happens now? Does he – or they – come here? Do I have to find a way to go there?"

"Relax, miss, it's been taken care of," the Chief assured her. "They're all being transported here on the mailboat, which is picking them up in Portsmouth. We're sending a boat down to ferry them up here from the Ditch. But when the mail's called over this afternoon, your fella can go with you if he likes."

"That's wonderful, thank you!" Laura exclaimed. Then she made an effort to compose herself, which included letting out a breath that felt like she might have been holding it since last night. "I imagine, sir, you'll be wanting to interview me now? About the wreck, I mean?"

"That's really no longer necessary," the Chief said. "We know who you are and how you got here, and that you're alive and well, and we got all the other details we needed from the Portsmouth crew. And Hazel says you're staying with her, so we don't need to find a place for you here. But before you go, we recovered some personal items from the wreck yesterday. You might want to take a look and see if anything belongs to you. They're out in the boathouse."

The Chief and the other Coastie led Laura and Hazel to the boathouse. Albert followed after he'd availed himself of a mug of what he considered to be some of the finest coffee on the island.

Laura spotted her trunk as soon as she walked into the boathouse. "This is my trunk!" she announced, going over to it. "And it's still locked!" she added with a meaningful look at Hazel, though she refrained from mentioning aloud that this meant her money pouch was probably intact. "And that one over there is Marshall's!" she said, pointing it out.

"Well, I'd say this here's your lucky day!" Hazel said. "Somebody up there must be on your side."

"Except for the shipwreck," Laura said. "But then again, I made it to shore, didn't I? And I didn't lose, um, anything, nor get injured. So maybe I was meant to come here. It sure feels that way right now," she said with a smile.

"Albert, why don't you pull your truck up, and we'll load up those trunks," the Chief said. "Then y'all can be on your way."

Laura felt like she was riding on a cloud all the way back to Hazel's place, even though the trail was just as bumpy coming back as it had been going up. After Albert had carted the trunks into the house for them and headed off, Hazel helped her break the lock on her trunk, since she no longer had the key. The first thing she went for was the money pouch, which it turned out was both present and as full as she'd remembered.

"Hazel, I can pay you now!" she declared.

"Never you mind," Hazel said. "You just hang on to that for the time bein'. We can settle up later on if we need to, when you decide what you're gonna do."

"I think I already have," Laura said, surprised at the sudden realization. She shouldn't have been, though, as she also realized she'd been working her way up to it all along. "I want to stay here on Ocracoke. I know there are probably more opportunities in Charleston – but I love this place! And I'm sure Marshall will like it here too. If you'll have us until we can find a place of our own, that is."

"You're welcome to stay here long as you like," Hazel said, dabbing at an eye for the second time in as many days. "But are you certain that's what you want to do? This ain't as far south as Charleston, you know, and the winters can get pretty rough. And it ain't as fancy here as you're used to, and you'll always be a dingbatter here."

Laura laughed. "Because I wasn't born here, I know. But there are far worse fates, and my child won't be a dingbatter, right? And I don't care about being fancy, and I don't imagine the winters could be that much worse than the ones around Washington. We get nor'easters and all up there too, and our estate is on the Potomac River. Nope, I'm game for whatever this island wants to throw at me.

It's worth it."

"I hope so, for your sake. But what if your folks have a different idea about it?"

"Well... When I don't turn up in Wilmington, they'll probably find out I booked passage to Charleston instead, so hopefully they'll assume that's where I went. And it says 'Sheppard' on the ship's passenger manifest, not 'Boyd', so they shouldn't think Marshall was with me on the ship. And if they look for him in Alexandria and can't find him, they'll probably figure he went to Charleston to meet up with me. *And*, if they go so far as to look for us in Charleston, they won't find us there, and they'll probably figure we moved on to somewhere else. So I don't think they'll be able to get at me."

"That all sounds pretty good, but let me add one more piece to your little puzzle. From now on, 'Sheppard' is Marshall's new last name, and you call him 'M.B.', at least in public."

Laura nodded agreement. "That's a very good idea, Hazel! Don't worry, I'll talk him into it."

"Good. Well now, I guess you ought to go make yourself presentable before we head back to town. That hair of yours is a fright!"

~ ~ ~

Laura's trunk hadn't leaked as much as she'd feared. It must not have gotten fully immersed in the wreck. Some of her clothing would need to be washed and dried, but she'd been able to come up with a dry dress and a pair of sensible shoes – the only kind she'd be wearing from now on, she suspected. And if she fixed her hair just so, you couldn't even notice the bump on her head. When the mailboat came in later, she was confident she'd be looking as attractive as she possibly could for poor Marshall under the circumstances.

Hazel had recalled Boy while Laura was getting ready, and he was already hitched to the pony cart when she came out the front door – which she didn't bother to lock, since she knew Hazel never did. She had however hidden her money pouch under a floorboard she'd pried up in her closet. She wanted to trust her new neighbors, but at the same time she knew a thing or two now about human nature and temptation.

There was quite a crowd down at the Ditch when Hazel and Laura arrived. They left Boy and the cart on a side street. Hazel told the pony to stay put there, and she and Laura joined the crowd at the docks.

"The mail bein' called over's a big event here," Hazel explained. "It doesn't happen every day, and it ain't just about the mail. It's a chance for folks to meet up and gossip and whatnot. Hey there, Doc!" she suddenly called out, spotting the familiar figure hurrying away from the crowd. "Where you runnin' off to?"

"Hey, Hazel. Well, you heard Bill and Albert are hauling lumber from that wreck, right? A boy just ran down here and told me there's been an accident. He says nobody's hurt real bad, but I thought I better go take a look to be sure."

"An accident? What happened?" Hazel asked. A ripple of murmurs ran through the crowd as the news was passed along.

"Well, seems one of the trucks was on its way up here from the beach, and one was on its way back down to the beach. They were coming around a blind bend at the same time just up that road there, the boy said, and they ran into each other head-on."

"Do tell!" Hazel said, putting a hand over her mouth. "Well, you'd best get on with it then." To Laura she croaked, "Follow me," and hurried off without waiting.

She led Laura behind a tree across the road from the docks. When she was sure no one could see her, she suddenly doubled over and burst into laughter. Still holding a hand over her mouth to muffle the sound as much as possible, she let the tears run freely this time.

"Are you all right?" Laura asked. "You're laughing, right?" Hazel nodded. "Well, what's so funny?"

"I'm sorry," Hazel answered when she could speak again. "I shouldn't ought to be takin' amusement from the misfortunes of others. But think about it! There's but two automobiles on this whole dang island – and they crashed into each other! You said they need more rules and regulations for them things, and you're right! There's only two of 'em, and there's a hundred and one ways they could go, and they, they –" She broke out then into another fit of laughter, and this time Laura began giggling along with her.

"Oh, Lordy!" Hazel said, wiping her eyes when her current bout of merriment finally died down. "You said you and Marshall like history, right? Well, this is a right historical event, ain't it? The first automobile accident on Ocracoke Island! And you were here to witness it! And, and... And there was only the *two* of 'em!" she got out before she lost her composure yet again.

"Stop!" Laura said, doubling over herself now. "I can't take any more!"

"Well!" Hazel finally said, wiping her eyes again. "I guess they'll be usin' the ponies after all for that job now. Oh, lookee – here comes the mailboat! Come on, we'd best sober up and get on back over there now."

When the boat docked, they let the passengers off before offloading the mail – which of course Laura had no interest in on this day. She stood anxiously near the dock and tried to be patient as the shipwreck survivors filed ashore from the boat. A Coastie was there to direct them to his own boat, which would take them to the station, and they duly followed his instructions.

Marshall was the last one off the boat. As soon as she

spotted him, Laura called out to him and began frantically waving. He bypassed the Coastie and loped down the dock to meet her. The two embraced and said nothing for a long minute, quiet tears of joy running down Laura's face. Then she pulled back a bit and spoke up.

"Oh, Marshall! I thought I'd lost you!" she exclaimed.

"I thought I'd lost *you*!" he said. "We paddled all over in that lifeboat looking for you, but we couldn't find you anywhere!"

"I think I might have heard you calling me, but I couldn't do anything! I got thrown off the deck when it broke up, and I was busy trying not to drown in the waves! Then I got washed up on the beach here –"

"I know, they sent a message about that to the Portsmouth station! Are you all right? What about the baby? Is it –"

"The baby's fine. But look at you! And where did you get those clothes? That's some outfit you've got on there, sir!"

"They had a used clothing bin for shipwreck survivors at the station."

"Well, guess what – I have your trunk! Does that hurt?" Laura asked, gingerly touching his reddened face. "Are you hurting anywhere else?"

"No, I'm all right."

"That ain't nothin' a little salve won't cure," Hazel cut in. "I've got just the thing for it back at the house."

"Oh! I'm sorry," Laura said. "I've completely forgotten my manners! Marshall, this is Hazel. She took me in and cared for me after I washed ashore. She's the best and kindest woman you could ever want to meet!"

"Hazel, it's a pleasure to meet you! Thank you for taking care of Laura," Marshall said. "She means the world to me, you know," he shyly added.

"Nice to meet you too, you're welcome, and I'm glad to hear that," Hazel replied, but with a smile. "Now Laura, you two can ride the cart back to the house if you want. I can walk. It ain't that far."

"Can you walk for a short way, Marshall?" Laura asked him. He nodded. "Well then, thanks Hazel, but you go on and take the cart," she demurred. "I don't mind walking, and Marshall and I have a lot to talk about. We'll meet you at the house. Actually, I'm to call you 'M.B.' from now on," she said to Marshall. "And if you don't mind, you're going to be an O'Cocker, and a Creeker as well for the time being."

"An oh-what?" he inquired while Hazel quietly set off to get her Boy and cart.

"I'll explain on the way. Hazel's offered to put us up at her place until we can get on our feet." Laura took his arm and began leading him up the path toward the Creek. "Don't worry, her house isn't too far. It's just a ways up the road here – and it's right off Route 101!" she laughed.

Afterword

Thanks for reading these stories! I had fun writing them, and I hope you enjoyed reading them. If you did, please consider taking a few minutes to post a short review online. Reviews help increase an independently published book's visibility, and I'd greatly appreciate it. Thanks again!

Keep a weather eye out for the next Storm Ketchum Adventure! You might also enjoy Ketch's full-length Adventures – the novels that were the inspiration for these short Tales – if you haven't already read them. You can find them at your favorite retailer, and at my Web site:

www.GarrettDennis.com

You can also sign up for my Port Starbird VIP Reader List there, if you want to stay in the Storm Ketchum loop. And if you sign up, you can get a free e-book!

I reckon that's it for now, y'all. Maybe you'll see me somewhere on ol' Route 101 one of these fine island days, if there ain't a storm a-brewin'.

Meanwhile – Happy Reading!

Made in United States
North Haven, CT
25 April 2022

18536649R00157